MW00987993

dark obsession

BOOK THREE

VAMPIRE ROYALS OF NEW YORK

Dark Obsession
Vampire Royals of New York, Book Three
Copyright © 2020 by Sarah Piper
SarahPiperBooks.com

Cover design by Covers by Juan

ISBN-13: 978-1-948455-22-0

VAMPIRE ROYALS OF NEW YORK

Dark Deception

Dark Seduction

Dark Obsession

Heart of Thorns

TAROT ACADEMY

Spells of Iron and Bone

Spells of Breath and Blade

Spells of Flame and Fury

Spells of Blood and Sorrow

Spells of Mist and Spirit

THE WITCH'S REBELS

Shadow Kissed

Darkness Bound

Demon Sworn

Blood Cursed

Death Untold

Rebel Reborn

CHAPTER ONE

"This... is not... *happening!*"

The glass door shattered in a glorious explosion, casting the rose garden in a thousand sunlit shards.

Ignoring his bloodied hands, Dorian tore another chunk of stone from the hearth in the dining room and hurled it through the second door, obliterating it.

He grabbed another stone.

Another.

Another still.

In a matter of minutes, he obliterated the fireplace, then swiftly moved on to the furniture. The high-backed chairs. The oak table that had so recently hosted his brother Malcolm's traitorous gathering and—centuries earlier— their last meal as mortal men. The cabinets that held his mother's delicate bone china. The sideboard against which he'd so exquisitely taken Charlotte's... confession.

Charlotte...

In a blur of blood and terror, Dorian smashed through every piece of wood, punched through every wall. He tore down the paintings, decimated the china, laid bare the stone foundations behind the wainscoting. He ripped loose the floorboards, still dark with the blood he'd spilled at the council meeting—Malcolm's and the gray's alike.

Blood and death, brother. Blood and death.

No one came to ease his pain.

No one even knew he was there.

Malcolm was gone—he'd vanished from Ravenswood after Dorian had damn near ripped his heart out.

Gabriel was back in the city, following Dorian's command to hunt down Silas—the vampire who'd beaten Charlotte and left her for dead in a dumpster.

Aiden and Cole were out with the wolves, scouring the woods for more clues about the grays that had invaded their lands.

And upstairs, clear on the other side of the manor, the witch who'd delivered last night's most crushing blow tended to the woman who'd stolen Dorian's heart.

He couldn't face either of them.

So there he remained, breathless and alone at the epicenter of his own chaos. His wounds had already healed, but blood soaked his skin, soaked his clothes, soaked the memories that clung to the room like cobwebs.

The more he destroyed, the more haunted he became, tormented by thoughts of his utter impotency. First, as House Kendrick had slaughtered his family. Later, as his human lover had murdered House Redthorne's bonded witch. And last night, in the face of Isabelle's dire pronouncement, he'd broken apart once again.

Charlotte D'Amico belongs to hell. I suggest you make peace with that and say your goodbyes...

Fire. Dorian needed fire.

Hands trembling, heart thudding, he stalked into the kitchen and grabbed a box of matches and a half-case of rum one of his brothers had left on the counter.

There was no thought of reason, of safety, of worry for the rest of the manor. There was only the need to destroy.

Today, he'd burn it all, just as he'd wanted to do decades ago. Centuries ago. It was time for that abominable room and everything it represented to go up in smoke.

But when he returned to the dining room, he was no longer alone.

Aiden paced the ruins, looking almost as filthy and bloodied as Dorian himself.

Meeting Dorian's eyes across the disaster zone, Aiden cocked a smile and said, "If it's a new look you're after, Dori, a fresh coat of paint and some stylish window treatments would do wonders."

Certain his friend was uninjured after his hunt with Cole, Dorian returned his attention to the mission, grabbing one of the bottles and soaking the decimated table with booze.

"Shall I fetch the marshmallows, then?" Aiden asked.

"Leave me, Aiden. I've things to burn."

"Hmm. Don't think I will, mate. I've always loved a good bonfire. Not to mention..." He turned toward the battered wall behind him and tore down the last remaining piece of art—a vile landscape of a barren, volcanic wasteland called Mists of Darkness. "I *really* hate this bloody painting. Been trying to tell you that since the first World War."

"In case it isn't *painfully* obvious, I'm in no mood for your feeble attempts at distraction."

"And *I'm* in no mood to be flambéed, so whatever blaze of glory you've got your heart set on this morning, let's move it outside, shall we?" Aiden carried the painting out through the battered doorway and pitched it into the rose garden.

Seeing no alternative to his friend's annoyingly unwavering good sense, Dorian followed suit, hurling pieces of rubble out into the pale morning—splintered wood, broken paintings, priceless antiquities. With Aiden at his side, they made quick work of it, clearing the entire room in minutes.

Standing together in the garden before the giant pyre, they surveyed the wreckage of a past Dorian was more than ready to destroy.

"Unless you've got a speech prepared," Aiden said, "pass me the rum, you bloody arsonist."

Dorian sighed and handed over a fresh bottle from the case. Aiden took a swig, then emptied the last of it onto the pile, chucking the bottle in too. They poured out a few more bottles, then Dorian struck a match and touched it to the box. The moment it caught, he chucked the whole thing into the pile. The fire ignited at once—a rapturous blaze that seared his skin and soared up to the heavens.

They stood in silence for a long moment, watching the flames consume and devour, blackening the stonework at the center of the rose garden. The fractured bits of wood turned dark, the painted canvases curling in the heat. The fire surged, and one by one, the rose bushes ignited, glowing silver-white before turning to black ash.

There was something deeply satisfying about watching fire consume its kindling. Something pure and beautiful about the way it transformed light to dark, cold to heat, creation to destruction.

As the fire roared into the sky, Aiden peered into the empty husk formerly known as the Ravenswood dining room and sighed. "Nothing but pure potential now, is it?"

"I should've done it decades ago."

"Yes, and now that you have…" Aiden looked back to Dorian, his eyes darkening with a concern that quickly worked its way into Dorian's heart. "What's this really about? I'm guessing it's not just a new look you're after."

"What do you *think* it's about?" Dorian raked a bloody hand through his hair. "Sasha's been kidnapped. Charlotte's uncle is a demon—one who nearly killed her last night. Not to mention there's an army of grays on the loose. Have you already forgotten?"

"How could I? Did you see the way I impaled that poor bastard with a pole?" Aiden laughed. "History in the making, my friend. They'll probably write a song about me. A ballad with—"

"For fuck's sake, Aiden! How can you be so… so bloody *you* right now?"

"As opposed to what, Dori? Falling apart? Shall I find something else to torch, then? Massacre some poor, defenseless furniture?" He chucked an errant floorboard into the fire, an unfamiliar anger rising in his eyes. "Sasha is my *friend.* Forgive me for attempting to pull you off your *mind*-numbingly predictable path of self-destruction, but if you think my cracking a few jokes means I don't care about what's happening, then you don't know me at all, your *highness.*"

The words cut deep, and Dorian shrank before them, guilt gnawing through his chest.

"I didn't mean... I appreciate your... I'm..." Dorian closed his eyes, unable to find the words. The fire flickered and danced, throwing cruel shadows across his eyelids.

They reminded him of demons.

Of hell.

In a dark, defeated whisper he barely recognized as his own, Dorian said finally, "Charlotte's hellbound, Aiden. Isabelle found some sort of demonic claim on her soul."

The admission stabbed a fresh hole into his heart, and he opened his eyes to relay the witch's assessment, every word burning through him like the blazing fire.

She's demon-touched...

A dark shadow...

Promised to a demon lord...

"But that's..." Aiden's mouth widened in shock, abject horror dousing the anger in his eyes. "No. I refuse to accept it."

"As do I, but refusal doesn't change the fact that soon

—*very* soon, according to Isabelle—the woman I love will be…" Dorian's voice broke, and he turned away, unable to face his oldest friend.

A hush fell between them, broken only by the crackle of the flames and a lone mourning dove cooing in the distance.

It was a long moment before Aiden spoke again, and when he did, his voice had softened considerably. "There's another way, Dori. There's *always* another way."

"And if I had an eternity to find it, I'm certain I could. But I *don't* have an eternity, Aiden. I'm not even sure I've got a week."

"Have you told Charlotte about this?"

"I… I need more information."

"She has a right to know."

"Yes, and exercising that right means unleashing a thousand desperate questions I can't even *begin* to answer." Dorian sighed. He was wasting time—time he desperately needed if he had any hopes of breaking that demonic bond. "I'm sorry, Aiden. I need to go."

He turned away from the flames and took a step toward the manor, but Aiden stepped in front of him, a deadly warning flashing in his eyes.

"Whatever you're thinking," Aiden said, "it's a rotten idea."

"You've no idea what I'm thinking."

"You've got the look. You're about to do something reckless and impulsive that will either get you killed or—"

"No one ever won a war by staying home."

"No one ever won a war by himself, either." Aiden grumbled something beneath his breath, then said, "If you insist on marching to your doom, I'm coming with you."

"No. I need you to keep watch over Charlotte. Colin said she needs to be monitored hourly for symptoms of concussion."

"As will you if you don't tell me what you're up to."

Frustration surged in Dorian's chest, but he knew Aiden wouldn't let him off the hook. "I'm going back to the city to find some Rogozin hellspawn to torture. Surely one of them knows something."

Aiden beamed. "Brilliant! And... Not happening."

"Today is *not* the day to test me, Aiden."

"Nor is it the day to storm the demonic castle and pick off Rogozin's underlings." Aiden gripped Dorian's shoulder. "Not alone, not while you're half out of your mind with rage, and *certainly* not without—"

"A witch."

Both men turned at the sound of the sudden proclamation, and Isabelle stepped out through the broken doorway, her gaze stern as she picked her way across the glass-strewn path. If the sight of the demolished dining room or towering inferno alarmed her, she hid it well.

Fear spiked in Dorian's gut. "Is Charlotte—"

"She's resting comfortably," Isabelle said.

"Thank you for telling me," he said. "Aiden's going to look after her while I—"

"He's right, Dorian." Isabelle took a step closer, gazing up at him with the same beseeching look she'd given him the night of the fundraiser when he'd wanted to strangle Gabriel in the study. "You can't interrogate demons without someone who can bind them. They'll unleash hellfire the moment you make your presence known. Even if you manage to kill them before that, they'll simply jump into the closest human vessel and try again."

"Not to worry, Isabelle," Dorian said. "I've no need to kill them. Merely to prod their minds for a bit of information. If they happen to suffer in the process?" Dorian shrugged and glanced at his fingernails as if he hadn't a care in the world. "Ends, means, etcetera, etcetera."

"You mean to leave them alive?" Aiden asked. "So they can run straight to Rogozin and tell him what you've been on about? That we know Charlotte's uncle is one of them? That you're searching for a way to break her curse? Are you *trying* to paint another target on her back?"

Isabelle's eyes softened, and she let out a long, terrible sigh. "There *is* no way to break it, Dorian. It's not a curse— it's a binding contract."

"All contracts have loopholes," Dorian said.

"Not when they're forged by a demon lord."

The reminder cleaved Dorian's heart in two, igniting his rage all over again.

"Bloody *hell*, do you two think me a fool? Oh, *yes*, I'll just march in there straightaway and ask Rogozin's dim-witted servants to point me in the direction of the filthy miscreant who's cursed my woman to hell. *Excellent* plan!"

Isabelle glanced at Aiden, worry creasing her brow. "We weren't suggesting—"

9

"Understand something—both of you." Dorian jabbed a finger toward the second story of the manor. "That woman sleeping off a possible head injury in my bed? She is *everything* to me. If she's in danger, I'll stop at *nothing* to obliterate it— including finding a way to break an allegedly unbreakable demonic bind. But I will *not* bring her further harm by blundering my way through an interrogation that even a simpleton could handle. We need to know about Rogozin's plans, including the extent of Rudy's involvement and where they might be keeping Sasha. Absent a better idea, torturing a few useless demons is the fastest and most reliable route. If either of you find such methods unsuitable, I'll invite you to keep your commentary to yourselves and leave me to my work."

"You'll have to excuse him," Aiden said to Isabelle. "You'd think after all these centuries living among mortals, he'd be more of a people person by now, and yet…"

"I'm not a *person*, Aiden. I'm a vampire, and I've got important business to attend to. So if you'll excuse me—"

"You need me," Isabelle said. "I can subdue the demons and prevent them from casting hellfire. And when you're finished with the questioning, I can eliminate them before they reveal your actions to Rogozin."

"Banishment?" Dorian narrowed his eyes. Banishing demons was an extremely particular skill set—one most upstanding witches avoided. "I thought your gift was empathic magic."

"And I thought you were a people person. Seems we've both misjudged." She flashed a quick smile, breaking some of the tension. Then, sobering again, "I walk the dark path on occasion, Dorian. Doing so allows me to appreciate the light all the more."

"What I'm about to do is a direct violation of the Shadow Accords, not to mention an invitation to more bloodshed. Risking my own head is one thing, but I can't ask you to—"

"You're not asking. I'm offering," Isabelle said. "Besides, demon blood is almost as useful to me as yours. I could stand to restock."

"Restock. Right." Dorian folded his arms across his chest, scrutinizing her face for the lie. "Why are you doing this? And don't tell me it's got anything to do with your dwindling supplies, or even upholding your father's wishes for Armitage Holdings."

"I told you last night," she said. "When it comes to family obligations, there's a thin line between duty and imprisonment. Let's just say I'm ready to redraw that line for myself."

"Meaning?"

She held his gaze for another beat, assessing him as plainly as he'd been assessing her.

"I'm tired of wasting my considerable talents managing my brothers' affairs," she finally said, "and I've no interest in freelancing. For years, I've been searching for a vampire partnership that will grant me the freedom to explore a... Let's call it a non-traditional course." She met his gaze, her eyes fierce and formidable in the firelight. "My intuition tells me House Redthorne is not only tolerant of such an approach, but in desperate need of it."

Dorian couldn't argue with that. "I appreciate the honesty."

"That's all you'll ever get from me, Dorian. If you're looking for someone to pour sugar over shit and call it a cupcake, I'm afraid this is where we part ways."

Dorian almost laughed, but Isabelle was dead serious.

He looked at her with new eyes, his respect and appreciation growing. There were few people he trusted in this world, but Isabelle Armitage might soon become one of them.

"Very well," he finally said. "Gather your things and wait for me in the garage. I need a moment with Aiden."

Isabelle nodded, then headed back into the house.

Next to him, Aiden had his phone out, thumbs flying across the screen.

"Who are you texting?" Dorian asked.

"Gabriel. You need backup on this."

"You don't trust Isabelle?"

"Listen, Dori. Any woman who can put you in your place like that is a bloody godsend. But if she's busy muting and banishing demons, you'll need someone to pass you the fire poker."

"The… what?"

"Honestly. Did they teach you nothing at royal vampire school?" Aiden rolled his eyes. "Shoving a hot poker up a demon's ass is a two-man job."

"Thank you, as ever, for the visual. But Gabriel isn't…"

Dorian crouched down to retrieve another loose piece of wood, then whipped it into the fire. "The only reason he's even tracking Silas is that it gives him an excuse to avoid me at Ravenswood."

"Never thought I'd say this about Gabriel, but perhaps you don't give him enough credit."

"He's literally the *last* vampire looking to help me. Well, second-last, if we're counting the brother whose heart I nearly excavated."

"Lucky for us, torture is a game the whole family can play. And from what I hear, the cold-hearted little princeling is a real pro." Aiden finished up his text, then waited for the return message.

After what felt like an eternity, the phone finally buzzed.

"Well?" Dorian asked.

"He says to text him when you're close. He'll meet you outside the Sixty-First Street Station in—"

"Woodside?" Dorian got to his feet and dusted off his hands. "That's in Queens. Rogozin's territory."

"Precisely. Gabriel says Rogozin's got some sort of chop shop in the neighborhood."

"That's... that's actually a good lead."

"No one knows how to navigate the seedy metropolitan underbellies of the world like your baby brother." Aiden slipped the phone back into his pocket. "Right, then. You've got your witch, your assistant torturer, and of course—favorite among favorites—me, entrusted with looking after the lovely Ms. D'Amico, hoping like hell she doesn't wake up and ask me where you've gone. How I get myself into these escapades is beyond me, but you're welcome."

Dorian smiled, the crushing weight on his chest lifting just a fraction. "Thank you, Aiden. Truly."

"Just come back to me in one piece, you damned fool."

"I shall do my best."

"I mean it, Dori. I'm not redecorating the dining room alone. Ask anyone—I'm right terrible at blending textures and patterns."

"Good to know," Dorian said. Then, shocking them both, he hauled Aiden in for a hug, holding him tight. "Take care of my woman. And save me a few marshmallows—I'll be back before you know it."

CHAPTER TWO

If there was one thing Charley's years of thieving and con artistry had taught her, it was how to compartmentalize.

So when the sun dawned on a new day after the worst night of her life, Charley took a deep breath, reminded herself that Sasha was a total badass, and shoved everything else into that rusty metal box inside her.

A fear so sharp it shredded her heart.

A rage so blinding it made her tremble.

A loss so deep and dark it threatened to swallow her whole.

None of that shit would help Sasha. Right now, she needed to stay focused. Rudy was a demon, but he still had weaknesses. With Dorian's help, Charley would find them, exploit them, and get her sister back.

And then?

Rudy would burn.

It was that simple.

Ignoring the headache and the dull throb of the cuts in her mouth and on her hands, Charley wrapped herself in Dorian's sweatshirt and headed downstairs in search of strong coffee or a strong drink—either would suffice. Instead, she found Aiden, sitting alone at the table in the breakfast nook, his face smudged with soot, his gaze a million miles away.

"Aiden?" she said softly, taking a seat across from him. "Are you... Is everything okay?"

The air on the main floor was heavy with the scent of woodsmoke, and the vampire himself looked as if he'd just escaped a fire.

It took him a beat to respond, but when he finally looked up at her, a faint smile touched his lips, and he blinked away the haze from his eyes. "Ms. D'Amico. I thought for sure you'd sleep the day away. Are you feeling all right?"

"As well as can be expected. But..." She took a deep breath of smoke-scented air and narrowed her eyes, taking in his disheveled appearance. "Was there a fire?"

"In the rose garden, yes. Completely controlled, I assure you." He ran a hand through his hair, his fingers coming away with ash. "Dorian just needed to... clear out a bit of old junk. In with the new, as they say. How's your head?"

"Still attached to my body. I suppose that's something, right?" Charley closed her eyes and turned toward the window, basking for a moment in the sunshine streaming through the pane. "Where *is* Dorian, anyway? I tried to wait up for him last night, but I guess I kept passing out. I don't think he ever came to bed."

"He's in the city with Gabriel following up on another lead, but not to worry. I'm looking after you today, so anything you need, you just let me know."

The fact that Dorian had left without telling her stung, but she understood why he'd done it.

Dorian and Gabriel were vampires—damn near impenetrable. She was a fragile human, as weak and breakable as glass. Whatever lead they were chasing now, Charley would only get in the way.

With a deep sigh, she opened her eyes and met Aiden's gaze across the table. He was so calming, so kind. And last night, he'd risked his life for her—first in coordinating the art buy with Vincent Estas, then in fighting off those grays...

God. She was so grateful, yet she couldn't find a single word to express it.

"What is it?" he asked, his brow creasing with worry.

"I... I don't deserve your kindness, Aiden. This is... It's all my fault."

"Nonsense. You certainly didn't kick your *own* ass last night. As a matter of fact, you faced down some pretty terrible odds, and came out—well, slightly worse for the wear, but still. Here you are, head attached, as you've so keenly noted."

She wanted to return his smile, but she couldn't. Despite her best efforts at compartmentalizing, the guilt still burned in her gut. "I need to tell you something, Aiden. It's about my uncle and—"

"The sodding demon, you mean."

"Yes. He's also my boss." Charley's stomach churned, but she forced herself to continue. "He's an art thief—*we're* art thieves. We were plotting to rob the manor. To rob Dorian. His brothers. All of you. That's the reason all of this happened. The reason Sasha's missing, and you're stuck babysitting a chick with a possible head injury, and Dorian's out there chasing down who knows what, and..."

Before she could stop herself, she blurted out the whole story—how she and Dorian had met at the Salvatore auction, how Rudy had zeroed in on him after she'd mentioned the Whitfield, how she'd been running schemes her entire adult life.

Charley's shame and embarrassment were so immense, she was sure she'd combust. But through every terrible confession, the kindness in Aiden's eyes never dimmed.

"It's all in the past, Ms. D'Amico," he said when she'd finally run out of words. "No need to further torment yourself."

"Wait. You... you knew." Charley stared open-mouthed as the realization struck, but she shouldn't have been surprised. He was Dorian's oldest friend—and a damn good one at that. She suspected there weren't an awful lot of secrets between them.

"Cole as well," Aiden admitted. "Dorian's not one for gossip. He simply wanted us to understand the situation before we approached Estas."

Another flame of guilt licked down her spine, but Charley nodded. Her own mortification aside, it was good Dorian had told them. They had a right to know what kind of person they were fighting for. What kind of person had caused so much destruction.

"I'm so sorry," she said. "I realize those are just words, but for what it's worth... I know you're all risking a lot for me. I... I guess I'm still working on deserving it."

"Dorian is my brother, Ms. D'Amico, in all the ways that count. He loves you, he trusts you, and he's forgiven you." He reached across the table and took her hand, giving her an encouraging squeeze. "That's enough for me. Let it be enough for you as well."

She pulled her hand back and lowered her gaze, blinking back tears. "I want to. Really. I just... Sometimes I still can't believe he stayed, you know? It would've been so easy for him to walk away—to avoid all of this. He had so many opportunities to bail, but he never did. Not really."

"Nor will he." Aiden let out a soft sigh. "Dorian Redthorne is, among other things, a complicated vampire. I've known him for centuries—literal centuries. I've seen him through the worst moments of his life as well as the best. Through all of them, he's carried a darkness inside him that would utterly annihilate a lesser man... And then he met you."

"But that's the thing," Charley said, finally meeting Aiden's eyes again. "He's *not* dark, Aiden. He's *haunted* by darkness, he struggles with it, but the darkness itself—it's not who he is."

"No, it isn't." Aiden's eyes shone with affection. "And you're helping him remember it, I think. For that, I'm grateful to *you*, Ms. D'Amico."

Charley's heart ached, but she managed a small smile anyway. "Then as a show of your gratitude," she teased, "you need to call me Charlotte. Or Charley. Take your pick."

"Very well, Charlotte. But now, I should let you get back to bed. I promised Dori I'd look after you, and here I am, chatting your ear off." He rose from the table. "I'll come check on you again in a bit."

"Wait." She reached up and touched his arm. "Don't go. I… I won't be able to get back to sleep anyway."

"You must try, Charlotte. Dorian will be back later, and I'm sure he'll have good news. There's nothing more you can do right now."

"I need to at least *attempt* to figure this thing out. And to be honest, I could use the company… if you're up for it?"

Aiden held her gaze another moment, then finally nodded. "Very well. I'll put the kettle on, and you can tell me everything you remember about what happened last night. Perhaps we missed a clue."

Charley nodded. It was a good idea, especially now that her head had cleared a bit.

"Mind if I crash your little tea party?" Cole stepped in through the garage door, his face and flannel smudged with dirt, a rogue maple leaf dangling from his scruffy beard. Like Aiden, he clearly hadn't slept last night, but his smile was warm and genuine. When he shot her a quick wink, it filled Charley with hope and relief.

They were good men, Dorian's friends. And for reasons she still couldn't fathom, they'd taken her in and made her one of their own, faults and fuckups and all.

"How do you take your tea, wolf?" Aiden asked, brushing the leaf from Cole's beard.

Cole procured a small bottle of booze from his inside flannel pocket. "I'm easy. Straight from the bottle for me."

Aiden rolled his eyes. "That's whiskey."

"Well, it *rhymes* with tea, don't it? Right there at the end?"

"An artist *and* a poet?" Charley grinned, then held out her hand and gestured for the bottle. "We are *definitely* going to be friends, Cole Diamante."

CHAPTER THREE

Friends.

Charley let the word settle inside her, slowly warming her heart. For all the luxuries her lifestyle afforded, friends had never been one of them.

Until now.

It was yet another gift Dorian had brought into her life —one she wouldn't squander.

"The grays were confined to the alley," Aiden said, passing Charley a mug of English Breakfast tea. "There were no other reports of them in Manhattan last night."

"Not of grays, anyway," Cole said. "But I got word of something else. Remember that traffic clusterfuck we hit coming off the FDR?"

"Don't tell me it was more grays," Charley said.

"Worse." Cole took a swig of whiskey, then said, "Demons."

"You've *got* to be bloody kidding me," Aiden said. "What happened?"

"Turf war, apparently. I got a shifter friend in homicide. She told me the cops are calling it gang-related, but the bodies—nine of 'em—were charred to shit. No eyes, either. Cops thought it was a bomb or maybe even a chemical attack—that's why they were blocking everything off last night, searching the cars."

"Have they identified any of the bodies?" Aiden asked.

Cole nodded. "Four so far. Three are Chernikov's guys. One is Rogozin's."

"Why are demons fighting over turf in Manhattan?" Charley asked. "Isn't that vampire territory?"

"Indeed, it is." Aiden dumped some more sugar into his tea and frantically stirred, spoon clanking hard against his mug.

It reminded Charley of her sister, and her chest immediately tightened. Was Rudy feeding her a decent breakfast? What about coffee—did he get her the almond creamer she liked so much? Did she have any books to read? A warm bed?

"Shitstorm's brewin', my friends," Cole said, drawing Charley back to the moment just before the flood of worries swept her away. "Better get your umbrellas ready."

Forcing herself to refocus, Charley poured a splash of Cole's whiskey into her tea, then said, "I don't know what's going on with the demons, but the thing about the grays is weird. You said there were no other sightings in the city?"

"None reported," Aiden said.

"They weren't even there when that Silas guy first blurred me into the alley," Charley said. "They showed up right after he dropped me in the dumpster. Literally a minute later."

"They must've been holdin' the fuckers somewhere close," Cole said. "Probably had 'em right there in the building. If that many grays had come in from outside, you would've heard trucks or something."

"It was definitely a setup," Charley said. "The timing is too perfect otherwise."

"But if your uncle wanted you dead, why go to so much trouble?" Aiden asked. "Why not order Silas to do it? Or why not do it himself, for that matter? He certainly had the opportunity."

"There's a lot about last night that doesn't add up." Charley took a deep drink of her spiked tea, trying to put all the strange, mismatched pieces together.

First of all, Rudy had allowed Silas to rough her up, which left visible injuries. Rudy *had* to know Dorian would notice them and question her about what happened. What if he got suspicious? This close to the big day, something like that could throw a wrench into everything. It was a sloppy move for a pro thief like her uncle, and it made no sense.

Then there was the matter of the gun. Between Rudy and his vampire buddy, they had all the supernatural power they needed to keep Charley in line, yet he still felt the need to flash that weapon.

And what was the deal with his watch? When she'd

inadvertently torn it from his wrist, it revealed his terrifying black eyes. But didn't most demons look human? And if demonic entities took over human bodies as vessels, why did *demon* Rudy still have all of *human* Rudy's mannerisms and memories?

Charley shared all of this with the guys. The longer she spoke, the more outlandish it all sounded.

"Bloody hell," Aiden said, shooting a worried glance at Cole. "Rudy isn't just a vessel. He's a host."

"A host?" Charley tightened her hands around the mug, trying to remember what Dorian had told her about demons the day he'd given her the supernatural crash course. "So Rudy's basically letting a demon hitch a ride?"

"It's the best of both worlds, really," Aiden said. "Rudy has access to the demon's power, and the demon has access to a physical body, which he can use as he sees fit, and claim fully when your uncle dies."

"But if that's true," she said, "it still doesn't explain the gun."

"Perhaps he just wanted to frighten you."

"That's just it. Rudy's *addicted* to power. If he had something more than that weapon, he would've relished the chance to use it against me, even if he'd only intended to make Silas compel me later. He gets off on terrifying me."

"What are you suggesting?" Aiden asked.

"I think there's something wrong with him. Like, maybe his power is fading or something. It might explain why he's becoming so unhinged. I'm telling you, guys. He never used to be so sloppy and erratic."

"I suppose it's possible. I've never encountered a host before." Aiden looked to Cole. "You?"

"Nah, but I don't get out much. Matter of fact, hangin' out with *you* fuckers is the most excitement I've had in decades."

Aiden lifted his mug and smiled. "Cheers, then."

"There's something else," Charley said. "At one point, Silas said he wanted to end me right there, but Rudy called him off. He said something about how I wasn't theirs to end."

"Do you think he was referring to the grays?" Aiden asked.

"I did at first, but that makes no sense. Rudy doesn't want me dead at all. He needs me—he still thinks I'm helping with the Ravenswood job. Otherwise, why use Sasha as leverage if he was only going to let the grays kill me before the heist?"

"So either Silas changed the play at the last minute," Aiden said, "or they were simply trying to frighten you."

"That's a hell of a risk just for a scare. If those grays had gotten into the dumpster..." Charley shuddered, then reached for the whiskey again. Right now, it was the only thing steadying her nerves. "Anyway, why did they want me to see the grays at all? They'd have to know I'd freak out, right? Rudy wants me focused on the job, not questioning my sanity."

"Which means he probably assumed Dorian would compel you to forget the gray attack," Aiden said. "Rudy's a demon host working with vampires. He must know Dorian isn't human. He must've known all along."

"Then he's also assuming I *don't* know Dorian's true nature." Charley let out a bitter laugh. "Rudy probably thinks I'd run away with my tail between my legs if I knew vampires existed."

"Your uncle underestimates you, Charlotte," Aiden said. "A mistake he'll live to regret, I'm certain."

"You two got some nice theories," Cole said, "but something tells me this ain't about you, Charles."

Charley cocked an eyebrow. "Charles, huh?"

"Just tryin' it out," Cole said with a teasing smile. "You good?"

"Actually, yes. I like it."

"Figured you would." Cole topped off her tea with another splash of whiskey, then took another swig. "Anyway, it *was* a setup—you got that right. All so those demonic dickheads could watch us in action."

"I'm not following," she said.

"Right before you and Red split up, he was ambushed by a Rogozin demon and two Duchanes bloodsuckers, yeah?"

Charley nodded. "That's how I ended up alone outside Perk. Dorian was dealing with the ambush, and I ran ahead to find Sasha. That's when Silas tossed my ass into the limo."

"They knew your man was close," Cole continued. "Knew he'd track you down as soon as he dealt with his attackers. They just needed enough time to threaten you, scare you shitless, and dump you in that other alley, where the grays were already on standby."

"They wanted to see how we'd deal with the grays." Aiden's eyes widened with the realization. "Like a football team watching their rivals' old games."

"Which means those sonofabitches are planning something even bigger," Cole said. "And now they know just what we're bringing to the party."

"Do you have any idea where Rudy might be holding Sasha?" Aiden asked gently. "Any other properties aside from his residence? Other associates who might have a place for them to hole up?"

"She could be anywhere, Aiden. Especially now that we know he's a demon. That opens up a whole new world of horrifying possibilities. God." Charley closed her eyes, willing herself not to cry. She'd been doing so well with the whole compartmentalizing thing, but all those fears and worries were doing their damnedest to break out of the box. "What if she's hurt? What if Rudy—"

Aiden gripped her hand, cutting her off. "Your sister is clever and tough, just like you. I've no doubts she's already making them rue the day they decided to mess with her. And just wait until *we* get hold of them. Talk about ruing the day."

When Charley opened her eyes again, Aiden gave her a soft smile.

"We'll find her, Charlotte. You have my word."

"I know," she said, if only because there was no room in her brain for any other possibility. Then, with a surge of renewed determination, "The original plan stands. We'll hit Estas' place in Woodstock tomorrow, see what intel we can find."

"Let's wait and talk to Dorian," Aiden said. "I'm certain he'll—"

"Try to talk me out of it, most likely. Unfortunately for *that* bossy vampire, I'm not the sit-home-with-my-thumb-up-my-ass type."

"No, I suppose you ain't." Cole bit back a laugh, his eyes twinkling with warmth. "Bet Red never saw you comin', did he?"

"To be fair, I didn't see him coming either." Charley smiled, but despite their kindness and willingness to help, she couldn't hold it. "Anyway, with Rudy's big demon reveal last night, and his connection to that Silas vampire, I'm more convinced than ever Estas has something on him. Maybe even something that can help us find Sasha."

"All roads lead back to the same scheming demons and traitor vamps," Cole said.

"And they all want me and Dorian dead." Charley lifted the mug to her lips, but it was empty. "Awesome."

"On the bright side," Aiden said cheerfully, "some couples have *nothing* in common. More tea?"

Charley passed over her mug.

"We need time to set up another buy," Cole said. "I came through with the cash last night—Estas trusts me now. So I'll lure him out for another sale, dick him around at the meeting, and give you and Red time to snoop."

"Perfect," Charley said. "When can you set it up?"

"We need to wait for Red. He's the bankroll here."

"Not to mention he'd bloody well beat Cole's ass if we went behind his back on this," Aiden said.

Cole laughed. "He'd *try*, anyway."

"Where *exactly* did you say Dorian went today?" Charley asked.

"Not to worry." Aiden forced a smile, then headed to the stove to put the kettle on for Charley's tea. "He'll be back soon enough. He's just... cooking up a little something in Queens."

CHAPTER FOUR

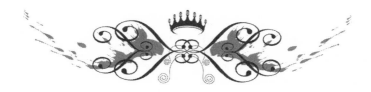

"Ah, there's nothing quite like the smell of fire-roasted demon." Gabriel took a deep breath and grinned. "Reminds me of that time in Paris. Do you remember, brother?"

"Summer, 1941?" Dorian laughed, adjusting the flame on the blowtorch to its highest level. "Goodness, I haven't thought of that trip in an age."

"Father always said French demons burned the hottest."

"And we certainly proved that, didn't we?"

"Several times, as I recall."

"Are you two fucking *crazy*?" The roasted demon in question—a vile, sniveling knob called Jordan, according to the embroidered patch on his mechanic's uniform—squirmed in his chair. He was already nursing third-degree burns on both arms, and blood leaked from a gash on his head, courtesy of his own tire iron.

To be fair, he'd swung first. And that was only after they'd walked in on him terrorizing a young woman in one of the auto detailing bays, his hellspawn brethren cheering him on from the sidelines.

If Dorian had any thought of going easy on the demons today, he'd lost it the moment he'd seen *that* sick little show.

Between Isabelle's quick work with the binding magic and Gabriel's quicker work with the tire iron, none of the assholes had a chance. After ensuring the woman wasn't physically injured, Dorian compelled her to forget the demonic torment and escorted her outside to safety.

By the time he returned, Isabelle and Gabriel had everything under control.

Now, all five of the demons they'd found here were doubly bound—chained to metal chairs strategically positioned on top of devil's trap sigils Isabelle had painted in vampire blood. The measures eliminated all possibility of escape—bodily or otherwise.

The chop shop itself was proving to be the perfect torture chamber—a mid-sized operation posing as a legitimate auto mechanic and detailing business chock full of power tools and sharp, heavy implements. Isabelle had spelled it to appear closed and gated from the outside, leaving them to do their business undisturbed.

It really had been a bloody brilliant idea.

"*He's* definitely crazy," Gabriel said to the demon now, arcing his thumb at Dorian. "Me? I'm just bored." In a blur, he grabbed the blowtorch from Dorian's hands and raked the flame across the demon's thigh, cutting clear down to the bone.

The demon howled in agony, his screams echoing off the concrete floor.

Music to Dorian's ears.

He no longer cared about Accords violations, or demonic retribution, or his own dubious moral compass. These bastards reported to Rogozin, which meant they were connected to Estas, who was connected to Rudy, who'd kidnapped the sister of the woman Dorian loved.

Furthermore, if Dorian followed the chain of command from Rogozin up through the levels of hell's top management, he'd eventually reach the demon lords—one of whom was under the mistaken impression he had a claim on Charlotte's life.

Dorian was more than eager to set that particular record straight. If he had to brutalize a few hellspawn minions in the process? Well. Who said mixing business with pleasure was a bad thing?

"Aiden was right," Dorian said brightly. "Torturing demons is *definitely* a two-man job. Mind if I give it a go?"

"By all means." Gabriel passed him the blowtorch, the mirth in his tone a stark contrast to the ice in his gaze.

Not since childhood had Dorian felt so connected to his little brother. As much as Dorian had judged him— despised him, even—he was certain if he looked in the mirror now, he'd find the same frigid determination in his eyes, the same cold cruelty that had earned Gabriel such a merciless reputation in Las Vegas.

Perhaps it should've bothered him—how close he felt to his own darkness. His own savagery.

Instead, it only fueled him.

He grabbed the demon by the throat and brought the flame to his eye, melting it in an instant.

"Stop! *Stop!*" Jordan bellowed, piss soaking through what was left of his torched pants. "I'll tell you anything! I swear it!"

"That's what you said fifteen minutes ago," Dorian reminded him, unrelenting in his torment. The skin around the demon's eye socket blistered and blackened, smoke wafting up from the wound. Fat, juicy tears leaked from his remaining eye.

"I mean it this time!" he cried. "Just... God, please stop! Please!"

Dorian finally backed off. "*God*? You're a demon, for fuck's sake. Show some self-respect."

The demon turned his head and spit out a mouthful of blood, but offered no witty comeback, no threats, no curses.

Demons could withstand unfathomable amounts of pain, but now, he was utterly broken.

Perfect.

"What does Rogozin want with Duchanes vampires?" Dorian asked, handing the blowtorch back to Gabriel.

"I... I don't know," he panted.

"So you and your friends *haven't* been cavorting at Bloodbath—a known Duchanes establishment?"

"Point of clarification, brother," Gabriel said, "Bloodbath is a *former* Duchanes establishment. Your friend at the NYPD made certain of that."

"Very true, Gabriel. Thank you."

"Do I *look* like the club-hopping type? *Fuck.*" Jordan slid partway off the chair, his ruined eye still smoldering, his legs trembling. "All I do is work. If I'm not here working on the cars, I'm running my ass all over Queens like a fucking errand boy."

"What sort of errands?"

"Drop-offs, pickups—shit like that."

"Dorian!" Gabriel gasped and pressed a hand to his chest, his voice laden with mock concern. "I believe he's referring to… to drug trafficking!"

"Rogozin has lots of different businesses," Jordan said. "I don't ask questions. I just do what I'm told."

"Were you doing what you were told when you kidnapped a teenaged girl?" Dorian asked.

"What? Look, I'm not saying I'm the most upstanding citizen, but kidnapping a girl? No. No *fucking* way."

"Right. Because you have so much respect for women?"

"Look, that bitch you saw in there? She had it coming. Her brother tried to welsh on his deal, and—"

"Now *that* was *definitely* the wrong thing to say." Dorian grabbed the torch and scored a fresh gash across the demon's chest, carving his flesh open from one shoulder to the other. "Women are not property to be bartered in deals."

"Fuck! *Fuck!* I know. I'm sorry. I'm so sorry. Fuck, man, I've never been more sorry in my life. I swear."

Dorian returned the blowtorch to Gabriel. "You're doing a lot of swearing today, Jordan, but not a lot of sharing. So tell me—what is Rogozin's relationship to House Duchanes?"

The demon remained silent.

Dorian glanced at Gabriel, who took a step closer with the torch.

"Come *on*!" Jordan cried. He was fading now, his breathing becoming more erratic. He'd lost a lot of blood already, and the pain alone was likely enough to drive his human vessel into unconsciousness, even if the demon himself could withstand the agony.

He was still lucid, but Dorian knew they didn't have much time.

"*Duchanes*," Dorian said again.

"Look, Rogozin doesn't waste his time with vampire bullshit," the demon said. "Duchanes? Yeah, I seen him around, but he's not part of the crew."

"You're certain? Certain your boss isn't working with Duchanes vampires to break a few more demons out of hell? Build an army, perhaps?"

"I told you—Rogozin doesn't give a fuck about vampires. Doesn't give a fuck about bringing in more demons either. Our numbers are rock-solid."

Dorian smacked him twice on the ruined cheek. "Slightly less solid after today, perhaps."

"You don't get it. If Rogozin wanted an army, he'd fucking build one. Meat-suits are a dime a dozen in this city —everyone's looking to make a deal."

"If he doesn't want more demons, then what is he after?"

"Same as every other supernatural in this city."

"Fae pussy?" Gabriel blurted out.

Dorian rolled his eyes. "Must you *always* be so uncouth, brother? Honestly."

Jordan spit out another mouthful of blood. "Rogozin wants territory."

"Where? Manhattan?" Dorian asked.

"Nah, that's bloodsucker domain. Too much trouble. Rogozin wants to expand our enterprise in the boroughs, maybe set up shop in a few more states."

"*Chernikov's* territory?" Dorian glared at him, shocked at the revelation. The two factions had a lifelong rivalry, but going after Chernikov's holdings was a suicide mission, even for the most powerful demons. "Rogozin wants to make a play against bloody *Chernikov*?"

The demon shot him a one-eyed glare, his silence all the confirmation Dorian needed.

"Is he looking to start a war?" Dorian asked.

"Look, you didn't hear it from me, okay? But Chernikov... He's been ramping shit up in a big way. Pushing his guys to close more deals, giving them quotas for souls. Rogozin doesn't like it."

"Well, Chernikov is top dog for a reason. You don't get there by resting on your laurels, Jordy."

"This is different. Bigger."

"How?"

He clammed up again, lowering his gaze.

Dorian was nearly out of patience. "What do you know of a man called Rudy D'Amico?"

The demon's face paled behind the wounds. "I... nothing. I mean, I'm not—"

"Are you familiar with a vampire called Silas?"

"Who?"

"Were you or were you not involved in the kidnapping of the human girl? One who's safety and wellbeing are *extremely* important to me?"

"Look, guys. I don't know where you're getting your intel, but all this shit is *way* above my pay grade. I never heard of a vampire named Silas. And all I know about D'Amico is he's some kind of demon thief who's got a lead on something the boss wants *real* bad."

Dorian's heart sputtered. Was he referring to Charlotte? To her soul? Was it Rudy who'd brokered the deal with the demon lord, selling out his own niece for a better position in hell's ultimate army?

"*What* something?" Dorian demanded.

"Again, above my pay grade."

"Is there anything *not* above your pay grade, you worthless fuck?" Dorian kicked his chair, and the demon flinched. "You report directly to Rogozin, do you not?"

"So?"

"Who does Rogozin report to?"

"The fuck you think?"

"I *think*," Dorian said, leaning in close, "you and your brethren should've spent less time stealing cars and more time studying the Shadow Accords. If you had, perhaps you would've known to show some deference to me today, and you'd be walking out of here with your balls still attached. Alas…"

Dorian nodded at Gabriel, who cranked up the flame

and shoved it near the demon's crotch, just shy of his most prized possession.

"I don't know their names!" Jordan cried, desperately inching away from the terrible blue flame. "They're demon lords, okay? They don't fuck around with our business. They're just a bunch of stuck-up cocksuckers who never leave hell. Half the guys say they don't even exist."

"And how does one communicate with a demon lord?" Dorian asked. "Assuming they do, in fact, exist—which is more than I can say for your cock if I don't like your answer."

"You don't communicate with them, man! They communicate with *you*, if and when they choose. But I told you— they don't give a rat's ass about anyone here on the earthly plane, so if you're after a hot date with the elites of hell, good fucking luck."

Dorian exchanged another quick glance with Gabriel, who nodded in return. They were on the same page. The interview was officially over.

"Thank you, Jordan," Dorian said, "for your *utter* uselessness. I'm afraid this is where we part ways, by which I mean we'll now be parting your essence from your vessel."

"What? But I told you everything I know! I cooperated! Let me go!"

"Let you go?" Dorian laughed. "What *ever* would I do for lunch? Torture leaves me quite famished, I'm afraid."

"Why are you doing this?"

"Should we tell him, brother?" Dorian asked Gabriel, unable to deny the urge to further taunt the bastard.

"Give him the multiple-choice answers," Gabriel said. "I love making them guess."

"Oh, very well." Dorian let out a put-upon sigh. "Why am I doing this, Jordan? Is it… A—because I'm the vampire king, B—because I'm hungry, C—because I *can*, or D—all of the above?"

"What? I don't—"

"Tick-tock, Jordy. Best guess." Dorian flashed a benevolent smile, and without awaiting Jordan's final answer, sank his fangs into the demon's neck.

The bastard fought hard for a moment, but Dorian truly *was* B—hungry, and in the span of thirty seconds, he drained his prey dry.

Just before the heartbeat finally stalled out, Dorian tore the body from its chains and launched it into the wall, unlocking its soul from the temporary prison of the devil's trap.

Thanks to Isabelle's handiwork, before the body even hit the floor, the demonic essence evaporated, exorcised to oblivion in a swirl of smoke.

The corpse turned as black as tar.

With a mouth full of blood and a vicious grin, Dorian looked to Gabriel and said, "Well don't just stand there, brother. Bring in contestant number two."

CHAPTER FIVE

Five vanquished demons and an ocean of rancid blood later, Dorian and Gabriel were no closer to finding Sasha, uncovering Rogozin's grand scheme, sussing out Rudy's angle, or learning a damn thing about Charlotte's mark than they were when they'd begun this dreadful day.

But one thing was certain.

Among the warring demonic factions of New York City, *someone* needed to get his story straight.

Wiping the last of the foul-tasting demon blood from his mouth, Dorian said, "Chernikov suggested at our meeting —quite convincingly—that Rogozin had been working with dark witches to open the demonic portals and flood the city with demons. But if *these* pricks are to be believed, Rogozin's got an entirely different modus operandi, and Chernikov is the one building up his armies."

"That's the thing," Gabriel said. "I *did* believe them."

"As did I."

"Maybe they're just not privy to the boss' master plan."

Dorian shook his head. "You don't plan an operation of that magnitude and leave out your key enforcers. Something isn't adding up."

"You think Chernikov's bullshitting you, then?"

"Oh, he's absolutely bullshitting me. The question is... what about? And to what end?" Dorian toed one of the blackened corpses at his feet. "The only thing I'm certain of is that he desperately wants the Mother of Lost Souls. As long as he believes I can procure it for him, he'll string me along by the balls for an eternity. How can I trust a word from his greasy mouth?"

"So what's our next move? There's another Rogozin stronghold a few blocks down—a butcher. That could be... fun."

"I'm not sure it would net us anything new." Dorian sighed, the stress of the last twenty-four hours finally catching up. He missed Charlotte. After all the bloodshed, all the burning flesh, all he wanted to do was go home to her, crawl into bed beside her, and let the warmth of her body and the sweetness of her scent take him someplace infinitely better.

But he couldn't. Not yet.

"We need to clean this up," he said, glancing around the bloodied garage. "Burn it, spread a rumor it was Chernikov demons. Better to let them fight it out amongst themselves."

Gabriel nodded. "We need to clean *us* up too. Bloody hell, these creatures are *disgusting*."

The brothers washed up in the men's room, eradicating

all traces of demon blood. Then, with Isabelle's help, they obliterated the devil's traps, burned the corpses, and torched the interior with a magical fire no one would see from the outside until the place was nothing but ash.

A lot of trouble, perhaps, but better than the alternative —having Rogozin show up at Ravenswood, demanding answers Dorian had no intention of providing.

Back out on Sixty-First Street, the sun shone bright overhead, casting their trio in a wash of unforgiving light.

Dorian winced, immediately stepping back into the shadows. His eyes throbbed, his mind going hazy.

That the copious amounts of demon blood he'd ingested hadn't been enough to stave off such sensitivity was surprising and concerning on its own. But worse?

Gabriel had shown the exact same response.

Dorian turned to him, eyes wide with surprise. Dorian had been experiencing similar symptoms for months, but it was the first evidence he'd seen that his brother was suffering a similar fate.

"Gabriel, are you—"

"All good." Gabriel forced a smile, but his eyes still held an echo of pain. He reached into his shirt pocket for his sunglasses and quickly shoved them onto his face.

Dorian wanted to press the issue, but they were no longer alone. A woman strolled by on the sidewalk, her long black hair fluttering in the breeze. She flashed a warm, flirtatious smile at Gabriel, blood rushing to her cheeks.

"Hello, love," Gabriel said smoothly, returning her smile.

She held his gaze another beat but continued on her way.

"I can help," Isabelle said when the woman had finally passed. She reached for his hands, just as she'd done with Dorian the night she'd recharged his magical tattoos, but Gabriel jerked away.

"I appreciate the offer, Isabelle, but I'm fine." Then, turning his attention to the raven-haired beauty's vanishing backside, he grinned and said, "Just a bit famished. Nothing I can't fix with a quick... *snack*."

"Gabriel," Dorian said, "I don't think—"

"Fear not, brother. I always ask nicely." He clapped Dorian on the back, and then he was off, chasing after the woman with all the cockiness his heartbreakingly good looks afforded.

"I apologize," Dorian said to Isabelle. "My brother is a bit touchy when it comes to witches. He's never quite forgiven himself for needing them."

"Please don't apologize. Gabriel's feelings toward me are merely a symptom of a much deeper issue. *Issues*, actually. He's... got a lot of inner work to do."

"I suppose you would know." Dorian smiled, but a new wave of sadness rose inside him. Trying to hold on to a connection with his brother—even one brought about by something as dark and brutal as torture—felt like trying to hold on to the wind itself.

As for the torture...

Dorian sighed. He had no love for demons, and he'd do

it again in a heartbeat if it meant protecting the people he cared about.

But out here in the bright, beautiful afternoon, surrounded by the rush of cars and pizza delivery bicycles and parents pushing strollers into their favorite shops and bakeries, his stomach churned nevertheless.

"Isabelle, what happened in there..." Dorian shook his head, shame heating his skin. "I don't know how much you saw or heard, but I—"

She held up a hand, cutting him off. "It's not my place to judge, Dorian. I said I'd have your back, and I meant it. But if we're going to continue working together, I'm afraid I do have *one* condition."

Dorian closed his eyes, already knowing what she was going to say.

Knowing he'd hate it.

Knowing she was absolutely right.

"Is this the part where I beg you for a sugar-covered shit-cake and we pretend everything's all right?" he asked.

"No, Dorian." She took his hands, imploring him with her wise, penetrating gaze. "This is the part where you go home and tell the woman you love the truth about her soul."

CHAPTER SIX

"Dorian?" Charley sat up in bed, blinking as her eyes adjusted to the darkness. "What... what time is it?"

Her vampire was sitting in a chair at the bedside, dressed in nothing but a pair of black silk pajama pants. Her gaze trailed up along the smooth, rigid planes of his abs and chest to his beautiful face, where she could just make out his features—the sharp lines of his jaw, the sweep of dark hair that fell over his forehead, the soulful eyes that glittered in the darkness.

Damn. Dorian Redthorne truly was a marvel. Day or night, Charley would never tire of looking at him.

But she could tell, even in the pitch black of the bedroom, something was wrong.

"After midnight," he said softly, then came to sit on the edge of the bed, so invitingly close the heat from his bare chest radiated against her skin.

"I missed you," she whispered.

"Charlotte, I..." He cupped her face, his eyes glazing with emotion. "I need to tell you something. It's important."

"Did you get a lead on Sasha?"

"No. This is... something else. I... It's..." He trailed off into a heavy sigh, his breath stirring the hair around her face.

She waited for him to continue, but he seemed totally lost, adrift on his own dark thoughts.

"I thought you'd be back this afternoon," she said, doing her best to hide the new fear coursing through her veins.

Dorian seemed to be carrying enough of it for both of them.

"I'm sorry. I... I had business in the city. I meant to return straightaway, but then I decided to pick up a few things, and after that I was just... driving. Trying to clear my head, but I..." He was looking right at her, but somehow *not*, as if he'd floated away to another realm and left his body behind.

"You're here now. That's what matters." She ran her fingers through his hair and down along his jawline, and he closed his eyes, leaning into her touch and letting out a soft hum of pleasure.

"You've *no* idea how much I was looking forward to that," he whispered.

"Me too." Charley continued stroking his skin, her thumb running back and forth over his earlobe. "How long have you been home? You should've woken me up."

Dorian turned and pressed a kiss to her wrist. "You needed the rest. Besides, I quite like watching you sleep. It calms me."

"Hmm. I can't decide if that makes it sound less creepy or more."

"Oh, I can be *very* creepy when properly provoked, Ms. D'Amico." Dorian winked, then wrapped her in his arms, holding her so tight it almost hurt to breathe.

Despite the light teasing, he was still so tense.

What are you not telling me?

Charley traced her fingers over the taut forearm wrapped around her midsection, noticing the stark contrast of his tattoos—the magic that allowed him to walk in the daylight, among other things. "They look darker tonight."

"I fed this morning. Not to worry—just a few sodding demons."

"Demons?" Alarm shot through her limbs, and she wriggled free from his iron grip to gaze up at his face. "What happened?"

"It doesn't matter, love. It's over now."

But it *wasn't* over—that much was obvious. His jaw was tight, his eyes haunted by a new darkness that hadn't been there last night, even after everything that had happened with Sasha, Rudy, and the grays in the alley.

"Dorian, please don't shut me out. Not now. We said no more secrets."

He cupped her face again, his touch as delicate as a feather. "It's not my intention to shut you out, Charlotte. I'm simply... I want to protect you. I *need* to protect you, and protecting you means showing some discretion with—"

"Bullshit." Charley glared at him, frustration rising in her voice. "Look. I realize you're an immortal vampire and I'm a weak human and you've got this whole overbearing, overprotective thing going on, and don't get me wrong—I appreciate it. Especially when you're hauling me out of dumpsters and beating off grays. But *this*?" She traced her fingertips over the wrinkle of tension between his eyes, then moved down to his chest, placing her hand flat against his bare skin. Beneath her touch, his heartbeat thrummed. "Whatever you're feeling, whatever you're going through, you don't have to protect me from it."

Dorian reached up and grabbed her hand, holding it firm against his chest. "You're *not* weak, Charlotte. Not by a long shot. But I'm not going to add to your nightmares just to momentarily unburden myself."

"I'm not afraid of your pain. Only of losing you to it."

He held her gaze a few more beats, then finally relented. "Gabriel and I interrogated some of Rogozin's demons today, hoping to net a bit of useful information. It was... unpleasant, to say the least. We left none alive."

"What happened?"

He closed his eyes and shook his head like he was trying to loosen whatever terrible memories had gotten stuck inside.

"Through all those gruesome hours," he said, "all I could think about was coming home to you. Coming home to *this* moment, right here. To your soft skin, to your perfect... *everything*." He drew her close again, burying his face against her neck and inhaling her scent. "You are the only good thing in... I can't..." His voice crumbled. "I've done things, Charlotte. Dark, *terrible* things I don't wish to bring home to the bed we share. Please don't ask me to."

The pain in his voice nearly broke her heart. She knew it'd cost him something to admit even *that* much—something she wasn't sure he'd meant to lose.

"I'm sorry," she whispered, because in all the things he *hadn't* said, the truth shone as starkly as if he'd written it in blood.

Whatever Dorian had done today, whatever brutalities he'd administered, whatever hell he'd put himself through... He'd done it for her.

She closed her eyes and lay her head against his chest, taking comfort in the strong, steady beat of his heart. Dorian slid his hand into her hair and stroked her head, and they held each other close, seconds turning to minutes, time slowing to grant them this momentary reprieve.

When the darkness finally began to abate, Dorian pulled back and glanced down at her face, his gaze sweeping to her mouth. The warmth had returned to his eyes, chasing off his earlier torments.

"How are you feeling?" he asked. "Any pain?"

"I was a little sore this morning, but I'm actually doing okay. Colin did a good job patching me up. I was hoping to thank him, but I didn't see him around today. Is he staying somewhere else?"

"I'm afraid Colin is still spending most of his time in the

crypts. My father left a number of medical journals in his laboratory there, and—"

"Wait. Your father had a medical lab? In the *crypts*?" Charley laughed. "That's what I get for skipping the official tour."

"The lab isn't part of the official tour. But if you'd like, I could put in a word with the owner." He brushed a powder-soft kiss across her lips and whispered, "I hear he likes you."

"Don't tell my vampire boyfriend. He's kind of the jealous type."

"Your vampire boyfriend is *definitely* the jealous type."

"Why do vampires even need crypts? I never understood that."

"They're a holdover from the original manor in West Sussex—all part of Father's re-creation. He used them for his own special projects—his medical research, mostly. Ironically, Augustus Redthorne *is* down there—what's left of him, anyway. Probably the only vampire in history to be interred in an actual tomb."

"Really?"

"He died there, Charlotte. We simply allowed him to remain."

"But... How did he die? I mean..." Charley sighed. They'd never really talked about his father's death, and she wasn't sure if that fell into the realm of dark things he didn't want to discuss tonight.

But before she could change the subject, he said, "My

father thought he'd found a way to reclaim his humanity. A cure for vampirism."

Charley gasped. "There's a cure?"

"So long as you're okay with the side effects. Namely, death within a matter of months."

"Holy shit," she breathed. "And your father... he discovered this cure?"

"He did."

"But... but what if someone found out? Couldn't your enemies use it against you? I mean, they could totally wipe out the vampire race!"

He held her gaze, his own stern and severe, his silence once again speaking volumes.

Demons, rival vampires, human hunters... Any number of enemies would probably *kill* to get their hands on that cure.

The realization blasted her in the face.

That's why he hadn't mentioned his father's lab before.

He hadn't trusted her.

But now...

She glanced up into his eyes again, and he nodded once, almost imperceptibly, as if he could read her thoughts.

He trusted her—with his life.

Just as she'd trusted him with hers.

Tears blurred her vision, but she quickly blinked them away. "How did the cure kill him?"

"It worked—well, technically speaking. It *did* cure him. But absent the magic and power of vampirism, he went through a rapid aging process. It was as if his body was trying to catch up with its sudden human reality. He was in his sixties when he turned. By the time he took the cure, he was nearly three hundred years old."

"Three hundred," she whispered. "That's... wow."

"It's a lot to wrap your head around. Some days, I barely manage it myself."

Charley touched Dorian's face, marveling once again at his existence. He would always look *exactly* the same. Ten years, fifty, a hundred—he wouldn't age a day.

How was it even possible? Even now, after everything she'd seen and experienced, she still couldn't believe it.

"So there's truly no going back?" she asked.

"Becoming a vampire isn't a costume, Charlotte." Dorian closed his eyes, his voice dropping to a dark whisper. "It's a life sentence. An *immortal* life sentence."

"Do you ever wish... I mean, if you *could* go back. Be human again—no side effects. Would you?"

"There was a time... I thought..." Dorian shook his head. "I've been a vampire for well over two hundred years —almost the entirety of my life. The truth is, Charlotte..." He opened his eyes again, their honey-brown depths threatening to swallow her whole. "I don't know how to be anything else."

"Neither do I."

Pain flickered through his gaze, but he quickly shut it down, forcing a smile. "Of course not. You've only ever *been* human."

She'd been referring to her life as a thief, not her life as a human, but Dorian must've thought she was talking about becoming a vampire—rather, about *not* becoming a vampire.

They'd never really talked about it. About what came next. Everything had happened so quickly between them— from lust to love in a blink. Deep love. *Real* love. The kind Charley used to think was a fairy tale.

And now…

God. Why did everything have to be so complicated? She was in love with a vampire. A fucking vampire! And Dorian was right—she'd only ever been human. Even if she survived her uncle, even if nothing bad ever touched her again, Charley would eventually die.

But Dorian wouldn't.

Charley's head spun. She wasn't ready for this conversation. Wasn't ready to think through the implications. She wanted to explain herself anyway, if only to take back the pain she'd inadvertently caused him, but before she could find the words, Dorian was moving on.

"Aiden tells me you've got a plan for our friend Vincent Estas," he said.

"He told you that, huh?"

"Among other things."

Charley tensed for the fight. "If this is the part where you try to talk me out of it, forget it. Not happening."

"I suspected as much," he grumbled. "And if I had any doubts, Aiden drove the point home with a quote. Let's see if I've got it right… 'Charlotte isn't the sit-home-with-her-thumb-up-her-ass type, you git.'"

"He's right, Dorian. You need me on this, and—"

"*And* I've already put Aiden back in touch with Estas to set up Cole's next art buy, so no need to draw your sword just yet."

"Really?"

"If all goes well, it looks like we'll be able to go in on Tuesday."

"Not tomorrow?"

"We need time to work out all the details. We can't leave anything to chance, right?"

Charley nodded. As anxious as she was to get her hands on Estas' intel, she knew damn well the importance of contingency planning. Besides, she was just grateful Dorian was backing her up on this rather than ordering her to stay home while he and the boys snuck out for another epic caper.

"Is that what you wanted to talk to me about?" she asked.

"What's that?"

"When I first woke up. You said you had something important to tell me, but then we shifted gears. Was it about the Estas meeting?"

His eyes clouded over, and Charley swore the temperature in the room dropped ten degrees.

"I… I'm sorry." Dorian shook his head. "It was nothing —it can wait."

"But—"

"But *this* can't." He pressed another kiss to her lips, cutting off her protests. When he finally drew back, his smile was firmly in place again, his eyes sparkling with mischief. "I've brought you a gift."

Without waiting for her reply, Dorian rose from the bed and retrieved a large, ivory-colored gift bag from the dresser. When he turned on the bedside lamp, she saw that it was stamped with the logo from her favorite hair salon.

"What's all this?" Charley couldn't help but giggle as she dug into the bag, finding several bottles of her favorite shampoo and conditioner, along with at least two of every possible styling product imaginable.

She couldn't believe it. She hadn't been back to the salon since Rudy had cut off her cash flow. She had a small stash left at home, but she'd been rationing it out, trying to make it last as long as possible before she'd have to switch to the drugstore stuff.

"This is Julian Micheaux product," she said, as if he didn't know. "There's only one salon that sells it in the entire world."

"As I discovered today," he said.

"But how did you know this was my salon?"

He sat next to her on the bed again and grinned. "I'd tell you, but I'm afraid you'll find it even creepier than my watching you sleep."

"Let me guess. You called one of your rich-guy colleagues at American Express and had them pull my credit card statements? Because that's a little bit psycho."

"Bloody hell!" Dorian smacked himself on the forehead and laughed. "If only I'd thought of that, I could've saved myself hours of sniffing every bottle of shampoo in every posh salon in Manhattan."

"You... *what?*"

"Oh, it caused quite a stir, as you can imagine. It wasn't until the tenth salon or so when one of the stylists finally took pity on me. When I told her what I was looking for, and why, she and her colleagues became quite invested in my plight. I did my best to describe the scent, and after many, *many* phone calls and consultations with friends in other salons, we finally tracked the stuff down. Of course, by then I'd already become somewhat of a social media sensation—hashtag Sexy Sniffer, if you must know." Dorian rolled his eyes, feigning irritation. "*Preposterous.* But it was worth every embarrassing moment, because here you are, love. Smiling and happy in my bed."

Charley's eyes filled with tears. "You did all that. For me."

"For you? Goodness, no. Thanks to my efforts, Sexy Sniffer now has free haircuts for life at Julian Micheaux's salon—the only one in the world, I'm told." He laughed again, but then his eyes turned serious, and he brushed his thumb across her cheek. "I know it's hard being away from home, love. I thought you should have something nice— something familiar."

The thought of Dorian wandering the salons of New York in search of her hair products, sniffing all those bottles... It made Charley laugh. It filled her with so much warmth and affection, she thought she might burst.

And then it filled her with a blinding ache that nearly took her breath away.

All at once, the rusty box where she'd shoved her worst

fears and denials finally shattered, everything exploding out of her in a deep, broken sob.

So much for compartmentalizing.

"What's wrong?" he asked, suddenly alarmed. "Did I pick the wrong product line? I thought for sure I'd—"

"No, it's right. Everything is absolutely, *perfectly* right. It's..." Charley closed her eyes, tears spilling freely. "This is exactly the kind of sweet, over-the-top romantic thing I should be dishing about with Sasha. All I want to do is text her about hashtag Sexy Sniffer—but I can't. I can't, Dorian, because she's gone. She doesn't have her phone. I don't even know if she's okay, or... *God.* All day I tried to keep it together. Figuring stuff out with Aiden and Cole, waiting for you to come back, playing Midnight Marauder— anything to distract myself from freaking out. A hundred times, I grabbed my phone to call Rudy, but I was too scared. I don't know how he expects me to respond to all this, and what if I slip up and he realizes I know he's a demon? I can't risk pissing him off. Sasha's just a kid. She must be terrified."

Dorian removed the gifts from the bed, then pulled her into his warm embrace, holding her without saying a word as she completely fell apart.

It was the first time she'd allowed herself to lose control since Sasha had been taken, and through it all, his strength never wavered. She shattered in his arms, and he let her. He offered no false promises, no half-truths, no platitudes.

He gave her only love and support. Only the space to breathe.

And then, when she was certain she'd wrung out the last tear, she finally found the strength to look into his eyes again.

Dorian's lashes were wet with tears of his own—a sight that damn near melted what was left of her tattered heart.

"I know I can't make this better for you right now," he said, "but I won't allow you to face any of this alone, Charlotte. Not your uncle. Not the grays." He slipped beneath the blankets and turned her around in his arms, kissing the back of her neck. "I will slay *every* one of your demons, love. *That* is a promise."

She pulled his arm tight around her waist, and the last of her fears drained away as her body melted into his hold. It felt as if they'd been created for exactly that purpose—to fit together perfectly.

A tiny bubble of laughter rose up from inside—a ray of sunshine breaking through the clouds.

"What's so funny?" Dorian asked.

"I was just thinking about that night in the Salvatore closet."

"Hmm. One of my favorite nights. One of my favorite closets too."

"I never thought... I mean, you were just supposed to be this *really* hot guy with a dirty mouth. I thought it was just a fling, you know? But look where it got me."

"Are you saying you no longer find me attractive? Or dirty, for that matter?"

"No." She closed her eyes, focusing on the comforting rhythm of his heartbeat against her back. "I'm saying I'm in love with you. And the truth is, Dorian… I don't know how to be anything else."

Dorian tightened his hold and murmured something into her hair, but Charley was already drifting back to sleep, her worries temporarily evaporating in the strong, protective embrace of the vampire she loved.

There was so much he hadn't said tonight—so much he was still guarding close, desperate to protect her from the things he feared would scare her off.

But there was *nothing* he could say to frighten her. No situation too dark or gruesome, no confession too bleak, no secret too shameful.

Because through all the craziness and uncertainty, one rock-solid, unshakeable truth had emerged.

The vampire king didn't need to slay her demons. All he needed to do was stand by her side.

And *no* demon—in this realm or the next—stood a fucking chance.

CHAPTER SEVEN

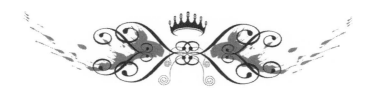

"I don't know whether to be mortally afraid of you, seriously impressed, or incredibly turned on."

Dorian stood on the front porch of Vincent Estas' home on the outskirts of Woodstock, watching in awe as Charlotte slid something she'd called a bump key into the front lock.

She was dressed head to toe in tight black clothing, a small leather satchel slung over her shoulder that held her tricks of the trade. Dorian had taken her into the city yesterday to retrieve it from a small storage unit in Chelsea where she kept her professional gear—gear she claimed she hadn't used in years. Not since she'd been promoted to the much more lucrative art scenes she currently worked.

Most recently worked, he silently amended. Those days, she'd promised him, were behind her.

Though he had to admit—she was damn good at her job.

Perhaps it's like riding a bike, he thought as he watched her wield the tools like some sort of heist-movie heroine.

But this *wasn't* a movie. It was an extremely dangerous mission with potentially deadly consequences. If Estas returned, or if any other demons showed up, Dorian would be hard pressed to defend against their hellfire.

Fortunately, Estas was currently occupied with Cole at a dive bar in town, discussing Cole's possible interest in another Egyptian statue. Because Estas seemed to believe Cole was a serious collector—and not altogether virtuous—he'd easily agreed to the meeting. Dorian would've preferred a more distant location, but on that point, Estas wouldn't budge.

With any luck, it would be a long negotiation, giving Dorian and Charlotte plenty of time to get the intel they needed.

Assuming it even existed.

Assuming it was kept inside Estas' home.

Assuming they didn't get caught.

Assuming Rudy didn't still have men watching their comings and goings from Ravenswood.

There were a lot of assumptions—a lot of risks. The only sure thing tonight was Charlotte, poised and confident, completely unfazed as she worked her magic on the door. She was truly in her element.

Now, she glanced at Dorian over her shoulder, a thin smile touching her lips. "Well, which is it, vampire king? Afraid, impressed, or turned on?"

He answered without hesitation. "Yes."

"Sounds to me like you're in the wrong line of work." She tapped the key with a small hammer, then turned it, easily unlocking the deadbolt. "We're in. Follow me, and remember, gloves on at all times. We don't know how smart Estas is or who else he's got on the payroll—no sense leaving behind evidence of our visit."

Dorian nodded, then sent a quick text to Aiden, who'd dropped them off and was now on standby in Dorian's BMW at a nearby park.

We're in. No issues so far.

Aiden replied with a thumbs-up.

Charlotte pushed open the door and stepped inside, Dorian close behind. The interior was dark, save for a dim light left on above the kitchen stove.

After listening for a moment to determine they were alone, she unzipped her satchel and exchanged the hammer and bump key for a flashlight, keeping the beam away from the windows and any reflective surfaces.

She really *had* thought of everything.

From the brief reconnaissance they'd done outside, Dorian knew the entire single-story space was less than a thousand square feet, with an open living and kitchen area up front and a bedroom, bathroom, and home office toward the back.

They headed straight for the office. It was sparsely appointed, with nothing more than a card table serving as a desk for a laptop and small banker's lamp. There was a cheap folding chair behind it, an empty waste basket, and one piece of art on the wall, with a set of cheap curtains hanging crooked over the windows. A small closet on the back wall held only a few coats and empty hangers.

"Doesn't seem like this is his primary location," Dorian said.

"He might be working out of the Fifth Avenue commercial space Aiden mentioned. Makes sense—there's not much room here to store the artwork."

"Aiden said the Manhattan space was being renovated."

"Probably just a front to keep passersby from nosing around."

"Excellent," Dorian said dryly. "Will we be breaking and entering there as well?"

Charlotte sighed. "You promised me, Dorian. You promised you'd keep your shit together tonight and your judgments about my life—my *former* life—to yourself."

"Forgive me." Dorian held up his hands in apology. "This is my first robbery. I'm a bit on edge."

"Well get *off* edge. We've got work to do." She set her satchel on the chair, then opened and booted up the laptop.

Dorian watched in scolded silence. It wasn't the crime itself that had him on edge. It was Charlotte.

After doing his best to get himself sorted after the Rogozin interrogations on Sunday—the epic shampoo hunt, a fruitless stop at his near-ruined Tribeca penthouse that only further enraged him, an hours-long drive through the mountains to get his head on straight—he'd returned to Ravenswood with every intention of telling her about the demon claim. But the moment he'd found her sleeping in his bed—a sight so perfect and right it was as if he'd been coming home to her for an eternity—all he could think was, *No. Let her have this one last night. One last night believing her soul is unmarred. Believing she's free.*

That one last night turned into the next, and the next, and here they were tonight, all the most terrible things left unsaid as they crept through the lair of the enemy.

The enemy who may very well be connected to the demon lord who'd made the claim.

Dorian didn't want Charlotte anywhere *near* Estas. Didn't want her anywhere near *any* demon—lord, crime boss, or bootlicking errand boy alike. But she was a fierce, formidable woman who'd no more sit on the sidelines than he would.

It was something he was learning, however reluctantly, to live with. To love, even, no matter how infuriated—and terrified—it made him.

"How are you holding up, vampire?" Charlotte asked, her face cast in the blueish light of the laptop screen.

Dorian didn't know how to respond.

The truth was… He wasn't holding up at all.

"If you're nervous and distracted," she said, glancing over at him, "it could—"

"No, I… I'm good. Carry on."

"Okay. Stay here and don't touch anything. I'm going to do a quick sweep of the bedroom, then we need to dig into these computer files. Be right back."

Though she was in the room directly adjacent to the office, and he was a vampire with superior senses, Dorian heard nothing—not so much as a footstep or creaking floor-

65

board. He marveled at Charlotte's skill, wondering just how many times she'd done this before, in how many homes and brownstones and penthouses and office buildings—all the places where people were supposed to feel safe and secure.

Dorian closed his eyes to clear his thoughts, reminding himself they weren't there to rob the home of some unsuspecting family. They were there—in the home of a fucking *demon*—to find information that would save Sasha's life.

When he opened his eyes again, Charlotte was back, standing right in front of him.

Her hair was pulled back into a tight ponytail, her copper eyes luminescent in the darkness. They glowed with a feverish intensity that made Dorian's heart beat hard and fast in his chest.

"You're dangerous, little prowler," he whispered. "And so... fucking... beautiful."

Instinctively his hands found her hips, the heat of her skin seeping through her leggings and his leather gloves. She slid her hands over his shoulders and leaned in close, allowing him this brief embrace.

She always felt so incredible.

Damn. They were so good together in every way.

With her breasts firm against his chest and her lips close to his ear, she whispered, "I'm just getting started, Mr. Redthorne."

Dorian was so turned on he couldn't even think straight. He'd never been able to keep a clear head with regard to Charlotte, but the intensity of their present circumstances only seemed to magnify his need, his cock suddenly throbbing. He pictured her on her knees. Imagined fisting that ponytail with his gloved hand as he slid into her hot, wet mouth...

Fuck.

With a firm grip on her hips, Dorian backed Charlotte against the wall. It was reckless and stupid and they did *not* have time for this, but he didn't care. Nothing made sense anymore. All that mattered now was her luscious lips, her warmth, the silky feel of her hair against his cheek as he pressed his mouth to her neck and licked her soft, creamy skin.

"What... what are you doing? Dorian, you... Holy *shit*, that's..." Charlotte's words slid into a soft moan as his teeth grazed her earlobe.

Dorian kissed his way along her jaw, slowly moving to her soft, satiny lips. She parted them easily, and he slid his tongue into her mouth, teasing her with soft strokes, grateful her wounds had healed so quickly. When she let out a sigh of abject pleasure, Dorian grabbed her ass and lifted her up, pushing her hard against the wall as her legs wrapped tight around his hips.

Fucking *hell*, he wanted to take her. Hard and fast, right there against the wall.

She wanted it just as badly—he could sense it. The scent of her desire, the warmth of her body, the yearning in her eyes... All of it called to him with a deep, carnal invitation he couldn't refuse.

He kissed her again, drinking in the taste of her. But

somewhere in the back of his mind, he knew this was a terrible idea.

He pulled back and met her gaze—dark and dreamy.

"What... What are we doing?" she whispered, slowly blinking away the haze.

It seemed they'd both come to the same inconvenient realization.

No matter how desperately they wanted to tear each other's clothes off, they couldn't. Not here. Not now.

Get a grip, Redthorne. For fuck's sake, your cock's going to get you both killed.

"I... I'm so sorry, love." He set her down, forcing himself to take a step back. "Heat of the moment. Won't happen again."

"No, it's... Me too. I shouldn't have... Let's just..." She reached up and tightened her ponytail, blowing out a long breath. "Right. Back to work, then."

Charlotte retrieved a small external hard drive and a cable from her satchel and connected it to the laptop. With a deftness that made FierceConnect's Silicon Valley-educated developers look like preschoolers trying to jam square pegs into round holes, Charlotte navigated through the file manager, searching through everything from the demon's vacation photos to his rather extensive porn collection.

"Busty Bollywood Babes aside," she said, "looks like Estas is marginally smarter than I'd given him credit for. There's nothing professional on the laptop."

"So this was a waste of time?"

"Hardly." Charlotte dug into her bag again, this time procuring a stethoscope.

Dorian laughed. "I'm all for playing doctor, love. But didn't we just narrowly avoid another clandestine closet interlude? Perhaps we can revisit this game later."

She looped the device around her neck, eyeing him flirtatiously. "Behave yourself, and we'll see what your future holds."

With that, she turned toward the art on the wall—a knockoff Monet in a plastic frame that had been painted to look like wood. She lifted it and set it on the floor, revealing a wall safe.

"You've got to be kidding me," Dorian said. "Estas is a high-ranking Rogozin demon and a multi-million-dollar black-market art dealer, and he's got a wall safe?"

Charlotte shrugged, adjusting the stethoscope over her ears. "I said he's *marginally* smarter than I'd thought—not a genius by any stretch. Besides, how often does a demon living in the woods get robbed?"

"Fair point." Dorian watched with twisted fascination as she pressed the stethoscope's chest piece to the safe and listened, spinning the combination dial this way and that.

After no more than a minute, a smile lit up her face. "Bingo."

The safe door swung open.

Dorian's jaw damn near hit the floor. "Did you really just do that? In sixty seconds, no less?"

"Can't say dear old Dad never taught me anything useful."

"No, I suppose you can't." Dorian shook his head, feeling as if he were trapped in a very long, disturbing, and slightly erotic dream.

But it was real. All of it. The scent of Charlotte's unfulfilled desire lingering on the air. The sound of her heartbeat, calm and steady as she focused on the task at hand. The dim glow of the computer screen. The swish of her ponytail as she efficiently rifled through the safe.

"Hello, beautiful," she finally said, slowly turning toward him. Her eyes danced, her energy buzzing and alive with some new victory. She held a large, mustard-colored interoffice envelope—the kind used for staff memorandums before email had rendered them obsolete.

In large black letters across the top, someone had scrawled two names:

RAVENSWOOD / D'AMICO

Charlotte opened the envelope and tipped its contents into her gloved hand, catching a flash drive, a passport, and a folio of first-class airline tickets.

Thumbing through the passport and tickets, she said, "Passport's a forgery. It's Rudy's picture, but the name says Joel Irwin. The tickets are in Irwin's name."

"Where to?"

"São Paolo. One-way, connects in Miami. Heading out in... wow." Charlotte's brow creased. "The twenty-seventh? That's just two days after he plans to hit Ravenswood."

"Is that odd?"

"Very." She flipped through the stash again, shaking her head. "First of all, Travis is Rudy's go-to forger, but this isn't his work—I don't recognize it at all. It looks like Rudy's doing this behind his back, going through Estas instead. And there's no return ticket. If Rudy's not coming back, who's handling the payout?"

"How do you mean?"

"Normally after a big score, the crew stashes the artwork in a storage unit in Jersey or Pennsylvania, then everyone lies low for a few weeks. After that, the boss does an inventory, figures out the initial payout for the crew, and then contracts a guy like Estas to fence it. He'll either sell it piecemeal, taking a commission on each sale, or he'll buy the whole lot for a set price and sell it off on his own time. The whole process can take months—sometimes longer."

"So maybe the Brazil trip is Rudy's way of lying low," Dorian suggested.

"No. Something isn't adding up here. My gut says Rudy's not planning to pay out at all. He wouldn't leave that kind of detail to anyone else."

"You think he's double-crossing his crew?"

"Looks that way. The thing is—I don't know who the crew even *is* this time. When he first brought me in on Ravenswood, he said it was a side project between him and Travis, and that our usual guys weren't involved. He was adamant that I not discuss it with anyone else."

"But others *are* involved," Dorian said. "All that surveillance of my property, the spies at FierceConnect…"

"Exactly. But I have no idea who they are. Rudy's a demon. For all we know, Rogozin is his crew."

"The spies who interviewed me were human."

"Maybe they had watches or something that hid their true nature. Rudy had us fooled, didn't he?"

Dorian sighed. She was right. They had no way of knowing what they were up against. No idea who—or what—might show up at Ravenswood for the planned heist.

No idea who might be holding Sasha hostage.

Dorian kept that last bit of worry to himself.

"We'll figure it out, love," he said instead. "This is just a starting point."

She grabbed her phone and snapped a few pictures of the tickets and passport, then slid them back into the envelope.

"Let's check the digital files." She plugged the flash drive into the laptop, navigating to the directory and clicking through the drive's folders. "*Shit.* The drive itself isn't encrypted, but the folders are—I can't open them or copy them over, and we can't just take the drive—Estas will get suspicious if he knows it's missing."

"*Ha!*" Dorian pointed at her and grinned. For the first time since he'd crossed the threshold into this place, he actually had something to offer—something she needed. "I can crack the encryption."

Charlotte arched a *very* sexy eyebrow. "So not only are you a video game nerd, you're a hacker? Since when?"

"Since University. Well, the most recent go-round."

"I thought college was all about drinking and getting laid."

"Not for nerds. We've got a special track."

"Well, well, well." Charlotte's smile lit up the dim room. "Now *I'm* the one who's impressed."

"Offering me a spot on the crew, are you?"

"At this rate, we'll be able to start our own."

"Assuming we don't get hell-roasted by a demon tonight. Cheers, then." Dorian got to work. After just a few moments of tech wizardry, he was able to crack the encryption on the folders. "It appears the files themselves have a slightly stronger encryption, so we'll need to deal with that back at Ravenswood."

"Good. Let's just copy everything onto the external drive so we can get the fuck out of here. We've already overstayed our welcome."

He did as she asked, then passed the flash drive back to her to return to the envelope.

"Anything else of interest in the safe?" he asked as she put everything back in order.

"More envelopes like this one—all different names. I'm sure it's all fascinating stuff, but we don't have time to go through it." She closed up the safe and re-hung the painting. "We need to get moving."

"It's too bad, really. We didn't even get a chance to try out the closet." Dorian knocked on the back wall behind the coats.

The *thunk* that greeted him in return was hollow and deep.

He knocked again. Same echo.

"That... doesn't sound like a solid wall," Charlotte said, slinging the satchel over her shoulder.

"It most certainly does not." He shoved the coats aside and ran his hands along the wall until he found what he was looking for—a recessed handle hidden in the shadows. He gave it a tug, and a small, chest-high door the same shade as the wall creaked open, revealing a rickety stairwell that led down into utter darkness.

The scent of rot and piss was overpowering, making his eyes water. Charlotte nearly gagged.

"I *really* should've kept my hands to myself," he grumbled.

Charlotte grabbed her flashlight and shone it on the stairs, illuminating a narrow passageway just wide enough for one person. The walls were made of cement, the stairs black with mold.

The moment the beam of light hit the landing at the bottom, a faint moaning sound emanated up from the chamber, followed by a metallic scraping that sounded like the rattling of a cage.

"Dorian?" Charlotte gasped and glanced up into his eyes. All the color drained from her face.

He knew immediately where her mind had gone.

"I'll go investigate," he said. "You stay here and—"

"No. We're in this together, remember?"

He slid his hand around the back of her neck and held her gaze, a thousand questions poised on his tongue.

What if it's Sasha?

What if it isn't?

What if it breaks you?

What if I can't put you back together again?

But in the end, he said the only words she'd listen to. The only ones that mattered.

"All right, love." He reached for her hand, squeezing tight. "Together it is."

And then he took a deep breath, crouched through the low doorway, and led her down into the abyss.

CHAPTER EIGHT

Blood and death, brother. Blood and death…

Cole's words echoed again through Dorian's memory as he and Charlotte descended into the darkness, the pungent air damn near choking them both.

Charlotte's heart rate was completely erratic, fear and adrenaline flooding her bloodstream until he hardly recognized her scent.

Please, he thought, recalling Sasha's bright blue eyes, her smile. *Please let this be* anything *but that beautiful, vibrant girl…*

"Dorian." Charlotte gripped his arm, her body trembling as they reached the lower floor and the situation came into view.

A long worktable covered in papers and books and supplies. A high-backed wooden chair. A cabinet of jars and bundled herbs. Two squat, grimy windows near the ceiling, hidden from the outside with brush and debris.

And there, in the back corner of the room, a cage.

Behind the metal bars, he saw the pale shapes in the beam of Charlotte's flashlight, stark in their utter nakedness. Two bodies huddled closed together, their backs to him, flesh blackened with bruises and burns. Broken ribs protruded from the skin. On the floor beneath the cage, a pool of blood and piss shone wet in the darkness.

"Grays," he said softly. "Just grays."

A stifled sob escaped Charlotte's mouth. Dorian couldn't tell whether it was one of horror or relief. Maybe both.

The grays could've just as easily been her sister— starved and beaten. Tortured.

Dorian pulled her close, and she buried her face against his chest, warm tears soaking his shirt. "It's all right, love. It's not her."

"I thought... Just for a minute, you know?"

"Wherever Sasha is, we *must* keep the faith that she's unharmed, and that we'll find her very soon." He pulled back and cupped her face. "Can you do that for me? For Sasha?"

Charlotte nodded resolutely, blinking away the last of her tears.

Certain she was all right, Dorian turned and knelt before the cage, his stomach twisting at the sight.

He had no idea how long they'd been there, but they were both emaciated and broken, cowering before the flashlight beam. They didn't have the strength to break free. Didn't have the strength to even try.

The first time Dorian had encountered the grays, he and his family were living under House Kendrick's rule. The vampire king—Evie's father, George Kendrick—ruled his sirelings with an iron fist. He kept his own cages of brutalized grays—a personal petting zoo whose captives were regularly trotted out to torment the new Redthorne slaves. Sometimes, he'd set them loose in the woods, allowing them to chase Dorian and his brothers while he watched from atop his favorite stallion. Other times, he'd use them as a warning. *This is what becomes of the Kendrick sirelings who disobey me.*

He'd forced Dorian to torture them. To make them bleed. To make them suffer.

Only then would his brothers receive fresh blood. Only then would the Redthorne vampires be allowed to survive another day. Another week. Another year.

And through it all, his father watched in silence, never once criticizing the king's methods. Never subjected to them himself.

To Dorian, the grays had always been monsters.

But now, looking at these poor, broken creatures through the rusty bars of the cage, how could he see them as such?

They weren't monsters. They were *him*—what he would become in his purest form, absent the magic of a bonded witch and a steady diet of fresh blood.

With a deep sigh, he rose and grabbed the wooden chair, shattering it against the floor. Picking through the broken pieces, he dug out the sharpest, gripping it in a tight fist.

"Turn around, love," he said, and Charlotte did as he asked.

Kneeling once more before the cage, he staked one, then the other, swiftly ending their misery. They vanished into a pile of ash, falling on his shoes like the season's first snow.

"It's done," he whispered.

Charlotte joined him at the worktable, and together they searched through the pile—pages of handwritten notes and sigils, ingredient lists, spells.

Witchcraft.

Dorian picked up a cracked leather grimoire and thumbed through it. There was a dedication spell engraved on the inside cover; its author had signed her name in blood.

"Jacinda Colburn," he said, tossing the book onto the table as if it burned his skin. "Duchanes' bonded witch."

"The one who made the poison that nearly killed you?" Charlotte asked sharply. "And the resurrection amulets for the grays?"

"It would appear this is her laboratory. One of them, anyway."

"Why would Jacinda do such a thing?"

He recalled what Duchanes had said the night he'd attacked Dorian and Charlotte in Tribeca.

Witches can be rather clever when sufficiently motivated...

"I'm... not sure she had a choice," Dorian said. But before he could further speculate on Jacinda's motives, his cell phone buzzed.

"It's Cole," he said, scanning the text.

No deal yet. Apparently Estas is having a party tonight. I'm invited, but you two ain't.

"Um, Dorian?" Charlotte said. "We've got a problem."

Dorian heard the sound of car doors slamming outside, followed by heavy footfalls on the front porch.

"We've got two," he said, as a new text buzzed in from Cole.

We'll be there in 5 minutes, maybe 10. I can play this part all night, but you & Charles need to get the fuck outta there. NOW.

Dorian's heart dropped. He would've loved to do just that.

If only a half-dozen drunk and disorderly Russians hadn't just filed into the cabin. Their boisterous laughter and crass commentary assaulted his ears.

Demons. Every last one.

"Stay here," he whispered urgently. "I'll lead them back outside, then you can make a run for it. Text Aiden to meet—"

"Are you insane? You can't take that many demons alone. They'll fry you!"

Fucking *hell*, she was right, and Dorian didn't have time to argue.

Without another thought, he shoved Charlotte into the darkest corner of the basement, positioned himself in front of her, and sent Aiden a series of rapid-fire texts.

Trapped in basement.

Demons inbound.

Give me a distraction — lure them out.

And then, as the first demon stepped into the office overhead and shouted in Russian for his comrades, Dorian sent out his final plea.

15 seconds or you'll need a bloody Hoover to get us home.

CHAPTER NINE

Charley had just enough time to suck in a shuddering breath before the night fucking exploded.

Literally.

It lit up the sky through the filthy basement windows, rattling the entire cabin. Upstairs, the demons scattered, shouting orders at one another, running from the back of the cabin to the front.

In the surrounding woods, fire crackled through the trees.

"Thank you, Aiden," Dorian said, just as the demons returned to the office, undoubtedly heading right for the basement chamber.

A few feet above Charley's head, one of the windows shattered. Dorian grabbed her and covered her with his body, shielding her from the raining glass as someone smashed out every last shard.

"A Hoover? Really?" Aiden leaned in through the

opening and held out his hands, gesturing for Charley to grab hold. "Bloody dramatic, Dori. Even for you."

"Get her out of here." Dorian gave Charley a boost, launching her into Aiden's awaiting embrace. "I'm right behind you."

Aiden hauled her out through the opening and into the smoke-filled backyard. Still on her hands and knees, she turned around and peered through the window just in time to catch two demons charging down the stairs, heading right for her man.

Dorian and Charley locked eyes, his gaze full of fiery determination.

"Go!" he shouted.

She didn't get the chance to refuse. She felt Aiden's firm grip around her midsection, and then the ground tilted, spinning out from under her.

When the vertigo passed, she was standing with Aiden in front of Dorian's BMW at the park.

Dorian was nowhere in sight.

"We can't leave him there!" she cried. "The demons—"

"I'm going straight back for him. But you need to leave, Charlotte." He opened the car door and practically shoved her inside. "Drive back to Ravenswood and wait for us there. *Now.*"

"Aiden—"

Before she could say another word, Aiden was gone.

Charley gripped the wheel so tight her knuckles turned white. As a human, she knew damn well she didn't stand a chance against demons. She didn't even know how many they were up against.

But it didn't matter. She wasn't about to let Dorian and Aiden die on *her* watch.

"No vampire left behind, dickheads." She peeled out of the park, jammed on the gas, and sped off into the night.

Charley came to a stop on the road in front of the cabin, her eyes wide with shock.

In the brief but excruciating minutes since Dorian had shoved her out that window, a war had erupted on Estas' property.

The backyard and surrounding woods were a disaster zone of flaming trees, roiling smoke, and broken bodies.

Demons fought grays. Grays fought each other. Behind a thick screen of smoke, Charley could just make out the blurred movements of the vampires double-teaming a gray the size of a refrigerator. Lower to the ground, a massive black-and-gray wolf lunged at a charging demon, taking him down on impact.

Cole.

Charley quickly took in the scene, trying to decide what the fuck to do. Charging into the fray on foot was pointless —she'd be killed in a heartbeat. She had no weapons, no protective gear—nothing but the car itself.

With the refrigerator finally down for the count, Dorian and Aiden spun around to face their next foe—a vile red-headed demon glaring at Dorian as if she wanted to set him on fire.

Charley gasped, realizing the demon was about to do just that.

Hellfire.

The demon smirked, and suddenly Dorian dropped to his knees, clutching frantically at his chest.

"I don't *think* so, bitch." Charley hit the gas and headed straight for the backyard. Plowing through a knot of grays, she smashed into the demon head on, sending her flying into a tree.

Charley leaned across the seat and opened the passenger door. "Aiden! Get in!"

Aiden hauled Dorian to his feet and tossed him into the passenger seat, then whistled for Cole. He opened the back door just in time for the wolf to leap in, then jumped in after him.

Dorian coughed, struggling to catch his breath. The scent of smoke and burning flesh filled the car.

Three more demons were heading straight for them.

"Drive!" Aiden shouted.

Charley didn't need to be told twice. She slammed the Bimmer into reverse and backed out onto the road, then rocketed the fuck out of there.

Seconds later, a pair of headlight beams blasted through the back window.

"We've got a tail!" she said.

Aiden turned around to look. "Keep driving. They'll fuck off eventually."

Charley nodded and gave the car a little more gas, zooming them up a steep mountain incline. They'd just crested the top of the hill and began their descent down the backside when the next fucking obstacle course came into view.

"What the hell is *that*?" She downshifted, slowing the engine. In the curve of the road a few hundred feet ahead, a cluster of pale, writhing bodies blocked the way.

"More grays," Aiden said. "They're everywhere."

Behind them, the headlights reappeared, quickly gaining ground.

"Don't stop," Aiden said. "We'll have to go through them."

But she couldn't—there were too many. A head-on impact at their current speed would either set off the airbags, flip the car, or worse—send it careening off the side of the narrow mountain road.

But they couldn't stop either. Not unless they wanted to be hell-roasted by those demons.

"Hold on, boys." Charley whispered a quick prayer to anyone who might be listening and switched the car to rear-wheel drive mode. As they hit the curve, she cut the wheel and smashed the accelerator, forcing the Bimmer's back end to drift forward. They slid into the curve sideways, clipping a few of the grays with the rear bumper before Charley jerked the steering wheel back in place and corrected course.

The smell of burning rubber filled the air.

Clear of the worst of them, she hit the gas on the

straightaway and blasted the fuck out of there, glancing into the rearview just as the demon car behind them plowed into the grays.

Whether they flipped into a ditch or sailed right off the fucking mountain, Charley wasn't sticking around to find out.

When they finally cleared the worst of the danger, Cole shifted into his human form—a sight she wouldn't have believed if she hadn't caught it in the rearview.

"Cole?" An insane laugh escaped her lips—the kind that could only come from saving one's friends from a demon attack, surviving a few near-death experiences, and watching a wolf transform into a naked man, his bare ass gracing Dorian's fine leather seats.

Cole clapped a rough hand over her shoulder and gave her a shake. "Charles. Ain't you a sight for sore eyes."

"One more minute and you would've been a sight for *dead* eyes," Aiden said. "Bloody hell, Charlotte. Thank you for *completely* ignoring my request to return to Ravenswood."

"What did I tell you?" Charley wriggled her thumbs. "These babies were not made for sticking up my ass."

The guys laughed, but Dorian only coughed.

She reached over and placed a hand on his thigh, his muscle twitching beneath her touch. After a beat, he covered her hand with his, squeezing tight.

Charley *finally* let out a breath. It felt like she'd been holding it ever since she'd seen that ginger bitch drop her man with hellfire.

Thank God he's okay…

"Do you think the demons will come after us again?" she asked, casting another glance in the rearview.

"Not if they want to keep their cocks attached," Aiden said. "Chasing us off the property is one thing, but none of those demons want to launch an all-out assault against the vampire king. My guess is they're regrouping, though. Definitely reporting back to Rogozin tonight."

"That doesn't sound good," she said.

"It ain't," Cole said. "But we certainly didn't start *that* fire."

"Technically, we did," Aiden said. "Rather *I* did, when I blew up the propane tank and turned Estas' little party into a barbecue."

"You ask me, this fight was a long time comin'," Cole said. "And we ain't the ones who let loose all those grays. Hell, even the demons didn't know what the fuck hit 'em— that was an outside job. So if Rogozin's got something to say about the shit that went down back there, he knows just how to find me."

Charley sighed. "That's what I'm worried about."

"After tonight?" Cole cracked up. "Pretty sure *Rogozin* should be worried about *you*."

Charley smiled, but she didn't let herself relax until they'd finally come to a stop in front of Cole's cabin. Tucked into the woods at the end of a long dirt road, it felt like another world—safe and protected, far removed from the craziness they'd just escaped.

"You're sure they won't retaliate?" Charley asked again. "Maybe you should come back to Ravenswood tonight."

"Your concern is real touching, Charles," Cole said. "But I got this place surrounded by wolves. Anyone tries to pull any shit—demon, vampire, gray, *or* human—they're in for a world of hurt." He got out of the car and lit a cigarette, taking a deep drag. If he realized he was still buck-ass naked, he didn't seem to care. "You all comin' in for a drink? I got just the thing. Special home brew—it'll put hair on your balls."

"Yes, but will it put *balls* on your balls?" Aiden opened the car door and stepped outside, more than a bit unsteady on his feet. "I seem to have left mine back on that mountain. Charlotte, where on *earth* did you learn to drive like that?"

"That's... a *really* long story."

"You know what's good for long stories?" Cole blew a plume of smoke into the night sky, then grinned. "My special home brew."

Charley laughed. "That actually sounds—"

"Charlotte and I are heading back to Ravenswood tonight," Dorian said sharply. It was the first he'd spoken since she'd picked them up, and though his voice was still hoarse, his tone left no room for argument.

Charley swallowed hard. Why did she get the distinct feeling she was in deep shit?

"You sure?" Cole asked. "I got the green stuff too. Might help get the taste of hellfire out of your lungs, Red."

Dorian coughed again, shaking his head. "Another time, perhaps."

"Suit yourself." Cole leaned in through the driver's side window and gave Charley a fist bump. "Catch you later, Fast and Furious. And hey—go easy on our boy here. I realize Red's a grumpy ol' *fuck*, but it's been a while since that antique heart of his saw so much goddamn excitement."

Charley laughed. "I'll do my best."

When the guys were back inside, she finally turned to Dorian, meeting his gaze across the front seat. It was only a couple of feet, but suddenly, it felt like a mile.

"You okay?" she asked softly, reaching for his face. "I don't like that you're coughing."

"And while we're on the subject of things we don't like..." He grabbed her wrist and glared at her, his golden-brown eyes igniting with anger. "You've got thirty seconds to explain what the *fuck* you were thinking back there."

CHAPTER TEN

"I don't need thirty seconds, vampire," Charlotte said. "I can do it in five."

Dorian seethed. The anger burned through him as readily as the hellfire. "*Well?*"

Charlotte narrowed her eyes, her pulse thudding beneath his touch, a wild energy buzzing through her veins like electricity. Dorian sensed *all* of it—every beat, every rush, every richly layered scent.

It made him dizzy and hungry and desperate to kiss her, but it wasn't enough to spare her Dorian's wrath.

She'd bloody near gotten herself killed tonight—more than once. And for what?

"*You,* Dorian Redthorne," she snapped, jerking free of his grasp. "*You're* why. And I'd do it again in a hot second, no matter how much it pisses you off. So if you're going to lecture me about—"

"Aiden *specifically* told you to drive back to Ravenswood and—"

"In case you haven't noticed, I don't do well with orders. Not outside the bedroom, anyway."

His own blood flared at the thought, but he was still too mad to do anything about it.

Scratch that. He was *furious*.

"You never listen, Charlotte. You put yourself in danger at every turn. You risked your life coming back for us tonight, and—"

"And it's a damn good thing too. If I hadn't, you, Cole, and Aiden might be dead."

"*Highly* unlikely. Maimed, perhaps. But—"

"That demon bitch tried to incinerate you! She dropped your ass like a hot stone! I saw you fall and all I could think was—"

"You shouldn't have seen that." Dorian clenched his jaw, doing his best to hold back the torrent of curses he wanted to unleash. "You shouldn't have even *been* there, Charlotte. If anything had happened—"

"Something *did* happen! You almost died!" She curled her hands into fists and closed her eyes. "*God*, Dorian! You're the most obstinate, demanding, pig-headed vampire I've ever met! Does it ever get old, acting like you're untouchable?"

"You tell me. You're the one who seems to have a death wish. Either that, or you've spent so much time at Ravenswood, you suddenly believe you're immortal."

She opened her eyes to look at him again, her gaze fiery. "I know I'm not immortal. And contrary to what you might think, I *don't* have a death wish. But when someone I love is in danger? You bet your immortal bloodsucking *ass* I'm going to fight for them."

"It won't do anyone a damn bit of good if you're dead."

"So I should do nothing? Is that what you would do?"

"We're not talking about me. We're talking about you."

Tears of frustration brimmed in her eyes, her copper irises glittering in the darkness as she continued to glare at him. Glare *through* him.

When she spoke again, her voice trembled with passion.

"My sister was taken, Dorian, and I wasn't there to protect her. A demon very nearly incinerated you tonight—so yes, I took a risk. I did what I had to do. You can call it reckless or a death wish or batshit crazy if you want to, but that won't change how I feel. It won't change the fact that I'd do it a hundred times over if it gave me even a *one* percent shot at keeping you safe."

"Those are *impossible* odds."

"One percent is still a chance, Dorian. One I'll take over the alternative every damn night of the week."

The tears finally spilled, streaking down her cheeks and cracking through the last of Dorian's anger.

Charlotte was only fighting for the people she cared about.

For Sasha. For Cole and Aiden.

For him.

Hadn't he sworn to do the same? Hadn't he *been* doing the same? As a king, as a prince, as a mortal man... Dorian hadn't always succeeded at keeping his loved ones safe, but he'd damn well tried.

He was *still* trying.

How could he take that away from Charlotte?

"You're... right," he finally managed, letting out a deep sigh. His lungs had finally healed—something he could only appreciate because of her. "I owe you a thank you, Charlotte. And an apology." He reached out and cupped her face, brushing away her tears with his thumbs. Through a soft smile, he said, "I suppose I'm still getting used to the idea that I can't keep you in a bubble. With extra padding and a bevy of armed guards, locked away in a castle, surrounded by a moat filled with sharks. And lava. And perhaps a few crocodiles, just to be safe. Oh, and a German Shepherd. I hear they're *fierce* protectors."

This finally got a smile in return—a sight that instantly made up for all the arguing.

"I'd say that makes you a paranoid, overbearing psycho," she said, "but the truth is, I'd do the same thing for my sister."

"Sasha would no more allow it than you, but... point taken."

Charlotte nodded, but her smile was already fading, her eyes clouding with worry. "This night was a complete fucking disaster, and it's all my fault."

"We couldn't have known Estas was planning a party, or that someone would flood the woods with more grays."

"I should've planned for the possibility, though—for *all* possibilities. That's how it works." She shook her head, admonishing herself. "You were so worried about me risking my life, but what about you? You risked your life fighting off those demons. You risked your life just walking in there with me tonight, and what do we have to show for it? The grays might've been an outside job, but our little smash-and-grab wasn't. Estas knows *exactly* what we're up to now. How long until he clues Rudy in and we're totally fucked?"

"Not happening. We left nothing behind. The demons found us in the basement—most likely, they'll assume we were after the grays. Jacinda may already know we're onto her about the amulets—it's not a stretch to believe we tracked her to Estas' place."

"Dorian, I left the external drive plugged into the damn laptop." She leaned her head back against the headrest and rolled her eyes, a defeated sigh escaping her lips. "Amateur move, D'Amico. Total *fucking* amateur."

"The drive? That's what you're on about?"

"My father's probably rolling over in his grave."

"Really? Over this little bit of plastic and circuitry right here?" Dorian retrieved the drive from his pocket and handed it over. "And Aiden thinks *I'm* dramatic."

Her eyes went wide, a smile breaking across her face as she stared at the thing in disbelief. "Are you *serious* right now?"

"It would appear that I am."

Charlotte laughed and set the drive on the dash, then

surprised the hell out of him by crawling out of the driver's seat and maneuvering into his lap, straddling him. Sliding her hands over his shoulders, she grinned again and whispered, "Dorian Redthorne, I could *kiss* you."

"Ah, but what a fall from grace." Dorian ran his hands up her thighs and gripped her hips, returning her smile. "The fearless, death-defying, *heartbreakingly* beautiful Charlotte D'Amico lowering her standards to kiss an obstinate, demanding, boar-headed—no, wait. It was pig-headed, wasn't it? An obstinate, demanding, *pig*-headed vampire—"

She cut him off with a kiss that stole his breath away, igniting a fire inside him that'd been smoldering for days. Her thighs clamped tight around him, and she slid her hands behind his neck and fisted his hair, the familiar press of her body bringing him back from all the darkness they'd endured tonight.

Her mouth was soft and warm and inviting, and there he lingered, tracing the contours of her lips with his tongue, nibbling and teasing, savoring the sweet taste of a kiss that was rapidly working him into the best kind of frenzy.

There was no hiding her effect on him. In a matter of seconds, he was as hard as steel, his cock aching beneath her.

"Dorian," she breathed, rocking her hips and rubbing against his length, driving him absolutely wild.

He tightened his grip on her hips, wishing like hell they were already naked. All he wanted to do was drive his cock into her hot, hungry flesh.

All he wanted to do was make her come.

But despite their mutual carnal appetites, something held Dorian back.

He knew Charlotte was upset about Sasha—about everything that'd happened tonight. As much as he wanted to give in to this impossibly hot moment, he wouldn't take advantage when she was feeling so vulnerable.

"Charlotte," he whispered, pulling back to catch his breath. "We don't have to do this right now. I understand it's—"

"I want to." She leaned forward again and pressed a searing hot kiss to his neck, then captured his earlobe between her teeth, her breath hot on his skin. "I need this, Dorian," she whispered, running her tongue along the shell of his ear. "You're the only thing that can make my mind stop spinning."

A shiver rolled through his body.

"I can... certainly... distract you," he panted, doing his damnedest to stay focused, but bloody *hell*, that hot, soft tongue of hers was making it nearly impossible. "But it's not... going to... solve..."

"I don't care." She pulled back, her voice breaking with emotion. "I'm barely keeping it together. Everything inside me hurts, Dorian. It fucking hurts."

"I know, love." He traced his fingertips over her eyebrow. He knew he could bring her to ecstasy, but right now, he wished he could simply erase her anguish.

"If you can take me away from this for even five lousy *minutes*," she said, "I want it. Please don't say no."

Dorian's resolve crumbled. In that moment, there was nothing he'd refuse her.

"Five lousy minutes?" he teased softly. A lock of hair had come loose from her ponytail, and he tucked it behind her ear, pressing a kiss to the corner of her mouth. "I think we can do a bit better than that."

She was already reaching for the button and zipper on his pants, freeing him.

"You're certain?" he asked.

Charlotte nodded, smiling again despite her pain. "Yes, Mr. Redthorne. Make me forget, just for a little while."

And just like that, Dorian was gone, lost to her desperate whispers, her eager touch, the warmth of it as she fisted his cock and stroked him just... *fucking hell*... just right.

"Charlotte, you... I'm going to... You need to... slow *down*," he finally managed, worried he wouldn't last five lousy *seconds*, let alone five minutes.

But she was relentless. Hungry. *Insatiable*.

"I need you inside me," she breathed urgently. "Don't make me beg. Not tonight."

"As you wish."

In the tight space of the car, Dorian helped her out of her leggings and panties, but there was no time to remove anything else. Naked from the waist down, she straddled him again, then sank down onto his cock, wrapping him in her soft, seductive heat.

For one brief moment, she stilled, her body pulsing around his cock in time with her heartbeat.

Dorian touched his forehead to her shoulder and sighed. She felt so bloody perfect, he wanted to weep.

They hadn't been together like this since before Sasha was taken, and even though it had only been a few days, he was absolutely *starved* for her. After everything he'd recently endured—fighting off the grays in the alley, carrying her wounded body out of that dumpster, watching Colin stitch her up, bearing the weight of Isabelle's crushing proclamation about her soul, torturing Rogozin's demons, the fight at Estas' place tonight—being inside her felt like a safe haven, a respite from every last one of life's torments.

If Dorian could've stayed there for an eternity, he would have.

But Charlotte was already moving again, rolling her hips to bring him in deeper, desperate to lose herself to this momentary pleasure.

"More," she demanded. "I want more of you."

Wrapping a hand around her throat, he pushed her backward, her shoulder blades hitting the dash. The new angle of her body gave him even deeper access, and he thrust inside her, making her gasp. He slid his other hand beneath her shirt, running it up her taut stomach, then palming her breast. Beneath the lace bra, her nipple rose at his touch.

Charlotte closed her eyes.

"Fuck, yes," she breathed. "Don't stop."

He had no intention of stopping. Not if Cole and Aiden emerged from the cabin and caught them in the act. Not if the grays returned and surrounded them. Not if the very pits of hell opened up and swallowed them whole.

The thought of hell reminded him of the demon mark, setting his heart ablaze.

I will not let you go, Charlotte D'Amico...

He fucked her deeper, harder, but it still wasn't enough. Bringing her upright on his lap again, Dorian hooked his hands around her shoulders and pulled her down hard against him, thrusting to meet her desperate writhing, driving into her wet heat again and again, giving her everything she wanted.

It was so hot, so intense.

Already his fangs throbbed, aching to break through, aching to sink deep into her flesh.

Please don't ask me to bite you, love. I won't be able to say no...

Dorian was damn near delirious with the thought, but Charlotte wasn't looking for the bite tonight. Only his cock, which she claimed with a wild, feverish desperation, as if she could ride him to some distant, foreign shore where nothing bad could ever touch them again.

The fog of their breath coated the windows, hiding them in their own private paradise.

And still, they didn't stop.

Kissing. Teasing. Touching. Fucking. Devouring.

"Charlotte," Dorian moaned, his balls tightening, so fucking close. Wherever she'd gone, he'd fucking follow, chasing her through all the darkness to the very edge of that achingly beautiful precipice.

He slid a hand between them, seeking her clit. At his touch, Charlotte let out a cry of pleasure, her body tightening around him like a fist.

"Fuck," she whispered. "Right there. Right... *God*, Dorian. You always know how to... *Yes*..."

"That's it, love," he murmured, quickening his touch. "Come for me. Let me feel you *break*."

"I'm so close. I'm... *Dorian*! *Fuck*!" She gasped and dug her fingers into his shoulders, her whole body shuddering as the orgasm took hold. A pink blush rose on her cheeks, her mouth parted in sheer ecstasy, a thin sheen of sweat glistening on her brow.

Dorian couldn't take his eyes off her.

She was stunning—like an immortal goddess. And in that moment, he wished she truly *was* immortal.

He couldn't bear the thought of a world without her.

Couldn't bear the thought of *his* world without her—not even for a single day.

He brought his mouth to hers, capturing her final moans in a kiss. She writhed in his lap, and he dragged his lips down to her chin, to her throat, lingering in the hollow above her collarbone, drinking in the taste and scent of her skin.

"My vampire king," she whispered dreamily, her body clenching him tight, and Dorian was *gone*.

"That's...I'm... Fucking *hell*, woman!" He came hot and hard inside her, marking her. Claiming her. Reminding himself that she *belonged* to him, as surely as he belonged to her, and no one—*nothing*—would shatter that bond.

Not Estas.

Not Rudy D'Amico.

Not Alexei Rogozin.

And *certainly* not some pathetic demon lord lurking in the bowels of hell.

As the last, blissful tremors finally receded, Dorian stilled inside her, once again sensing the pulse of her heartbeat, the perfect heat, the softness.

She smiled at him in the darkness, and he lifted a hand to cup her face, holding her as if she were the most delicate summer rose on the vine.

Emotion welled in his chest.

"Tell me you're mine, Charlotte," he said suddenly, desperate to hear her say it. "Promise me you'll *always* be mine."

Another smile ghosted across her mouth, and she closed her eyes and touched her forehead to his, her breath warm and sweet on his lips. "I'm yours, Dorian Redthorne. Always."

Dorian closed his eyes, letting her soft voice echo through his mind and shore up his heart, as if her own impassioned declaration could break the curse that bound her to another.

The curse he'd yet to tell her about.

"I love you," he whispered, and there in the quiet, intimate space of the car, the truth of those words—the depth of them—finally set him free.

He would tell her about the demon mark tonight because she deserved to know.

But in the end, the confession wouldn't matter.

One way or another, Dorian would hunt down the beast who'd claimed her.

And one way or another, he'd destroy him.

Even if he had to destroy himself in the process.

CHAPTER ELEVEN

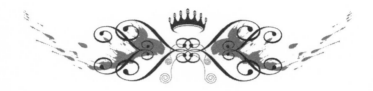

They drove back to Ravenswood in silence, Charlotte lost in her own thoughts, Dorian struggling to find the words for his.

He was no closer when the massive stone manor finally came into view. No closer when he pulled into the garage, navigating the BMW to the dark corner in the back. No closer when he turned off the car, listening to the familiar tick of the engine.

The sound used to bring him comfort; it'd always meant he was home. That however terrible and black the day had been, he'd survived it. That somehow, he'd made it back to the one place that always brought him solace.

Now, the sound reminded him only of a bomb counting down to its brutal detonation.

Next to him, Charlotte let out a deep sigh, her shoulders heavy with some new weight.

Neither of them made a move to exit the car.

"There's something you're not telling me," she finally said, her voice impossibly soft in the confined space. "I can always tell when you're holding back."

"Between you and Aiden," he teased, "I'm afraid I'll never be able to hide anything again."

"Are you still upset with me about tonight?"

Dorian brushed his knuckles across her cheek and shook his head. He could no more stay mad at her than he could imagine spending an eternity without her.

"Then what is it?" she asked.

Then what is it... The ultimate question. There were so many thoughts colliding in his head, all he had to do was reach out and pluck one from the ether.

It's that I'm so in love with you, I feel as if my heart might burst.

It's that I would die before I let him take you from me.

It's that I can't bloody exist without you, Charlotte D'Amico...

"When I say you're *mine*, Charlotte," Dorian said, "do you have any idea what that really means?"

A faint smile touched her lips. "That you're a possessive, overbearing caveman? A trait I'm learning to love about you, but—"

"It means you're my heart. My soul. My absolute... *obsession.*" Dorian closed his eyes. Bloody *hell*, how had it even happened? Wasn't he the one who'd sworn off love forever?

He recalled that first night with her in Central Park, when he'd compelled her to forget the Chernikov demon attack. Even then, when she was merely a sexy, feisty stranger he'd ravaged in a closet, he'd wanted so badly to protect her from the darkness of his supernatural existence.

Little did he know then, she was already on a collision course.

"Losing you..." Dorian's throat closed on the words, but he shook his head and swallowed hard, forcing himself to continue. "It would *end* me. Do you understand?"

Her smile faded, and she turned away from him. "I'm not the one who's lost. Sasha—"

"Will be found." He reached for her face, turning her toward him once again. "And her tormentors will be brought to their knees, kept alive just long enough to look upon the face of their executioner, who will show them *no* mercy."

A soft sigh. Another smile.

Both melted him.

"My very own vampire hero," she said, "charging in to smite my mortal enemies."

"I'm quite adept at smiting mortal enemies. If only it were as easy to vanquish the *immortal* ones."

Her brow furrowed, and she opened her mouth to question him, but Dorian spoke first.

"You're right, love. I've been keeping something from you. Dodging it for days, trying to find a way around it, but there *is* no bloody way around it." He was still holding her face, and he forced himself to keep his touch steady, knowing this moment wouldn't get any easier. Not for either of them. "Isabelle... She's an empathic witch. She can sense things about people—about our souls."

"Right. She mentioned something about it the other night when she was trying to do a locator spell for Sasha. Has she found something?"

"This isn't about your sister, Charlotte. It's about you. You're..." Dorian closed his eyes, wishing he could hold onto this moment for just one more minute. One more *second* before he spoke the words that would shatter her world.

But time, as it so often did, had finally run out.

"When she was helping Colin heal you," he said, "she found an anomaly in your energy. In your soul."

"An anomaly?"

"You're... you're demon-touched. I suspect that's why vampire compulsion doesn't work on you—his claim essentially invalidates it. Perhaps only the demon himself can manipulate your mind. You were promised to him, and you... Somehow the mark... It's all just... Bloody *hell*." He was making no sense, all the words tangling up inside, his own terrifying thoughts bleeding into Isabelle's interpretations until he could no longer find the beginning or the end of this dreadful story.

"I don't understand what you're saying, Dorian. Demon-touched? A claim? *What*?"

"You're bound to a demon lord, Charlotte. Someone promised you to him. And according to Isabelle, the end of your term is... quite near."

"But... but what happens then?" Her voice was a

SARAH PIPER

broken whisper, her eyes wide with the same horror coursing through Dorian's own veins.

He did his best to explain, as Isabelle had explained to him—that Charlotte belonged to a lord of hell. That she would either die and become a vessel…

Or live and become a slave.

The *demon's* slave.

Every word sliced through Dorian's mouth, as if he were spitting out broken glass. He couldn't tell which hurt worse—forcing those sharp, jagged-edged words through his lips, or seeing the raw fear and pain in her eyes as she tried in vain to make sense of them.

"I don't know which lord," he continued, "nor how to find him, nor how many demon lords even exist. I don't know who brought this cruel fate upon you. I don't know how much longer we have until the demon attempts to collect on his claim. But I do know this, Charlotte… I will *not* rest until I find a way to break this abominable curse."

She turned away from him again, her breath shallow, her heartbeat as quick as a rabbit's caught in a snare.

Rage boiled up from inside—at the demon, at hell, at whoever had made this promise.

Charlotte was *not* for sale. Not for trade. That such a bright, vivacious human soul could be so carelessly bargained away was a fucking abomination.

After an eon, she finally turned to face him again, her lashes wet with tears, eyes wide in the darkness. In a pained whisper that nearly gutted him, she said only, "And what if you can't?"

Dorian reached for her hands and brought them to his mouth, pressing soft kisses to her palms. When he glanced up at her again, his own eyes blurred with tears, his voice shattering, his heart damn near exploding with the force of his conviction. "Then my last act upon this *wretched* earth will be to sign away what's left of my soul. I will follow you to the depths of hell, Charlotte, because I love you, and I'll continue to love you—in this realm or the next—for however bloody long eternity lasts."

CHAPTER TWELVE

You're bound to a demon lord, Charlotte...

The words echoed through Charley's nightmares, chasing her down every dark alley, into every fiery pit. She couldn't escape them; even as Dorian held her in his strong embrace, tucked into his bed hours after they'd returned from Cole's cabin, everything about his confession haunted her.

A demon claim. A slave of hell.

It all sounded so ridiculous and impossible—like something out of a low-budget horror movie. But she'd seen the fear in Dorian's eyes when he'd said the words. She'd felt the desperation in his touch.

However impossible, it was real. *All* of her nightmares were real.

And all of them—Sasha's kidnapping, her father's murder, the attack by Rogozin's guys when she was a kid, the demon mark—could be traced right back to Rudy.

Charley might not know the specifics, but she was sure of it now.

Her uncle was a conniving, murderous, demonic shitbag who deserved to fester in hell.

The question was...

What the fuck was she going to do about it?

There was something supremely hopeful about the smell of coffee on a crisp fall morning, and when Charley made her way down to the kitchen, the dark shadows that had haunted her all night finally began to shrink.

Taking in the sight, she couldn't help but smile.

Sunshine. Coffee. Friends. The vampire she was madly in love with.

It felt like the universe was conspiring to give her a second chance at a better day. Was there anything more promising?

"Good morning, beautiful." Dorian rose from the table in the breakfast nook, where he, Aiden, and Cole had been huddling over a pair of laptops, a tablet, and enough print-outs to wallpaper the kitchen.

"*There's* our little speed demon," Cole said, winking as Dorian came to press a soft kiss to her cheek. The wolf mimicked a crazy steering maneuver at the table, nearly knocking over his mug. "Thought maybe you'd snuck off to the racetrack to practice your sweet-ass moves."

Charley laughed. "Coffee first. Sweet-ass moves later."

Dorian handed her a freshly brewed cup, then wrapped his hand around the back of her neck and smiled softly—a look that was just for her.

Are you all right, love? he seemed to be asking. *I'm right here with you.*

She read it all in his eyes, and in response, she nodded and let out a slow breath, the last of the night's tension evaporating.

Of *course* he was right there with her. And he always would be.

For however bloody long eternity lasts...

It was a promise, a vow, and it gave her so much strength, she felt as if they could accomplish anything.

Charley smiled again, warmed by the coffee and the support. No matter how cold and dark the night had seemed, the sun had found a way to rise again.

So maybe, Charley could do the same.

With one more adoring glance for her man, she joined their friends at the table.

"I'll be back with you in just a moment." Dorian pulled the phone from his pocket. "I need to check in with Isabelle."

"Everything okay?" Charley asked.

"She's planning to go to bat for us with Armitage's senior staff in an hour. They're reviewing FierceConnect's latest counter-offer."

"So there's a chance the acquisition might happen after all?"

"We're not sure. According to Isabelle, her brothers are still keen on selling to Duchanes, but she's hoping to change their minds. Regardless of what they think of our offer, I still want everything to look legitimate if Rudy sends in additional investigators. With Aiden and me working out of the office this week, I don't want to arouse suspicions."

Charley nodded, grateful he'd thought of it.

As Dorian headed out to make the call, she turned her attention back to the paperwork spread out before her.

"I take it these are the Estas files?" she asked, skimming through a page of what looked like bank account numbers —probably for the buyers Rudy had already lined up for the Ravenswood art.

"Took a bit of doing," Aiden said, "but Dorian was finally able to crack the file encryption and get us set up. We've just started sorting through it. Perhaps you can tell us what these numbers mean?"

He turned his laptop around so she could see what he was looking at—a spreadsheet containing what appeared to be random numbers and dollar amounts.

But Charley knew they weren't random at all.

"They're bids," she said. "And the codes in the right-hand column are serial numbers to track the pieces they're fencing. There should be a master sheet for the artwork somewhere."

Cole handed over a few printed pages from the pile in front of him—a list of the Ravenswood artwork she'd cataloged for Rudy, complete with the corresponding serial numbers that matched the ones in the spreadsheet.

"How does all this fit together?" Aiden asked. "Seems fairly complicated."

"With a major score like this, dealers will often line up buyers in advance," Charley said. "When there's more than one potential buyer for a hot piece, they'll take bids or even early deposits. There's probably a list of names somewhere —they keep everything in separate files to make it harder to put together."

"Lucky for us," Cole said, "we got you on the job."

"That, and they're getting a little careless," Charley said. "Seems like this job has *everyone* on edge—not just Uncle Psycho." She tabbed through the open files on the laptop until she found what she was looking for, then turned the screen back toward Aiden. "These are probably our bidders."

"Those traitorous little shites," Aiden said, a note of surprise coloring his voice. "Most of these knobs are high-ranking officials from other supernatural factions—vampire houses, witch covens, demons, shifter packs. The gang's all here."

Charley shrugged. "Estas is a demon. And don't take this the wrong way, but a lot of you guys are *loaded*. It makes sense he'd hit up the supernatural community first."

"He's not hitting them up because of the money," Aiden said. "He's doing it because they believe the pieces have occult value. Witches in particular are known for purchasing rare art and antiquities. Anything from the home of the vampire royal family is bound to be in high demand, especially so soon after the death of the last king."

"So all these fuckers know Ravenswood's about to get robbed?" Cole shook his head. "Can't trust anyone these days."

"Precisely why I don't." Dorian had just returned from his call, and now he settled into the chair next to Charley, his brow creased with new concern. "Present company excluded, the world is full of cutthroats and sellouts. It's no wonder Father kept his circle small."

"Dori." Aiden laughed. "Your father's circle was a straight line. He didn't even talk to his own family."

"Probably for the best."

Beneath the table, Charley gave Dorian's thigh a gentle squeeze. "Did Armitage reject the counter offer?"

"Not yet. Isabelle's been reviewing their financials with the CFO all morning. Apparently, they've discovered some serious anomalies they haven't been able to reconcile."

"Lemme guess." Cole picked up the tablet and woke it from sleep mode. "Armitage's little mini-mages are embezzlin' from the old man?"

"The opposite, actually," Dorian said. "Billions of dollars in venture funding no one can trace, siphoned into top-secret projects the C-level staff know nothing about. Isabelle has stumbled into a real mess."

"Take heart, then," Aiden said with a grin. "Perhaps the Redthornes aren't the most dysfunctional supernatural family on the eastern seaboard after all."

Dorian rolled his eyes. "We can always count on you to find the silver lining."

"It's what I live for."

"Yeah, about that..." Cole blew out a deep sigh, then passed the tablet to Aiden. "Think I just found some shit even *you* can't turn into sunshine."

"What the hell is... Oh, dear." Aiden's eyes widened as he scrolled through the documents. There was no smart-ass commentary, no bright-side banter, no *nothing*. He was silent for so long, Charley started to worry something had actually broken him.

"Out with it," Dorian finally prompted.

"It would seem Vincent Estas is more than just Rogozin's dirty art dealer. He's also a demonic contracts manager." Aiden's mouth twisted into a scowl. "And *this* lifelong opus of debauchery and malfeasance belongs to one Rudolpho D'Amico."

Charley's heart leaped into her throat. "Is that how he became a host? He made a demon deal?"

"I'm not sure about the host part," Aiden said, "but he definitely made deals. Lots of them—starting when he was just a teenager. It's all here—all of his requests. All the relevant documentation."

"A *teenager*?" Charley couldn't believe it. "That means he knew Rogozin when..."

Her words trailed off before she could finish her sentence, and the old fears knocked around inside her, squeezing her lungs tight.

Don't struggle, D'Amico bitch...

Dorian slid his arm around her, pulling her close. Even without the words, he knew exactly where her mind had gone.

Charley leaned on his shoulder, trying to keep her breath steady.

If Rudy was involved with demons that far back in time, then he *damn* well knew Rogozin was a demon when he'd dragged Charley and her father to that abandoned pizza joint on Long Island.

Not so tough when Daddy's not around, are ya?

Aiden continued to scroll, shaking his head in disgust, though his eyes held a touch of sadness. "It seems your uncle was quite... desperate."

"For money, right?" Charley scoffed. Wasn't it *always* about the money with him? "Rudy was obsessed with it long before we got into the family business. He resented my father because Dad always managed to get better jobs than him. Even if it was just a minimum-wage gig at the auto parts store, Rudy always had something shitty to say about it."

"Charlotte, it's..." Aiden sighed and exchanged a heavy glance with Dorian, then passed over the tablet.

Charley couldn't bring herself to look at it. She didn't want confirmation of what Rudy had traded away in exchange for all that cash.

She was pretty sure she already knew.

You're bound to a demon lord, Charlotte. Someone promised you to him...

Dorian took the tablet and read through the file, a dark

sigh escaping his lips. "I don't think money was the source of your uncle's resentment toward his brother, love"

"Then what was it? My father spent most of his life in a dinky little trailer park. It's not like he had anything to envy."

"Apparently, there *was* one thing."

"His piece-of-shit Toyota?" Charley let out a bitter laugh, but the look in Dorian's eyes was dead serious.

"Your mother, Charlotte."

"My... *what*?"

In Dorian's rich accent, the words felt completely out of context. The suggestion that her mother—a woman who'd marched unceremoniously out of their lives decades ago and never looked back—could have anything to do with this demon business was beyond absurd.

But no one else seemed to think so. Especially not Dorian, who looked at her as if his own heart was breaking over the revelation.

The coffee in Charley's stomach turned to cement.

With trembling hands, she took the tablet and scrolled through the files and photos, each one punching a fresh hole in her chest.

Her mother's records—aliases, addresses, personal details. Thousands of emails between her and Rudy. Transcripts of online chats—declarations of love, arguments, apologies. Pictures of the woman from the time she was in junior high all the way up to more recent shots—pale and gaunt, cigarette dangling from her mouth, barely recogniz-able as the formidable mother in Charley's memories.

There were other pictures too.

Charley's parents dancing at their high school prom, and then her mother making out with Rudy in the limo afterward.

Rudy and her mom holding hands on the beach a few years later, her father nowhere in sight.

Rudy and her mom snuggling together in the booth at the diner around the corner from their trailer park, years after that.

Her mom in some seedy motel bed, covering her face with her hands, a smile peeking out from between her fingers.

Her mother.

Her uncle.

Holy shit.

They'd been having an affair for decades—starting when they were in high school, long before Charley was even born. Putting this together with what Charley knew of her parents' history, she figured her mom must've bounced between the two brothers for most of her teen years and into her twenties before finally marrying Charley's dad.

And then, she continued bouncing, keeping Rudy on the sidelines the entire time.

According to a particularly heated email exchange, Rudy had even assumed he was Charley's father at one point, but a paternity test later proved him wrong.

Thank fucking God.

Charley didn't want to read the emails. Didn't want to see the photos. But she couldn't look away.

The truth revealed itself, one little file at a time.

Rudy had been in love with her mother forever. Obsessed with her. And she strung him along through all of it, making promise after promise, only to push him away again the minute someone better or richer or more interesting came along.

It was still going on; the most recent photos were taken at an apartment complex in Florida—her mother's place, she assumed—just a few months ago.

Briefly, she wondered if her mother had asked Rudy about her and Sasha.

And in that moment, the faintest pang of sympathy struck her heart.

She hated herself for it, but she couldn't deny it. Because beneath all the revulsion Charley felt toward her uncle, she understood his pain—the soul-crushing emptiness of a desperate, lifelong chase for the affection of a woman who couldn't care less.

"He blames me," Charley said. "Sasha too. He says it's our fault my mother didn't choose him. That if she hadn't gotten herself—and I quote—knocked up with those empty-headed little sluts, she would've run away with him in a heartbeat." Charley set the tablet down. "I can't believe he managed to keep this secret for so many years."

"He had some help," Dorian said.

"That's what I don't get. Why does Estas even *have* all this personal stuff? Why would Rudy give it to the demons?"

"It's part of his file—his agreement," Dorian said. "If

Rudy made a deal with Rogozin in hopes of winning over your mother, the demons would've wanted to know everything about her."

"Why?"

"Demons can't force someone to fall in love any more than vampires can compel true desire. They can only force the circumstances that might bring people together. By knowing everything there was to know about your mother, the demons could ensure Rudy was always on her path."

"Someone should've clued them in to the fact that my mother is incapable of love. Would've saved everyone a lot of time."

"The demons wouldn't have cared. They prey on the desperate, and they don't offer guarantees."

"So Rudy became a demon host, binding himself to hell for eternity, just for a *chance* with my mother?"

"The file doesn't include the specific terms of his contract, but yes, I think that's a fair assumption. It's like he also performed other duties for Rogozin as well. Errands, introductions, criminal acts. When it comes to demon deals, the possibilities are endless."

"Where's the rest of the contract?" she asked.

Dorian shook his head. "We've got files from one flash drive. This is likely just the tip of a very large, very dark iceberg."

"Charles," Cole said, halfway through another stack of papers on the table. "Was your daddy's name Paul D'Amico, by any chance?"

Charley nodded, her heart stalling out as Cole passed over the stack.

"What is it?" Dorian asked.

"It looks like... copies of my father's will." She flipped through several pages of legalese. "Two different versions. In one version, he left everything to me. The penthouse, the artwork, his liquid assets—all of it."

"But you said most of his assets went to Rudy," Dorian said. "Unless—"

"Version two is a forgery. That's how Rudy got his hands on everything." Charley's insides burned with anger. She wanted to kick herself for not realizing it sooner. "I should've known my father wouldn't have left me high and dry like that, but at the time, I was just so out of it... I didn't question anything."

"You were heartbroken," Dorian said gently. "Of course you didn't."

"Does the name Travis ring any bells?" Cole asked, picking up another sheet of paper. "Looks like he's the one behind the forgery. Named here as an interested party—a human contractor brought in on the One Night Stand job and retained for Ravenswood."

"Travis?" Charley sucked in a sharp breath. "But we didn't meet him until about a year after my dad died."

"According to this," Cole said, turning to another page, "Whenever Estas sells something from One Night Stand, Rudy and Travis pocket the proceeds. Looks like they've got a similar deal set up for Ravenswood."

Charley glanced down at the forged will again, tears

blurring her vision as the bitter truth burned through her heart.

Rudy and Travis were behind her father's murder.

She'd known. Deep down, she'd *always* known. She just hadn't wanted to believe that her uncle could orchestrate the killing of his own brother.

But the forged will said it all.

Hell, a *lot* of things had said it all. They'd been saying it all—*screaming* it—for years. She'd just chosen to ignore it, shutting away her doubts and fears like she always did.

The confirmation was shocking, but Charley wasn't surprised. Not really.

Now, in the darkest parts of her heart, there was only room for one response.

Terror.

"Rudy had my father killed," she whispered. "What's to stop him from doing the same to Sasha?"

"*We* are," Dorian said firmly.

"All of us," Aiden said, and Cole nodded too. "Charlotte, we're going to get her back—safe and whole. You have to believe that."

"Listen to me, love." Dorian gripped her shoulders, gazing into her eyes with so much conviction, Charley had no choice but to believe what came next. "Regarding your uncle's connection to Rogozin, his fixation on your mother, as well as his involvement in your father's murder—I know it's a lot to take in. But factually speaking, *nothing* has changed from a day ago or even five years ago. He's been keeping these secrets the entire time. The only difference is we know about them now, which means we can do something about them. But only if we stay focused, and only if we don't lose hope." He leaned in close, whispering softly against her ear. "Everything is going to be all right. I *promise* you."

Charley nodded. Dorian was absolutely right, and his firm, no-nonsense attitude was just what she needed right now.

"Something else ain't adding up here," Cole said, pulling another file up on one of the laptops. "There's a separate spreadsheet with two *very* high bids for the same piece of art. Actually, it looks like these are wire transfers— they're connected to offshore banks. Twenty million bucks apiece."

"Twenty million?" Dorian asked. "For the same piece?"

"Serial number 87206."

Charley scanned through the master list of the artwork. "It's not here. There must be another file somewhere. Try searching for the number directly on the computer. I'll see if I can track down the bidder names."

"Is that typical?" Dorian asked. "Two payments for the same piece?"

"Not at all." Charley reached for the second laptop, paging through the files. "Bids are one thing, but deposits and transfers mean a sale is pending. Estas and Rudy are either getting *very* sloppy, or they're planning a double-cross."

"Or both," Aiden said.

"Found it." Charley scanned through yet another list—

names connected with banking details and wire transfer amounts—twenty million each. "And the lucky buyers are... Alexei Rogozin and Nikolai Chernikov."

"You've *got* to be joking," Dorian said, leaning in for a closer look. "Estas works for Rogozin. He's playing his own boss against their top demonic rival?"

"I got bad news and worse news," Cole said, tapping the screen on the other laptop. "Bad news is—that's exactly what he's doing. From some of the correspondence here, it looks like Estas and Rudy were banking on 87206 to bring in a lot of early bids from the supernatural community. They'd planned to auction it off before the robbery, but then two buyers elbowed their way to the top."

"Rogozin and Chernikov," Charley said.

"Yep. But here's the kick in the ass," Cole said. "Neither of them know the other guy's in the mix. Estas and Rudy promised 87206 to *both* buyers, demanding full payment in advance. Well, they got it. Now the demons are cranking up the heat, getting desperate for a confirmation that the artwork has been secured. No wonder your uncle's all twisted up, Charles. The demons want it *bad*, and Rudy and Estas aren't even sure it's here. It wasn't on your list."

"That's the *bad* news?" Dorian sighed. "What's the worse news?"

"87206?" Cole reached into his pocket for his whiskey, then dumped a healthy dose into his coffee mug. "It's the Mother."

"The mother?" Charley asked. "Is that... Oh, *no*." She

dropped her head into her hands as the realization finally dawned. "You're talking about the Mother of Lost Souls."

"Bingo," Cole said. "You know her?"

"The night Rudy and Silas nabbed me in the alley, they asked me about it. *Shit*—I completely forgot. Rudy got all stressed out when I said I hadn't seen it."

"Is it any wonder?" Dorian asked. "They've already sold it to two different buyers. One of whom has been pressuring me for the same damn statue for months."

"Chernikov?" she asked.

"The same." Dorian slammed the laptop shut. "He's been stringing me along this entire time, promising to deliver intel on Rogozin in exchange for this dreadful sculpture, knowing damn well Rudy was planning to steal it from me anyway."

"Hedging his bets," Aiden said. "Can't exactly blame him. Augustus promised it to him more than two centuries ago, and it never materialized."

"Guys. What's the deal with this Mother of Lost Souls piece?" Charley asked. "What's so special about it that two powerful demons are willing to fork out twenty million bucks for it, sight unseen?"

The three of them exchanged a loaded glance.

Charley was more confused than ever. "Do you even *have* it? I never saw it here."

"Be glad for that," Aiden said with a grimace. "The Mother has a face—"

"Don't say it," Dorian warned.

"—only a mother could love," Aiden finished anyway.

"Seriously?"

"It was the perfect setup, Dori. Admit it."

"I'll admit nothing." Dorian rose from his chair and held out a hand to Charley. "Fancy a walkabout, love? I think it's time we give you the rest of the tour."

CHAPTER THIRTEEN

"Everything about this place belongs in a movie." Charlotte grinned, her eyes wide as she stepped out of the elevator. "Crypts. Actual, legitimate crypts. Honestly, Dorian. Next you're going to tell me you all sleep in coffins when I'm not around."

Dorian laughed, trying to see everything through her eyes. He supposed it *was* a bit gothic and macabre—a secret network of tombs running beneath the manor, protecting the royal vampire family's closely-guarded secrets.

Secrets Dorian was about to reveal to the human he loved.

It wasn't how he'd imagined bringing her down here for the first time—that particular fantasy involved leading her into the darkest, most secluded tunnel, chaining her to the iron wall mounts, and tearing her clothes free with his teeth, one little scrap at a time until she was wet and hot and begging for...

Bloody hell. He forced the thoughts from his mind, willing his cock to behave.

Unfortunately for him and Charlotte both, circumstances had called them here today for another reason.

"Right this way, then," he said, leading them toward the chamber that had served as his father's laboratory.

In the short time since Dorian's last visit, Colin had managed to make it completely his own. Dorian's gaze skimmed over the organized chaos on the central stone slab—beakers and test tubes, vials of blood in a centrifuge, two microscopes, and stacks upon stacks of their father's journals, all of them teetering precariously toward a spill.

At the center of the tabletop, the demonic book they'd unearthed with the sculpture sat unopened, black and ancient. Even at a distance, it raised the hairs on Dorian's arms.

It felt like a warning.

Yet behind it all, Colin stood oblivious, his face glued to one of the microscopes.

"When you said your father had a lab down here," Charlotte said, "I didn't picture it quite so literally."

"Complete with the resident mad scientist," Aiden teased. Then, raising his voice, "Good morning, Colin. I see you're spending your nights wisely."

Colin was so lost in his work, he didn't even acknowledge their presence.

"We've brought you a trade, brother." Dorian approached the stone table and set down a small cooler of blood bags he'd brought from upstairs, courtesy of the local clinic. "Breakfast in exchange for a peek at the old Mother."

It was a few more moments before Colin glanced up from his work, his breath catching as he finally noticed the company.

"Dorian?" he asked calmly. "Have you seen Father?"

Dorian narrowed his eyes. "Are you all right, Colin?"

"I... of course." Colin blinked away the confusion. "I meant Father's other... centrifuge. I seem to have misplaced it."

His eyes were red and glassy, his long hair unkempt. In that moment, he looked so much like Augustus, Dorian's heart nearly stalled.

"When was the last time you fed?" Dorian asked.

"Or showered?" Aiden asked. "Goodness, Colin. You've become the literal troll under the bridge."

Aiden wrinkled his nose and took a step backward, but Colin was oblivious to the teasing.

He blinked again, still trying to process the sight before him.

Then, as if gripped by a sudden mania, he darted out in front of the table, attempting to block whatever he was working on from view. "Charlotte! I... Good evening. Rather, good morning. I... I wasn't aware Dorian wanted to show you around today. I would've... tidied up a bit."

"It's all right," Dorian said, concerned about his brother's frazzled state. "We won't be long. We're just here to see the sculpture."

Colin continued to blink.

"The Mother of Lost Souls?" Dorian prompted. "It would seem she's captured the interest of not just Chernikov, but Rogozin as well."

"Mother of... Lost Souls? The sculpture?" Colin snapped to attention, finally breaking free of the strange, work-induced trance. "Why didn't you say so?"

Dorian tried not to sigh. "You really need to eat, brother."

"And I will," he said with a familiar, dimpled smile that filled Dorian with relief. "As soon as I get you sorted down here."

He made his way through the disaster area to the shelves beyond, retrieving the bundle from the nook where they'd stashed it after Dorian and Cole had unearthed it.

"Here we are, then." Colin cleared a space at the end of the table, then unwrapped the sculpture.

It was just as ugly as Dorian remembered.

"So she's the woman who's got our demons all hot and bothered, huh?" Charlotte asked. "May I?"

Colin stepped aside to give her access, and she immediately got down to business, studying the piece with an unbroken intensity that brought a smile to Dorian's face.

He loved watching her work, her left brow arched gently, bottom lip caught between her teeth. She reminded him of an archeologist, her fingers exploring every curve and contour for clues about the Mother's origins.

Holding the sculpture upright, she slid her phone from her pocket and snapped a few close-up shots, then glanced at her screen, zooming in for more clues.

"You're like the Sherlock of the Smithsonian," Cole said with a low chuckle.

"It certainly feels that way sometimes," she said, still examining the photos on her screen.

"Well, what do you think, Sherlock?" Aiden asked. "What do the most powerful demon factions in the city want with that crude, nipple-less abomination?"

"Still with the nipple fixation?" Dorian gave Aiden's cheek a playful smack. "Perhaps you ought to talk to someone about that, mate."

"Perhaps the artist should've paid more attention in anatomy class."

"Aiden's right." Charlotte glanced up from the phone, her brow furrowed. "The lack of nipples is the first clue something isn't right."

Cole laughed. "And if *that* don't belong on a T-shirt…"

"What do you mean, something isn't right?" Dorian asked.

"Hate to be the guy who has to break this news to Rogozin and Chernikov," she said, "but this piece is a forgery."

It took Dorian a moment to realize she wasn't joking. "You're certain."

"Look." She put her phone away and grabbed a pen from the table, using it to direct their attention along the edges of the statue. "See these lines? They're seams from a cast. The forgers likely made a crude mold from the original piece, then filled it with clay. And these tiny grooves here? They're from a knife, probably used to scrape off the excess and try to smooth out the lines. They added the stones and hair, and carved in some of the other details, but then they got sloppy—hence the missing nipples."

"*Thank* you," Aiden said. "Vindication never felt so good."

"The weight balance feels off too," she said. "There's just something odd about the whole thing. Where did you say you bought this?"

"I didn't." Dorian picked it up for a closer look, squinting as if that might help him decipher the evidence as easily as Charlotte had. "It wasn't a purchase. My father stole it from House Kendrick in the 1800s, right after he slaughtered them."

He and Colin told her the story—as much as they knew of it, anyway.

"So tracing back the known ownership line," Charlotte said, tapping her lips, "Kendrick is the first one duped. Then your father, who promises to retrieve it for Chernikov but instead keeps it hidden in a coffin in your backyard. Two-hundred-some years later, your father passes away, and suddenly Chernikov—along with another demon kingpin—are both vying for it again, to the tune of twenty million dollars each."

"That sounds about right," Dorian said.

"But in all that time, no one thought to have it authenticated?" she asked. "No one even questioned it?"

"Apparently not," Dorian said.

She shook her head, still puzzling through the mystery. "The odd balance, the sloppy workmanship, the strange history, the insane wire transfers... It's almost as if... Oh, fuck *me*."

Charlotte's eyes suddenly blazed with a look of sheer wonder and excitement that rivaled Colin's the day they'd found the demon book. Then, before Dorian could utter another word, she grabbed the sculpture from his hands, lifted it over her head, and dropped it onto the floor, smashing it to bits.

CHAPTER FOURTEEN

"Brilliant!" Aiden laughed. "I can't tell you how badly I've wanted to do just that."

Dorian glared at her as if she'd lost her mind. Which, obviously, she had. "Bloody hell, woman! Forgery or not, that statue was our only bargaining chip with—"

"The statue wasn't the bargaining chip, Dorian." Charlotte crouched down and retrieved something from the rubble—a long, slender object wrapped in an old cloth, dusty with clay.

When she got to her feet again, she swayed.

"Charlotte?" Dorian reached out to steady her. "Are you all right?"

"Yeah, just... just a bout of vertigo. Combined with a big helping of déjà vu." She took a breath and shook her head. "It seems to have passed. That was... weird."

"Has this happened before?" Colin asked, immediately snapping into doctor mode.

"No. Probably just a head rush."

"Or a side effect of your injuries." Concern tightened his brow, and he held up a finger, asking her to follow it with her eyes. "Any other symptoms these past few days? Dizziness? Headache?"

"Honestly, I think I just got up too fast. I haven't eaten anything yet today either, so that's probably not helping."

Colin sighed, but his eyes held only warmth and kindness for his newest patient. "Charlotte, as your unofficial vampire doctor, I *insist* you take better care of yourself, lest I be forced to put you on bedrest under the watchful eye of my brooding brother."

"Gabriel?" Dorian teased, wrapping an arm around Charlotte's waist. "As if I'd allow *him* to darken her doorstep."

"I'm *fine*," she insisted. "I'll grab something to eat as soon as we get back upstairs."

With a reassuring smile for them both, she slid out of Dorian's hold and brought the bundle to the stone table, where she unwrapped it with a delicate touch.

"Holy shit," she whispered, her eyes widening again as if the day just kept getting better and better.

"What is it?" Colin asked.

Cole peered over her shoulder. "Some kinda dagger. Old as shit. Good for stabbing, though. Nice and pointy."

"Old as shit," she repeated reverently. "And yes, definitely good for stabbing. A *lot* of stabbing, if the history is to be believed."

"*What* history?" Dorian asked.

"Our demonic pals aren't after the Mother of Lost Souls, guys," she said. "They're after the blade of the *Bessmertnym Soldat*—the Immortal Soldier."

"Fancy name for a rusty old relic," Cole said.

"This *relic* allegedly killed some of the highest-ranking generals in Napoleon's *Grande Armée* during the Battle of Borodino," she said. "Not to mention scores of secret police, government officials, thieves... It's hundreds of years old. Thousands, maybe—its origins were never confirmed."

She lifted the blade, still partially wrapped in the cloth, and passed it to Dorian for a closer look. The others crowded in around him.

"It's falling apart," he said, noticing all the notches in the blade.

"Considering its age and the method of storage, it's actually quite well preserved," she said, her eyes still sparkling at the find. "It was forged in the shape of a raven's wing—the notches are intentional. My *God*, the detail work is just exquisite."

"Did you say a raven's wing?" Colin asked.

"Yes, the motif is repeated here too." She pointed to a few etchings in the bone handle. "The raven was often associated with death and immortality. It was probably a symbol of power for the men who'd forged it—allegedly, members of one of the original Russian assassin's guilds."

"Where does the immortal bit come in?" Aiden asked.

"According to legend," she said, "this blade was given to the most skilled assassin in the guild—a man known only as the *Bessmertnym Soldat*. The Immortal Soldier."

"Immortal, as in, all of this is no more than a myth?" Aiden asked. "A story told to naughty children at night to frighten them into behaving?"

Charlotte shook her head. "Immortal because he lived forever. At least, his persona did. Upon his death, his greatest apprentice would take up the blade and the identity, continuing the legacy. At any given time, no one knew the true identity of the Immortal Soldier, or for how long each assassin carried the name. The soldier—and this dagger—killed hundreds. Thousands. It vanished from the records soon after the Battle of Borodino, but there were rumors it was smuggled into England, hidden in a piece of art created for just that purpose. No one ever knew which piece."

"The Mother of Lost Souls." Dorian shook his head, glancing at the broken shards still scattered on the ground. "All this time, I thought it was just another esoteric piece of art. Yet it was hiding something far more valuable."

"Obviously, Rogozin and Chernikov knew better." Charlotte set the blade back on the slab and paced the small chamber. "A few months ago, I would've told you this piece was the Bratva's holy grail. But Rogozin and Chernikov's organizations make the Bratva look like schoolyard bullies. And with so many supernaturals bidding on other pieces from your father's collection... No. This isn't just a Russian cultural artifact. There's something more to all of this."

"She's right," Colin said suddenly, emerging from the shadows with one of their father's anatomy books in hand.

"There *is* more to it. A *lot* more. In fact, it's not a Russian artifact at all."

"What is it, then?" Dorian asked.

He glanced at Charlotte, then cut his eyes back to Dorian, as if he wasn't sure how much to reveal.

"Speak candidly, brother," Dorian said.

Colin let out a long, slow breath, then said, "This blade was forged in hell by an ancient demon called Azerius."

Cole barked out a laugh. "Just when I thought there might be a dull moment around here, you Redthornes gotta kick it up another notch."

"Colin, how did you come to know this?" Dorian asked.

"It's only a hypothesis, but…" He set the book on the slab, then rummaged excitedly through one of the stacks of journals until he found what he was looking for. "Father's journals spoke of a cure for demons—a weapon that would essentially strip a demon's essence from his vessel and trap it for eternity. The journals are cryptic at best—the fanatical rantings of a madman at worst—and I'd assumed the weapon he referred to was an actual formula, not unlike the one he synthesized to cure vampirism."

"Isn't it?" Aiden asked.

"I think the weapon, in this case, may be literal." Colin flipped open the journal and pointed to a passage in the center. "Many of his entries have odd references to ravens, like this one: 'The wing of the raven shall cure the darkness as surely as the sunrise cures the night.'" He flipped past a few pages, then read, "'Black as a demon's heart, forged in the very same darkness, the raven's gift is the key to its

139

demise.' There are literally *hundreds* of notations like this."
Colin set the journal back onto the stack, then grabbed the
anatomy book he'd left behind. "At first, I couldn't decipher whether raven wings were part of the formulary, or a
metaphor, or some other clue. I set aside that mystery in
order to work on re-creating the vampire cure, but when
Charlotte mentioned the raven's wing, I recalled *this*
book."

He held it up so they could see the cover.

"Corvidae: Anatomy and Physiology," Dorian read.
"What does that have to do with father's rantings?"

"Corvidae is the family of birds that includes the raven."
Colin gestured around the lab. "In all of the anatomy and
medical books father brought back here, this is the *only* one
that doesn't deal specifically with humans."

"So?"

"Father didn't study birds, Dorian, or *any* animals for
that matter. He was obsessed with humans. Always."
Colin's eyes had taken on the crazed appearance of the very
madman they were discussing, sweeping the rest of them
up in the majestic wonder of it all. "Yet consider the name
he bestowed upon the manor."

"Ravenswood," Dorian whispered.

"You yourself thought Father had intended for us to
find the blade and the book. Perhaps you were right, and all
of this—the journals, the name of our very home—is all
part of the trail he left for us to follow. I didn't want to see it
at first, but it's all here, Dorian. Written on every page,
inked over the original text." He handed the Corvidae book

to Dorian. "The first entry was written from the ship, right after we set sail for America."

Heart pounding in his chest, Dorian opened to the first page, focusing on the black hand-written letters floating above the text.

"At long last the Blade of the Raven King is in my possession," he read. "Kendrick was a fool to confide in me its purpose and location, but I shan't make the same mistake. I confide in no one but this very parchment—not even my own sons—not until such time as I deem it necessary for them to know. This alone shall ensure the longevity of our great house."

"Keep going," Colin said, his dimples flashing in the dim light of the cavern.

Dorian cleared his throat and continued. "In the darkness that followed the turning of the Redthorne line, for many years did I pray for guidance, yet none heeded my call. Not until the demon Azerius came to me in my dreams did I see the faintest glimmer of hope. The white raven spoke to me thusly: 'So shall a demon cross your path who shall rid you of your tormentors and allow you to ascend to your rightful position as king in the name of your forebears. In return, he will ask you to retrieve for him a gift befitting the lord of demons. You will retrieve this gift from the manor of your oppressors, but you must never reveal it. For if the Blade of Azerius and the Book of Lost Souls were to fall into the hands of a lesser immortal, chaos shall reign eternal…"

Dorian glanced up from the book, his memory echoing

with the words his father spoke the night he'd buried the Mother of Lost Souls and the book in the coffins behind Ravenswood.

A gift befitting the lord of demons—may his eternal reign darken our doorstep only until we're ready to see the light...

Colin took the book from Dorian's hands and continued where he'd left off. "The very next evening, the demon Nikolai approached me in the tavern, and after introducing himself as a messenger of Azerius, there we discussed my plight, though he was already well aware of my desperate need."

"Chernikov," Dorian said, and Colin nodded.

"Only such a demon," Colin read, "with the help of his coven of dark witches, could have assisted me in destroying the ruling vampire family that enslaved my line. Yet this help did not come without cost; in return, he demanded the very gift Azerius had spoken of: a blade with the power to cure this world of demons as surely as I might one day cure it of vampires, for a single drop of demonic blood spilled by the raven's wing shall imprison his essence within it for eternity, never to return to conscious awakening, not even in a human vessel. Used against humans, it shall expel the human soul to hell, creating a demonic vessel requiring neither consent nor contract."

Colin gasped, his fingers skimming over the words as if he needed to absorb them by touch in order to believe them.

"So lemme get this straight," Cole said. "Your old man made a deal with Chernikov—via this Azerius dude—to wipe out the ruling vampire family and ascend to the throne?"

"It makes sense," Dorian said. "I've always wondered how father managed it. House Kendrick was well-guarded, and the entire family was home at the time of the murders. Father's version of events never made sense, yet he always refused to answer our questions."

"He said it on the first page," Colin said. "'I confide in no one but this very parchment—not even my own sons—not until such time as I deem it necessary for them to know. This alone shall ensure the longevity of our great house...' Though, I can't see how his secrecy ensured anything but resentment and confusion."

"So *this* is what bound him to Chernikov," Dorian said, lost in his own churning thoughts as he recalled the Russian demon's warnings. *His secrets are your secrets now, Dorian Redthorne...* "The two of them conspired to murder the royal family, and then escaped to America, where my father ascended as king and put in place the Accords that allowed Chernikov to expand his own criminal empire."

"And Rogozin," Cole said, "and every other demon shitbag to follow in their footsteps."

"What else is in the book?" Dorian asked Colin.

Colin skimmed through the rest, shaking his head. "Just more of the same—Kendrick confiding in him about the statue and the book, telling him about the blade, how it would make vampires the most powerful supernaturals on earth. Father doesn't mention the specifics of the Book of Lost Souls, or the details of the murder, or how he managed to convince Chernikov he didn't have the blade. After the initial entries, the rest are little more than praise for Azerius. It's as though Father thought he was some sort of demigod, or..." He flipped through the pages, quickly skimming. "The last entry is... Wow. He wrote this just days before his death."

"What does it say?" Dorian asked.

"Azerius, the Great White Raven, King of Kings, I remain, as ever, your faithful servant, yet I can no longer decipher what it is you're asking of me. I have followed your commands as best as I could interpret them. I have guarded your secrets. I have sacrificed so much in your name—spilled the blood of innocents, destroyed families, started wars—and yet a dark curse remains within my blood, a blight upon my house, my sons, our sires. It is, I fear, Nikolai's final revenge. And so, I ask of you—I *beg* of you, Azerius—grant me guidance in my final hours, so that I may know your will. So that I may end this and free my sons of this once and for all." Colin sighed. "That's it. The very last entry."

Again, Augustus Redthorne's final words haunted Dorian's memory.

Your brothers... you must find... genetic...

Was this what he'd meant? Some sort of dark curse on their bloodline? Nikolai's revenge? Dorian rubbed his hands over his arms where the tattoos beneath his shirt were already fading, despite his recent feeding on demons and cold blood bags, despite Isabelle's temporary spell.

Had Chernikov somehow caused this?

"In every answer lies a thousand more riddles," Dorian muttered.

Colin closed the book, and for a long moment, no one spoke. Deep within the twisted caverns beyond the makeshift laboratory, Dorian could hear the crumbling of rock, the faint dripping of water seeping into the cracks of the stone, the slow yet endless passage of time as it consumed the very walls around him.

In that moment, a profound sadness flooded his heart, threatening to carry him away.

Blinking back the sting of unshed tears, he took a deep breath and focused on the sound of Charlotte's heartbeat, a steady rhythm that instantly calmed him, reminding him of her life and vigor, her warmth.

He glanced up and found her already watching him, a soft smile curving her lips, her eyes full of something so rare and intense and beautiful, it made him believe—for just a moment—in divinity.

She held his gaze for another heartbeat, and something deep and profound passed between them.

Dorian hadn't the words for it, but eventually he turned away, as if looking into her eyes for too long would break him.

Colin put the Corvidae book back on the shelf, and Charlotte finally spoke.

"If the blade of the *Bessmertnym Soldat* was truly forged by the demon Azerius, and it has the power to not only eradicate demons on contact, but turn humans into vessels, it's no wonder Rogozin and Chernikov are so eager to acquire it."

"You know what's even more fucked up?" Cole said. "If this is true, all those high-ranking generals and police you mentioned *weren't* actually killed. They were turned into demons. For all we know, they're still around."

"The blade might have other powers as well," Colin said. "Perhaps Father left additional clues, but we just don't know at this point. I think we should err on the side of caution and assume we've only just scratched the surface of its abilities."

"It slices, it dices, it juliennes!" Aiden said exuberantly. Then, dropping into a deadpan that sent a chill down Dorian's spine, "And look, ladies and gentlemen. It opens the bloody hell-book too."

Dorian had been on the other side of the chamber, and now he turned to look at Aiden, standing behind the stone slab in the center of the room, the previously impenetrable Book of Lost Souls inexplicably opened before him.

His face was bathed in its magical silver light—a light that emanated from the very pages themselves, pulsing like a living thing.

Dorian could feel its eerie heartbeat in his own veins.

"Aiden," Dorian whispered. "How did you…?"

"I picked up the blade for a closer look," he said, "then set it down on top of the book, not giving it a second thought. The moment it touched the cover, the book opened of its own accord."

"Can you read it?" Dorian asked.

"I don't speak demon, mate. But I'm getting a definite One Ring to Rule Them All vibe here, so I think I'll just..." He glanced once more at the book, then took a few steps backward, shaking his head. "Right then. Who's ready for breakfast? Better yet—drinks? Shall we head back upstairs? Far away from the portal to Mordor and into the nice, cozy study instead? Excellent! I'll run ahead and start the fire."

He headed off in the direction of the elevator, but no one else made a move to follow.

Colin leaned in to inspect the demonic tome, his skin nearly blue in the strange silvery light. "I can't make it out either. It's... quite complex." He traced his fingers over a page but drew back as if the words themselves burned to the touch. "Whatever it is, it doesn't want to be read. Not by me, at least."

"Perhaps Isabelle might have some insight," Dorian said, heading toward the elevator with the others. "She'll be along later with an update on Armitage Holdings—I can ask her then. In the meantime, I think we should all... We should... I..."

Dorian's thoughts slid away, and a deep chill slithered through his blood, casting his skin in gooseflesh.

He felt a whisper against the back of his neck, then spun on his heel, only to be met with empty space.

"Someone walkin' on your grave?" Cole clapped him on the shoulder. "You look a little freaked, Red."

"No, I... I thought I sensed something. Someone. I..." He glanced around the area again, but there were no others. "I could've sworn someone else was down here."

Just the ghosts of the past, he thought, hoping like hell Augustus' spirit wasn't lingering. His father had offered little to them in life; Dorian had nothing left for the man in death.

Besides, Augustus' soul—what was left of it, anyway— was in hell. It was likely the only thing about their father that *wasn't* a mystery.

Shaking off the odd chill, Dorian pressed his finger to the blood scanner and opened the elevator, ushering Charlotte, Cole, and Aiden inside.

He turned back once more to look for Colin, hoping he'd join them for a meal, but his brother was already immersed in the next great puzzle, his eyes shining like twin lamps over the demon book, his mind percolating with possibilities Dorian could only imagine.

"Don't forget to eat, brother," he said softly, but he knew the words had fallen on deaf ears.

CHAPTER FIFTEEN

"Is that scotch?" Gabriel asked. "Thank you, brother. Just what the doctor ordered."

Dressed in dark jeans and a black leather jacket that still held the late morning chill, Gabriel marched into the study and reached for the glass Dorian had just poured.

Despite the smirk and the healthy pink glow in his cheeks, Gabriel's mouth was drawn tight, his eyes red with exhaustion.

"Impeccable timing, brother." Dorian relinquished the glass, then poured himself another. "Have you found something on Rudy?"

The group had just finished brunch, and now they gathered before the fire to review the last of the Estas files and day-drink themselves into a mild oblivion. At Dorian's question, all eyes were on the youngest Redthorne.

Gabriel took the chair next to Charlotte, downing a few healthy gulps of liquor. The booze and the fire seemed to relax him, and after a long moment, he finally said, "He opened a bank account in Brazil recently. Bought some property there as well—all in cash."

Dorian nodded. "That corresponds with what we've found in the Estas files."

"Beyond that, nothing more than what we already know. I've been trailing him the better part of four days, but he's been extremely careful. Aside from his residence on the West side and a few restaurants in the area, he hasn't ventured far. He seems a bit paranoid too. Constantly looking over his shoulder, jumping at every backfiring car. Something definitely has him on edge."

"Did you check the restaurants?" Dorian asked. "The staff? Other patrons?"

"Clean. And human—all of them. If he's conferring with demons, he's not doing it in person. While he was out, I searched his penthouse—nothing professional inside, and no signs of Sasha."

Charlotte sighed beside him, but still managed a faint smile. "Thank you, Gabriel. I appreciate your... All of this. I'm not..." She trailed off, her eyes misting with tears.

Gabriel softened at the sight. "We *will* find your sister, Charlotte. And wherever she is, I'm certain she's already got those motherfuckers taking her out to breakfast, listening to her *endless* stories, and catering to her every whim." He let out a light chuckle, then reached over and touched her hand, his eyes filling with a compassion Dorian hadn't thought possible of the man. "Please don't lose hope. You're carrying it for all of us—Sasha too."

Charlotte seemed just as surprised by the turn in Gabriel's normally brusque demeanor, and his words buoyed her, bringing a new smile to her lips.

For that alone, Dorian was beyond grateful.

"I do have other news, though," Gabriel said somberly, glancing back at Dorian. All the warmth left his eyes. "It's about Malcolm."

"Have you spoken with him?" Aiden asked.

"He's managed to evade me at every turn, but one of my sources spotted him entering and leaving Bloodbath on more than one occasion."

"I thought Bloodbath was closed down indefinitely," Cole said.

"To the public, yes," Gabriel said. "But House Duchanes still owns the building. They've been more careful due to the increase in police presence after the murders in the area, but they're still around."

"So our brother was spotted cavorting with Duchanes vampires?" Dorian asked.

Gabriel nodded. "As well as vampires from house Mirren."

"Mirren?" Dorian sipped his scotch, trying to place the name. "Doesn't sound familiar."

"Relatively new on the scene, though the older sires were around when Father first started making inroads here." Gabriel retrieved the phone from his jacket pocket. "Young vampire by the name of Dominic, and another my contact wasn't familiar with. He took these pictures."

"Dominic... Why do I know that name?" Dorian

SARAH PIPER

reached for the phone, glancing down at the screen. There were two vampires in the shot—one he didn't recognize. The other, however, made his blood boil. His face was partially obscured by the shadows, but there was no mistaking that smug, youthful arrogance. "For fuck's sake. Dominic was at the bloody council meeting."

Gabriel leaned his head back and sighed. "Fuck. You're right. I barely gave him a second glance that night."

"Nor did I. Just long enough to put him in his place." Dorian recalled the little twat who'd insulted him at that sham of a meeting.

House Redthorne is not united... How can you keep our communities safe and at peace when you can't even keep your own house in order?

Well. The boy had certainly pressed *that* advantage, hadn't he? Parlaying it right into a friendship with the one Redthorne brother who seemed to agree with him.

"Malcolm's gone full-on turncoat." Dorian tipped back his glass, wishing the alcohol would burn the taste of his brother's name from his lips.

"There's more. The bad kind of more." Gabriel slid a folded newspaper from his inside pocket and handed it over—today's Times. "Looks like our brother and his new friends have been doing a bit of midnight snacking."

A fresh hole burned through Dorian's gut, and he knew before he even finished scanning the article what he'd find.

CRIMSON CITY DEVIL COPYCAT STRIKES AGAIN

Two more bodies were discovered late last night in a dumpster in the East Village. Both victims appear to have suffered massive blood loss from puncture wounds at the neck and thigh. Police are not sharing additional details about the scene and are not speculating on the exact cause of the wounds but have released sketches of three suspects compiled from key witness reports. Suspects are to be considered armed and extremely dangerous. Anyone with information is asked to contact the authorities immediately. A midnight curfew remains in effect for all of Manhattan.

The first two sketches looked very much like the vampires in the photo Gabriel had just shared.

The third was a dead ringer for Malcolm, and the sight of it nearly brought Dorian to his knees.

All the bloody battles. The arguing. The cruel words. The threats and betrayals. The heartbreak.

And this is what it had come to.

"Witness reports can be unreliable," Dorian said anyway, tossing the newspaper back at Gabriel. "We can't assume—"

"I'm not assuming anything, brother. But we need to consider the possibility that Malcolm is... not himself."

Not himself. Dorian would've laughed if the thought hadn't so deeply gutted him.

Fifty years after Dorian had terrorized the city he so loved, chasing away his brothers in the process, Malcolm was following in his footsteps. Could Dorian honestly judge him? Was this savagery part of their so-called curse? Would all of them fall prey to it in time?

Who would be the next to succumb?

Gabriel, with those cold and calculating eyes, the anger always simmering just beneath the surface, desperate for an outlet?

Colin, swept away by his endless quest for answers, chasing their father's ghost as he sought, even now, to recreate the cure that would surely kill them all?

Aiden—kind, loyal Aiden—whose only fault was that he'd remained a friend to the family whose fucked-up history had damned him to the same cursed eternity?

Dorian caught his friend's gaze across the study, and the last of the breath rushed from his lungs.

In that moment, he wished his father were still alive, if only so he could tear the heart from his chest and watch the life drain from his eyes one last time.

"Oh, fuck," Charlotte said suddenly, dragging Dorian back from the precipice of his own darkness. She'd picked up the discarded newspaper, and now she stared at the sketches with a look of sheer horror. "I know this other guy."

"Are you certain?" Dorian asked.

"Couldn't forget the motherfucker if I tried." She dropped the newspaper and glanced up at Dorian, new anger rising in her eyes. "Your brother's new bloodsucking BFF is Silas."

"The vampire who assaulted you the other night?" Gabriel asked.

"Yep. And he's probably—"

Charlotte's phone buzzed in her pocket, cutting her off.

In an instant, all the color drained from her face.

She hadn't even looked at the screen yet, but everyone in that room knew at once who she'd find on the other end.

CHAPTER SIXTEEN

"Good morning, Charlotte." Rudy's face filled the screen, his fake smile making Charley's stomach lurch. "I was hoping we could chat about a few... family matters. Is now a good time?"

A good time?

What he really wanted to know was whether she was alone. Whether he could threaten her without witnesses.

She'd anticipated the question, though, and had scooted into the kitchen before hitting the answer button. No matter how she felt about him, Charley knew she needed to keep playing the game. Just long enough to get Sasha back, then all bets were off.

Along with your dick, you fucking coward.

He'd sold her out to a demon lord. He'd killed her father. Maybe he hadn't pulled the trigger, but he'd orchestrated the murder. He'd siphoned her inheritance into his own pockets, forcing her to become completely dependent on him. He'd had a lifelong affair with her mother. He'd threatened and abused her.

And he'd kidnapped her fucking sister—a beautiful, fiery young woman with a heart of gold and a contagious laugh Charley would give *anything* to hear again.

For that, more than anything else, Rudy was going to die.

As painfully as possible.

"It's a great time," Charley said now, forcing the words through the twin knots of rage and fear in her throat. "Dorian and Aiden are sequestered in the study dealing with FierceConnect business. I haven't seen the other three. I was just about to make some coffee."

Right. She was currently looking at Dorian, Gabriel, Aiden, and Cole, who were looming just out of sight of the phone camera, but Rudy didn't need to know that.

"How are things going at Ravenswood?" he asked casually.

"Everything's on schedule. Just trying to get things ready before the Hawaii trip."

"Excellent."

"Rudy..." Charley closed her eyes and blew out a breath, her patience cracking beneath the weight of her worry. Gabriel had said there was no trace of Sasha at Rudy's penthouse. So where the fuck had he stashed her? Why was he still acting so nonchalant about all this?

"Something on your mind, kiddo?"

"Where *is* my sister?" she finally asked—partly because she knew Rudy was expecting it—hoping for it, even—but mostly because she really needed to know. "Sasha has nothing to do with this. You *know* I'm not going to fuck up my end of the deal."

"I certainly hope not," Rudy said, "but as I told you before, I didn't get where I am in this world by skipping the necessary precautions."

No, you did it by kissing a bunch of demon ass and making deals using other people's souls.

"Is she okay?" Charley asked, fighting to keep the desperation from her voice. "Can I at least talk to her?"

"I'm so glad you asked." Rudy flashed a cruel smirk, his eyes lighting up like he was the damn fairy godfather about to grant her every wish. "I thought you might appreciate a reminder about why you're doing this. An *important* reminder, just in case you get any ideas about alerting Redthorne or the authorities."

Before Charley could utter a single reassurance, Rudy conferenced in a video call from an unknown number, and the screen switched to an image of a blank white wall without a single identifying mark or shadow to be found.

There was a muffled sound from the new caller, and suddenly the screen filled with a sight that made Charley go boneless.

She collapsed onto her knees on the kitchen floor, tears welling in her eyes. "Sasha! Baby, are you all right?"

"Chuck?" Sasha yawned and blinked the sleep from her

eyes. Her face was lined with sheet marks, but she seemed unharmed. "Oh, crap! I didn't miss a shift, did I? Hey, you okay? Why are you crying?"

Miss a shift?

Why are you crying?

Charley glanced quickly at Dorian, then back to the screen, her heart thudding against her ribcage. "Sasha, do you know what day it is?"

"Um… Sunday? Friday?" Sasha shrugged, then let out a cute giggle. "Who even knows anymore."

God, how Charley had longed to hear that laugh. To see that sparkle in her sister's big blue eyes. Her color looked good, her eyes bright, her skin unmarred.

It was enough to make Charley weep with joy.

But she couldn't, because for all the outward signs of health and vitality, something was *very* wrong.

Sasha wasn't just disoriented from sleep. She was on another fucking planet.

"Did they hurt you?" Charley asked, wondering how long she had before Rudy cut her off.

Fuck, what else should she say? What intel could she ferret out before Rudy figured out her game?

She took a quick screenshot, just in case there was a clue to be found later.

"Are you okay?" she tried again, attempting a more casual tone. "Where… What are you up to?"

"Hmm?" Sasha yawned again, but it quickly trailed into another laugh. "Why wouldn't I be okay? I've got Netflix and a fully stocked fridge. Are *you* okay? You're acting weird. Well, weirder than usual."

Charley forced a smile. "I'm good. I'm really good, Sash. So, um, who's there with you?"

"Just some guys I met at Perk. No, wait..." She wrinkled her nose, her brow furrowed in concentration. "Actually, I think I met them in class? Yeah, it was probably in class. Everyone is *super* nice. Hey, you should totally come over later!" Sasha beamed, then glanced at something across the room and nodded. "But listen, Chuck. I need to get going. We're just about to start an Originals rewatch, and Klaus Mikaelson waits for no woman. Call you later?"

"Sasha, wait! I—"

The call disconnected, and Rudy's evil face filled her screen once again.

"See?" he said. "The little bitch is just fine. No harm, no foul."

"*Fine*? She doesn't even realize what's going on!" Charley closed her eyes, willing herself not to freak out.

There was only one explanation why Sasha would be acting so bizarre.

They'd compelled her. They'd fucking compelled her to think being kidnapped and kept prisoner was totally normal. Fun, even.

Charley couldn't let on that she knew about vampire compulsion, but she had to say *something*. Rudy would get suspicious otherwise.

"Did you drug my sister?" she asked.

Rudy laughed that machine-gun cackle of his. "Why would you think that?"

"She seems to be taking this whole kidnapping thing pretty well."

Rudy let out an irritated sigh. "Has it occurred to you, Charlotte, that Sasha is simply content? That she's grateful to me for giving her all the things you couldn't?"

"Rudy, *please* let her go. You and I can work something else out."

"Big day's coming up, Charlotte. Keep up the good work, and you'll be reunited with your sister soon enough."

Charley did her best to keep her face neutral, knowing damn well Rudy had no intention of returning her sister. He was planning to leave the fucking country right after the heist.

But if he wasn't going to return her, what the hell was his end game?

She took a deep breath, forcing herself to stay calm. For now, compulsion aside, it looked like he was keeping Sasha relatively safe.

Charley had no idea how much longer that would last, but it was a start.

"Everything's on schedule," she said. "We leave out of JFK next Friday."

"Excellent. Hey, send me some pineapples."

Don't they have any in Brazil? she wanted to ask, but instead she could only nod. "Count on it."

"I *am* counting on it, Charlotte. Enjoy the rest of your day. I'll be in touch again soon."

Before she could utter another word, the screen went blank.

The phone slipped from her hands and hit the floor with a soft thunk.

Dorian was at her side in an instant, gathering her into his arms and pulling her to her feet. "You did great, Charlotte. Rudy didn't suspect a thing."

"They compelled her. They messed with my baby sister's mind."

"I know, love."

"I just want her back. Why the fuck can't we get her back?"

"Gabriel's going to try to trace the location of the other caller. In the meantime, we'll keep looking through the Estas files until we figure this out." He slid a finger beneath her chin and tipped her face up to meet his gaze. "My brother was right to tell you not to lose hope. Your sister may be under compulsion, but she can sense your love for her. She knows you're with her, Charlotte. She knows you won't stop fighting for her."

Charley nodded, comforted by his presence as much as his faith in her.

Seeing her sister again—alive and apparently safe—*had* bolstered her.

But more than that, it filled her with a cold and deadly determination.

Not just to find Sasha and bring her home safely.

But to end her uncle for good.

I can't wait to see you burn, Rudy D'Amico...

"Dorian," Aiden said suddenly, "do you mind if I borrow Charlotte for a moment? There's something I'd like to show her."

"By all means." Dorian pressed a soft kiss to the corner of her mouth. "But don't be too long. I start to miss her when she's—"

"Oh, for the love of..." Aiden rolled his eyes. "You two are bloody disgusting. Please, Charlotte, allow me to save you from this Hallmark movie moment before your teeth rot from the nauseating sweetness."

Grateful for Aiden's particular brand of humor, Charley laughed and took his offered arm, allowing him to escort her into the small sunroom at the back of the manor.

It was warm and bright, with curved, floor-to-ceiling windows that overlooked the infinity pool and the rolling hills beyond. Fallen leaves in reds, yellows, and browns carpeted the landscape, reminding Charley of some of her favorite things about this time of year.

Soft flannel shirts.

Fuzzy socks.

Hot caramel apple cider.

Sasha's endless quest for the perfect Halloween costume.

For a brief moment, her heart seized up again, but then she relaxed, deciding right then and there that she had nothing to worry about. Of *course* Sasha would be home for Halloween. In fact, maybe they could even talk Dorian into throwing a costume party at Ravenswood. Sasha would go nuts for it.

"Sasha adores this room," Charley said now, remembering how much her sister had gushed about it when she'd visited. "It's easy to see why."

Aiden smiled. "We spent quite a bit of time chatting in here between dips in the pool. She said it reminded her of floating in a big bubble."

"Sounds exactly like something Sasha would say."

"Here—this is what I wanted you to see." Aiden guided her over to the far corner of the room, where a small café table and two chairs were set up near the window. On the table, an antique chess set gleamed in the sunlight.

"Is this yours?" Charley asked, crouching down to admire the craftsmanship. The board was made of polished wood, but the pieces were antique ivory, each one painstakingly carved and painted with so much detail, they almost looked alive. "It's beautiful, Aiden. I've never seen anything like it."

"It was crafted in France in the Renaissance period, passed down to Dorian's mother through her family. She was a kind woman with the patience of a saint—as you'd expect from the woman tasked with raising those little hellions." Aiden laughed softly, his eyes glazing with memories. "Sometimes, when the boys were out with their father and I'd gotten lost in the shuffle, she'd take me into the sitting room, order tea service from the kitchen staff, and chat with me for hours, teaching me how to play. Years later, she gifted this set to me. It was one of the few possessions I cared enough about to bring with me to America."

"I wish I could have known her," Charley said, trying to

imagine what she looked like, what she sounded like, how she called Dorian's name when he was late for a meal.

"She would've loved you, as her son does." Aiden held her gaze for a beat before turning his attention back to the chess set. "Anyway, I haven't played in an age—Dorian doesn't play, and it's not easy to find a partner. But when Sasha expressed an interest, I thought... I mean, I wanted... I..." He closed his eyes and took a deep breath, clearly flustered.

Charley bit back a smile. She'd never seen him so off-balance before.

When he finally looked at her again, his cheeks had taken on a deep red blush.

"Sasha deserves to learn on a nice set, not some cheap plastic knockoff. That's all." He brushed off a bit of micro-scopic dust from the board, then rearranged some of the pieces, turning them just so. "I set it up last night. I want it to be ready for her when she comes back to us."

When, not if.

One little word, and it made all the difference.

"She's going to love it, Aiden."

"Yes, well... I just thought you should know we've *all* got an incentive to bring Sasha home safely. I can't very well play chess on my own, can I?"

The tears fell again from Charley's eyes, but now she was smiling, drawing Aiden in for a warm and grateful embrace. "No, Aiden. I suppose you can't."

"Right, then." He held her for just a moment longer, then pulled away and said, "Better get you back before that boyfriend of yours starts *missing* you and tears down the whole bloody east wing in a fit of love-induced psychosis. He really is a bit mad for you, isn't he?"

Charley bit back another smile. "I wouldn't have it any other way."

CHAPTER SEVENTEEN

Alone in Dorian's bedroom, Charley stared at the money she'd stacked on the dresser.

Five thousand two hundred and thirty-nine dollars.

Along with a hastily packed suitcase full of her remaining clothes, the tampon box where she'd stashed the money was all she'd grabbed from home the day Dorian had taken her into the city for her gear.

She didn't plan on returning to the penthouse without her sister. And when they *did* return—together—Charley would be damn sure she could take care of them.

The money was just a start.

"I hope you're not planning to keep that under the mattress," Dorian said, entering the room with a curious grin. "Do I even want to know where that came from?"

"I earned it," Charley said, with more than a little pride. "Rudy canceled my credit card, so I sold all the couture stuff in my closet. Not a bad haul, considering."

"What? When did this happen?"

"I found out that day I took Sasha to the movies—my cards were declined."

"Why didn't you tell me? I would've—"

"That's *exactly* why. You *would've*. And I didn't want you to—not with this." She sat on the edge of the bed, and Dorian sat next to her, his eyes full of concern. "It's not like I was going to let Sasha starve or end up on the street. I would've asked for help if things got that bad."

"I don't want things to get anywhere *near* that bad, Charlotte. You could've come to me with this. You can come to me with anything."

"I know—and I love you for that. It's just… It's hard to explain, but I knew if I dug deep enough, I could figure something out. And I did." Charley looked over at the pile of money. "I know it's not much—probably not even enough to cover the damage I did to your cars. But it's—"

"Bloody brilliant, is what it is. What *you* are." He smiled and reached for her face, gently running his fingers along her jawline. His touch was electric, and she shivered in its wake. "You're so much stronger than you give yourself credit for, Charlotte. I've always known it about you."

Charley shrugged. "Before I met you, I don't think I would've been able to do it."

"What makes you say that?"

"I've never considered myself particularly strong or clever. Sure, I know how to plan heists and run a good con. But to actually take a stand—no matter how small—against someone like my uncle? To find my way out of a jam?

Forget it. I was always too scared and insecure to even try." She gazed into his honey-brown eyes and smiled. "The thing is... You're right. I *am* strong. I've *always* been strong. Maybe it was something I learned by necessity after my mom left, or from growing up without money, or maybe I was just born to fight my way through life, regardless of the circumstances." She closed her eyes and shook her head, the old shame creeping back in. "Then I started working my father's game, and every damn time I put on one of those outfits—one of those *costumes*—I took on a new identity, and I lost another piece of myself."

Emotion welled inside her—a lifetime of regret bubbling back to the surface, no longer content to stay locked in its box. Part of her was terrified even *this* was another game— that she'd open her eyes and the manor would vanish around her, as if falling in love with Dorian had been nothing more than a role she'd played for someone else.

But when Charley opened her eyes again, the manor didn't disappear. She was still here, sitting on the bed with her vampire king, who looked at her with a mix of love and admiration that brought tears to her eyes.

"I thought I'd truly lost myself, Dorian," she said. "But you *saw* me—the first time you looked at me across the lobby in the Salvatore. It was in your eyes—that moment and every time you've looked at me since. You *see* me. You helped me find my way back."

"I will *always* see you, Charlotte. And if you lose your footing again, I will always help you find your way back." He took her face between his hands and drew her close, lowering his mouth to hers in a kiss that sealed his promise, warm and soft and decadent, every hot breath a reminder that this *wasn't* a role or a game. It was real, it was hers, and she wanted to hold on to it forever.

But it wasn't enough to simply want it.

The odds were stacked against them, and every day, they took another hit. Sasha's kidnapping. The Estas and Rudy connection. The grays and the dark witches working with Dorian's enemies. The mysterious blade of Azerius. Silas and Malcolm's newfound bromance. The demon lord who'd marked her.

Charley pulled back from his kiss and met his gaze again, knowing she couldn't put this off any longer.

She had to tell him what she'd been thinking about.

What she wanted.

Before she said another word, Dorian was grinning at her as if he already knew.

"And there it is," he teased, tracing his thumb across her eyebrow. "You're having a think about something."

"Busted."

"Tell me."

She climbed into his lap and straddled him, looping her arms around his neck. "I've been thinking about superpowers."

"Superpowers?"

"Yeah, like how you've got the whole compulsion thing going on, and the blurring, and vampire super strength."

"Don't forget I'm *devilishly* charming," he added, leaning in to nuzzle her neck.

"Oh, and humble too!" Charley ran her hands through his hair and gave it a gentle tug, forcing him to meet her gaze again. "You know what my super power is?"

"Do you need a list, then?" Still grinning, Dorian ran his hands along her thighs and said, "All right. You're the smartest woman I know—I think we've covered that already." He kissed her forehead, his lips making her skin tingle. "You're incredibly brave—a quality I *deeply* admire, even when I'm scolding you for being reckless." Another kiss, this time on her temple, lingering just a bit longer than the last. "You drive like you're on the racetrack, and you can crack a safe like nobody's business—a thing I've only just learned about you." His mouth grazed her ear. "You're passionate, funny, and *devastatingly* beautiful." Slowly, he kissed his way to her lips, his hot breath teasing her for just a moment before he claimed her in another kiss, deeper this time, a low moan vibrating from his chest. When he finally pulled back, his eyes were glazed. "And you do this thing with your tongue that I..." He blinked rapidly, his mouth curved in a seductive grin. "I'm sorry. What was the question?"

Charley laughed. "We were talking about my super-power, and then you got completely distracted."

"Maybe *that's* your superpower. Distracting me until I've melted into a useless puddle, then having your way with me."

"Good guess, but nope."

"What is it, then, Charlotte D'Amico? What is your superpower?"

Charley rose up on her knees and pushed him backward on the bed, pinning his hands above his head and collapsing on top of him. "I *adapt*."

"Hmm." He lifted his head just enough to bite her lower lip. "I rather like this adaptation."

Charley let out a soft sigh of pleasure. Dorian was rock-hard beneath her, and she wanted nothing more than to give in to the ocean tide of his impossible magnetism. She wanted to kiss her way down his incredibly sculpted body, take him into her mouth, and suck him until she'd had her fill.

She wanted to make him lose control, all for her.

But she needed to get this off her chest first. Needed him to know what she *truly* wanted—and to hear his real answer—before things got all tangled up in the heat of their insatiable cravings.

She wouldn't blur those lines. Not with this.

It was too damn important.

Charley rolled onto her hip beside him, and he turned to face her, propping his head up on his elbow, patiently waiting for her to continue.

"I told you how Sasha is obsessed with vampires, right?" she said. "But there's one thing that's always both-ered me about all those books and movies."

"Only one thing?" Dorian laughed. "I could write a dissertation on the factual errors alone, not to mention the sodding fools they cast in those roles. They wouldn't last a *day* against a real vampire."

"Agreed, but more importantly..." She blew out a

breath, still trying to find the words to express her desires. "The girl—the *human*—hardly ever gets to choose."

"Not true! What about that whole kerfuffle between the sparkly vampire and the teen wolf with the abs? It was practically a national sport. Team Sodding Fool or Team Bloody Idiot… I'm certain Aiden had the T-shirt. Utter embarrassment, if you ask me."

"I'm not talking about choosing a boyfriend, Dorian. I'm talking about choosing whether to become a vampire."

"But the human never *has* to choose in those stories. Someone always turns her in the end."

"That's my point. They turn her because she's on the brink of death and there's no other option. Or the enemy turns her against her will. Me? I'd rather have the choice."

His eyes turned serious, and he threaded a hand into her hair, gently stroking her head. "I won't let it come to that, love. No one will bring death to your doorstep."

"How can you make that promise?"

"I… Well, that is to say… I mean…" Dorian opened and closed his mouth a dozen times to answer, but there *was* no answer. Not for this.

"I want a choice, Dorian. Not when I'm taking my last breath. Not when I'm being chased by some insane enemy, whether it's a gray or a demon or even my own flesh and blood. I want the choice right *now*." Charley rose from the bed, her nervous energy making it impossible for her to stay still. "And I've already made it. Adapt or die, right? I'm choosing to adapt. I *always* adapt."

Dorian sat up in bed and met her gaze, but his thoughts were guarded. "Adapt to *what*, exactly?"

He knew what she was asking. He *had* to know. But he was going to make her say it out loud.

He was going to make her be brave.

Charley took a deep, steadying breath and got on her knees before him, taking his hands and lacing their fingers together. She knew that once she said the words, she wouldn't be able to take them back.

Whether he agreed with it or not, her desire would be out there in the ether.

Voiced.

In so many ways, confessing it out loud felt like blowing out the candles on a birthday cake, and both of them held their breath, waiting for it.

I wish, I wish, I wish...

"I want to become a vampire," Charley finally admitted. "I want you to turn me."

He stared at her, unblinking, the intensity in his eyes boring deep into her soul. He was silent and motionless for so long her knees started to ache, but Charley didn't dare move.

In all their late-night conversations, the whispers in the dark, the declarations and promises, this was the one thing they'd managed to avoid talking about. The one thing that probably mattered more than anything else.

It carried the risk of death and the promise of eternity in equal measure, and it was terrifying and life-altering, miraculous and impossible.

The night Silas assaulted her, Charley had said she was afraid to let the vampires heal her with their blood—afraid it might turn her. But deep down, she wasn't afraid of turning.

She was afraid Dorian wouldn't *want* her to turn. That he'd see her as this eternal burden—an immortal commitment he'd never signed up for.

But she knew now—her *heart* knew now—that wasn't the case. Whatever the reasons for his silence, it wasn't because he didn't love her.

For however bloody long eternity lasts...

When Dorian finally spoke again, his voice was low and dark. "There's a human saying," he said. "Something about how it's only in the worst hours of our lives that we discover who we truly are."

"I'm familiar with it."

"It's bullshit, Charlotte. The worst hours utterly *shatter* who we truly are. Then we spend the whole of our existence trying to crawl back to some semblance of our true selves. Putting the pieces back together? *That's* what shows us who we really are—the rebuilding of a life from its smoldering ruins. So what you need to ask yourself is this: You're on your hands and knees, love. Now how much fire and broken glass are you *really* willing to crawl through to get back?"

"As much as I have to, Dorian. Because this *is* the worst hour of my life. My sister's been kidnapped by the man who murdered my father, my soul's been claimed by a demon, and the man I love—the *vampire* I love—is facing threats from supernaturals I didn't even know *existed* a month ago, including one of his own brothers." Charley released Dorian's hands and cupped his face. "I am in *love* with you, Dorian. I'll stand by your side through anything, no matter what I have to crawl through to get there. After everything we've been through, how could you even doubt it?"

"I don't doubt your heart. I just don't think you realize what you're asking." He pulled away from her touch and rose from the bed, crossing the room to the windows.

She stood, watching him in silence as he stared out across the lands of Ravenswood.

"I think having a choice is better," she said.

"I know you do, but—"

"No, Dorian. Those were *your* words. When you told me about what happened with Adelle, you said you'd wanted to give her the choice about whether to turn. You wanted to honor her wishes."

His shoulders tightened, and he let out a deep sigh. "That was different."

"Why? Because I don't deserve the same choice? Because I'm—"

"Because what I felt for her doesn't even come *close* to what I feel for you." He finally turned to face her again, his eyes blazing. "Loving you… It *consumes* me. I can't lose you. I can't watch you go through the change, knowing there's even a *chance* you won't come out on the other side."

"Then I guess that makes you a fucking hypocrite,

doesn't it." She crossed her arms over her chest and glared at him, heat rising inside her like a teakettle about to blow.

"I beg your pardon, but—"

"You don't get to tell me you're ready to sign away your soul and follow me into the depths of hell over some alleged demon contract, but then turn around and say I can't follow you on *this* path—a path I'm actually choosing."

The fire in his eyes dimmed, but only a fraction. "You're looking for a way to beat your uncle, and I understand that. Being a vampire would give you the advantage. But—"

"This isn't about Rudy! Don't you get it? I've spent my entire life playing by other people's fucked-up rules. You made me realize it's okay to want things for myself. And what I want—not because of my uncle, not because of some demon lord—is to be with you. Not as a weak, terrified human who'll one day die and leave you behind, but as a *vampire*."

"Charlotte, you can't just—"

"You said signing your soul away to follow me to hell would be your very last act on this earth. Well, maybe becoming a vampire is *my* very last act."

"Wonderful. And if the demon comes to claim your soul next week?"

"Then I would've gotten a whole week to live under my own rules. To be something *I* wanted to be. To claim some-thing all for myself."

All the fire returned to his eyes, and he shoved a hand through his hair, pacing the room like a caged beast. "Have you given this more than a *moment's* thought? Do you have any idea—any *bloody* idea—what your life would be like as a vampire? You can never have children, or—"

"I've never wanted children."

"What about the part where you have to drink human blood to survive?"

That particular detail still made her a bit queasy, but she shrugged, feigning nonchalance. "It's a food source like any other."

In a blur, Dorian was in her space again, gripping her arm and jerking her wrist against his mouth.

Charley gasped at the sudden contact, her heart thudding, her skin heating at the touch of his lips.

The memory of the last time he'd bit her filled her with a dark, delicious ache.

"Do it," she whispered, daring him, *begging* him, trembling in anticipation of his exquisite bite.

Dorian dragged his lips over the sensitive skin, his tongue darting out to tease her. Then, with a wicked gleam in his eye, he whispered, "Are you certain?"

"I... I'm..." Charley closed her eyes, momentarily disoriented by the sudden shift in his mood, the air crackling between them. "Dorian, I... *Yes*. Just fucking do it. I'm—"

A sharp, unmistakable pain pierced her skin, and she cried out and opened her eyes, crimson blood dripping from her wrist.

Still gripping her tight, Dorian glanced up from the bite and met her gaze. His eyes were the color of the sunset, wild and unbidden. Behind a dark and desolate smile, her vampire bared his fangs, blood slick on his lips.

"Is this what you want?" he demanded. "To live your life as a monster?"

Tears welled in her eyes, but it wasn't from the bite or the arguing or even the very real possibility that he might not turn her.

It was because he was still punishing himself. Because he still thought he didn't deserve happiness or love.

There were no words to encapsulate how she felt about him in that moment. So she pulled out of his grasp, slid her hands into his hair, and kissed him.

Hard. Deep. Bruising.

When she finally pulled away, her mouth was coated in blood, her heart threatening to beat out of her chest. "I'm not afraid of you, Dorian Redthorne. When I look at you— whether you've got fangs or a smile or a broody scowl—all I see is the man who has my heart."

He lowered his eyes and shook his head, the fight draining from his muscles. "You may choose not to see the monster when you look at me, Charlotte, but that doesn't mean he's not here."

"You're wrong." She took his face in her hands, forcing him to meet her gaze again. When he did, his eyes were back to their golden glow. "I *do* see the monster. I see him as clearly as I see the man. It's who you are, Dorian. And *that's* who I love."

"Is this truly how you want to live your life?" he asked. "Consumed by an endless hunger, knowing at any moment you might snap? That you might catch a stranger on the street—an innocent person, a child—and end their life in a blink, all because you're having a bad day?" He twined his fingers into her hair, and a tear slipped down his cheek, his eyes filling with anguish. "That you could kill the very person you love more than life itself?"

"Is that what it's really like for you?" She touched her fingers to his lips, a knot of sadness tightening her throat. "No peace? No love? Not a single shard of light in all that darkness?"

"Charlotte, I..." He closed his eyes and kissed her fingertips, but didn't answer her question.

"This is my choice, Dorian," she said. "I've thought it through. And I'm asking you to help me—to turn me. If you say no, I—"

"You'll what? Ask one of my brothers?" he backed away again, the smoldering embers of his earlier anger igniting once more. "One of our enemies, perhaps? I'm sure you'll have no trouble finding a suitable sire. Vampires will be lining up for miles for a chance to sink their fangs into *you*."

Charley wanted to be pissed—to lob a few insults, to lash out as sharply as Dorian had.

But all she felt in her heart was disappointment, and a profound sadness that he just couldn't see things from her perspective.

"No, Dorian," she said softly. "I was going to say... If you don't want to turn me, I'll respect that as *your* choice, and I won't go through with it. I don't want anyone else to do it—it's you, or it's no one." She touched his face one more time and smiled, despite her sadness. "Whatever you decide... It doesn't change how I feel about you. Nothing ever could. You have to know that."

His eyes softened, but he didn't say a word.

Charley stretched up onto her toes and pressed a kiss to his cheek, lingering just a moment before turning away and walking out of the room.

She didn't wait to hear him speak his final answer.

She'd already read it in his eyes, and it broke her fucking heart.

CHAPTER EIGHTEEN

The rose garden was covered in a layer of fine black ash—
all that remained of Dorian's epic bonfire. Someone—
Aiden, he'd guessed—had hauled away the smoldering
remnants of the dining room and boarded up the shattered
glass doors.

Beneath the blackened ruins, the roses bloomed anew,
their perfect beauty unmarred by his tempestuous rage.

And there, standing upon the charred cobblestones,
cupping a blood-red bloom in her hands, was the woman
who'd claimed his heart.

In her haste to escape his overbearing ridiculousness,
she hadn't bothered with a coat or shoes. Dressed in a red
flannel button-down and faded jeans, auburn hair loose
around her shoulders, she looked to Dorian like the very
picture of autumn.

"Aiden told me you'd burned them," Charlotte said as
he approached, her voice touched with wonder.

"I did. Quite thoroughly, at that." Dorian took the rose from her hands and brought it to his nose, inhaling deeply. The scent would always remind him of Rosalind—the bonded witch who'd died in his arms, right in this very garden. "The rose garden was always Rosalind's favorite place. She tended to every bloom as if they were her own children. After her death, I tried to have the garden plowed under—the reminder was just too painful. But no matter what I did to destroy it—the plows, a flood, fire—the roses always returned."

"Rosalind," she whispered.

A light breeze ghosted through the trees, and Dorian's heart warmed as he thought of Rosalind's kindness. Whether or not she'd ever forgiven him, he hoped she was in a better place.

"The suite with the LaPorte painting—that was hers. It looks out over her roses. I've kept it up for her, changing out the artwork every few years, thinking maybe she… I don't know." He shook his head. "Sorry. I realize it sounds ridiculous."

"I think it's lovely," she said. "And obviously she's still with you. The roses are her way of letting you know."

"Even in the cruelest winters, they continue to bloom beneath the snow." Dorian's chest tightened, and he returned the rose to Charlotte, his eyes never leaving hers. "It's a remarkable sight."

Charlotte smiled, and he swore the roses surrounding them brightened.

He didn't think he'd ever stop marveling at the fact that

she'd come into his life at all. That she'd remained. Moments earlier, he'd worried he'd finally chased the warmth from her eyes for good, yet there she was, still shining like the brightest star in his sky.

"I look forward to seeing it," she said.

Look forward...

The words held so much promise, it terrified him.

Could he *keep* that promise? Could he tell her, beyond a shadow of a doubt, that when the first snows of winter blanketed Ravenswood, she'd be here to bask in the magic of it?

Or would she be in hell, serving the demon lord who'd claimed her?

"Charlotte, being a vampire..." Dorian closed his eyes, desperate to find the right words this time. Determined not to screw it up. "It *will* make you stronger. But it won't make you any less terrified."

"No?" She shared another smile, all for him, and took a step closer, the air carrying her sweet scent. "So you've always been fearless? Even as a mortal man?"

"I've never claimed to be fearless. The same things that terrified me as a man terrify me as a vampire—perhaps even more so."

Charlotte let the rose fall to the ground and looped her arms around his neck, her coppery eyes bright as she gazed up at him. In the barest of whispers, she said, "What are you afraid of, Dorian Redthorne?"

He closed his eyes, unable to bear the intensity of her scrutiny. Her kindness.

"I can't protect them," he confessed. "No more than I could back then."

"Can't protect who?"

"Any of them," he continued. "House Kendrick murdered half my family and turned the rest into vampires, and I couldn't do a damn thing to stop them. To save my mother and my youngest siblings, even to ease their suffering... And here in this very garden, Adelle... She killed Rosalind, and I..." Images of the past rushed at him from all sides, dragging him back into the depths of his despair.

Two hundred fifty years on this planet, and the story of his life had been written in the blood of everyone he'd ever loved.

Everyone he'd ever failed.

"I should've been able to protect my family," he said. "My witch. You. Sasha. Even Malcolm. And now we're facing a war with unknown enemies and ever-shifting alliances, and I've no guarantees any of you will be spared the same cruel fate."

"There *are* no guarantees in this life, Dorian. There never were."

She touched his face, and he opened his eyes, chancing another glimpse at the woman who'd turned his life upside down, who'd saved him, who'd made him believe in love.

"I want to give you *everything*, Charlotte. Everything your heart desires, even if those desires are... I just... I need a little time. The thought of changing you—of harming you... I know I didn't handle things well earlier. I'm sorry. I—"

She stretched up on her toes and pressed a kiss to his mouth, silencing the last of his mangled apology.

Her lips were cool from the chilly air, but her mouth was hot and inviting, and Dorian eagerly returned the kiss, deepening it with soft, teasing strokes until he finally coaxed out a moan of pleasure. Her heartbeat quickened, the familiar hum of her pulse entrancing him as they picked up where they'd left off in his bed.

He was always so hard for her, so ready to devour her, everything in him aching to be closer to her.

After a kiss that lasted an eternity, she broke for air, gasping through swollen lips that sent a fresh bolt of desire straight to his cock.

"Tell me you're mine," she whispered urgently, mirroring the words he'd so desperately uttered in the car last night, the swell of her breasts rising and falling in time with her ragged breath. Her flannel shirt had shifted sideways, revealing a black bra strap and the soft curve of a shoulder, and in that moment, all Dorian wanted to do was claim her. Bite her. *Fuck* her. Answer her demands with a litany of hot, hard thrusts that would eradicate every last doubt.

The utter baseness of his thoughts reminded him of their very first meeting.

The very first taste.

"I'm yours, Charlotte. Always." He captured her mouth in another bruising kiss and slid his hands under the curve of her ass, lifting her off the ground. She wrapped her legs around his hips, and he leaned back, relishing in the feel of her weight against his body, steadying him, anchoring him.

Right now, everything else could fucking *burn*. As long as Charlotte was in his arms, in his mouth, in his hands, nothing else mattered.

He carried her to the grass beyond the cobblestones and laid her on a bed of fallen leaves, unfastening her jeans and sliding them off with her panties. He stripped out of his own pants and boxers, then climbed on top of her, kissing her madly as he slid his hand between her thighs, seeking her endless warmth.

She was hot and slippery for him, her hips arching up to meet the urgent thrust of his fingers, her hands fisting the leaves at her sides.

Bloody hell, how he loved making her blush.

Making her moan.

Making her shatter.

She was close to the edge already, her body pulsing around his fingers as he thumbed her clit, her thighs trembling, her mouth parted as she gasped for breath...

But then she grabbed his wrist and stopped him, pulling herself up onto her knees.

"Not yet, Mr. Redthorne," she said, her voice hoarse, her eyes dark with a feral desire that told Dorian everything he needed to know.

She wanted—*needed*—to take control.

It was a demand. A test. A question.

Would he give this to her? Would he let her call the shots?

The flannel skimmed the top of her bare thighs, and Dorian ached to lower his mouth to them, to trace every curve with his tongue until he had her writhing once again.

She knew it, too. He could read it in her devious little smile.

But his answer, now and for the rest of eternity, was yes.

"Whatever you need, love," he whispered, holding up his hands, as if he'd just surrendered his very life. "Take it."

She reached for the buttons on his shirt, slowly working them open and pushing it off his shoulders as she kissed her way down his chest, leaving a searing-hot path in her wake.

"On your feet," she ordered, and he obeyed without question, standing naked before her as she knelt in the leaves and fisted his cock. "I've been wanting you to fuck my mouth all day."

She brought her lips to him and blew a soft breath across his flesh, then swirled her tongue around the tip, licking and teasing him as she continued to stroke him with her fist. Just when he thought he couldn't take another moment of the teasing, she moaned and closed her lips around him, taking him in so fucking deep it made him shudder.

"Charlotte," he growled, fisting her hair. "Keep doing that and I'm going to come right inside that dirty mouth of yours."

She looked up at him through her dark lashes, her eyes sparkling with mischief. Dorian's warning had only served to encourage her, and now she cupped his balls, teasing them as she sucked him in deeper, harder, her mouth so hot and wet and soft and...

"Fuck, I'm..." Dorian could hardly form words. "You're so... *Fuck*..."

She pulled away in an instant, his cock mourning the sudden loss of her lips. "Don't you *dare* come without me, Mr. Redthorne."

The look in her eyes went from mischievous to ferocious, a raging storm intent on utter destruction. Dorian was powerless in its path.

She dragged him down into the leaves and pushed him onto his back, climbing on top and straddling him.

Dorian barely had time to catch his breath before she fisted him again, guiding him inside her, claiming his cock with a single demanding thrust.

"Fuck me hard, Dorian," she breathed.

Dorian *hated* giving up control, but this was... *Bloody hell*, it was everything. Bare flesh on soft, wet leaves. A cool breeze caressing warm skin. The scent of fireplaces and fallen apples and the first bite of winter in the air. The perfect arch of her hips as she took him in deeper, her fingers digging into his shoulders, the faint hum of the blood racing through her veins.

Fuck yes, woman.

Dorian grabbed her hips, thrusting up as she ground down against him, their bodies colliding as they both fought for control. She took what she wanted, what she needed, rising onto her knees and then slamming back down again, her breasts bouncing inside the tight flannel, her fingernails scoring his flesh like claws.

Every thrust unleashed more of her inner wildness, her fierceness. She was getting close to the edge again, losing herself, ready to fall.

Dorian *wasn't* ready. He didn't want this fucking moment to end.

"Wait," he whispered. "Wait."

"*No.*" She gripped his face and leaned in close, her long hair spilling into his mouth, a dark fire burning in her gaze that only made him harder. "You said you *own* this pussy, Dorian. Prove it. Make it *hurt.*"

Fucking hell, the ferocity of her demands nearly made him come right there.

With a deep growl, he grabbed the back of her head and pulled her down against his mouth, licking and biting her neck, her jaw, her ear. He wanted to be everywhere at once, kissing her, sucking her, *consuming* her.

He slid his hands down her back and gripped her ass, bucking wildly against her willing flesh. Suddenly, he couldn't get in that pussy deep enough, fast enough, *hard* enough. Dorian was out of his mind with desire, his balls heavy and aching to unleash hell.

"You'll always be my bad girl," he breathed, then raised a hand and brought it down hard against the bare flesh of her ass. She cursed his name and begged him for more, and Dorian was happy to oblige, alternating hot, hard spankings with a soothing touch, pushing her to the very edge of her limits.

"You make me crazy in the *best* way," she breathed, still desperate for more. "I could *die* for this cock."

Fuck... that mouth of hers was going to deliver him straight into madness. He couldn't take it anymore. Not like this.

Dorian wrapped her in his arms and flipped them over, pinning her beneath him. Charlotte didn't fight him this time, didn't try to take back the control he'd ceded earlier. She raked her nails down his back and arched her body, and he tore her flannel open to reveal the luscious curves of her breasts, her auburn hair splayed out on the carpet of leaves like a flame, her cheeks pink and glistening, her mouth parted in ecstasy.

Charlotte was a vision.

He continued to fuck her—to *own* her—just like she'd commanded. Lowering his mouth to her nipple, he bit her through the bra, then pushed the lace aside and licked, soothing the sting of the bite before sucking her into his mouth, his lips caressing her skin while his tongue teased the stiff, rosy peak.

The first tremors finally rocked through her thighs, slowly building to a crescendo as she panted and thrashed beneath him, and Dorian felt the answering call in his own body, his muscles tightening, everything in him ready to burst.

He brought his mouth to hers and breathed her name, and the feel of her soft sighs against his lips pushed him over the edge, driving him to euphoria as he sank deep inside her, burying himself, losing himself, unraveling, and when she finally reached her own breaking point, their cries of passion were indistinguishable, their bodies wringing out every last drop of pleasure until they were utterly spent.

Sticky and exhausted and unable to form words, they collapsed side by side onto the leaves, closed their eyes, and chased the sound of their wild heartbeats into oblivion.

"I thought I saw them in the rose garden a little while ago, but I... Oh, for fuck's sake, Dorian!"

The words cut through the blissful haze, and Dorian opened his eyes and bolted upright in the leaves, just in time to catch Aiden's glare.

Next to him, Isabelle stared in equally embarrassed surprise, her eyes sparkling with a hint of laughter.

"Dorian?" Charlotte sat up next to Dorian, then gasped, frantically trying to cover herself with the loose flannel. "Shit! I mean, sorry! Hi! We didn't realize... Um..."

"We were just..." Dorian scrambled to reach for his pants without standing up and giving them both an eyeful. "My apologies, Isabelle. If you'll just give us a moment to... gather our things..."

"Take all the time you need, Dori," Aiden said. "I was *just* thinking... You know what this day is missing? The chance to make things *really* fucking awkward for everyone. And here we are, prayers answered! Well, you two carry on then." He turned Isabelle back onto the path and led her toward the manor. "I'll just escort our guest inside and see if we might find some bleach for our eyes."

With the intruders out of sight, Dorian and Charlotte dressed in record time, Charlotte doing her best with the now-buttonless flannel.

"Why are we always getting so rudely interrupted?" Dorian teased, sweeping her into his arms for one last embrace.

Charlotte shrugged. "At least Aiden didn't lecture you about taking your woman on a cruise or to a fancy hotel."

"True, but he also failed to mention the gold-plated dick. I'm not sure if I should take that as a slight."

"Let's just keep the dick between us, shall we?"

Dorian laughed and tugged a rogue maple leaf from her hopelessly tangled hair. "Another command I'm *more* than happy to oblige."

CHAPTER NINETEEN

"I'm afraid we'll need something stronger than tea for this conversation," Isabelle said as Aiden put on the kettle. Then, with a hopeful smile, "I don't suppose you have gin?"

"A woman after my own heart," Charlotte said.

Dorian, who'd been surreptitiously pulling leaves from his woman's hair while attempting *not* to develop a raging hard-on at the kitchen table, was happy for the distraction of a new task.

Slipping the last leaf into his pocket, he rose from his chair. "Drinks it is, then."

With Gabriel on a mission to trace the location of Sasha's call, and Cole back at his cabin to regroup with the wolves, that left Dorian, Aiden, and Charlotte to deal with whatever news Isabelle was about to drop into their laps.

Based on her comment about the drinks, he had a

feeling they'd be discussing a lot more than the ongoing delays with the Armitage acquisition.

He escorted everyone to the study, and while Aiden lit a fire, Dorian fixed two gin and tonics for the women, along with glasses of scotch for himself and Aiden.

Isabelle took a deep drink, then said, "After hours of brutal negotiations, my brothers have decided to sell Armitage Holdings to Renault Duchanes. I'm pushing for a legal challenge on account of my father's health, but that's where we stand right now."

"Well, we knew it was a strong possibility," Aiden said. "Duchanes has been courting the company for quite some time."

"This goes well beyond Duchanes," she said. "Remember the financial anomalies I mentioned earlier? On paper, Armitage Holdings has been bleeding cash for years, yet there always seemed to be funding for new projects. Until my father's health started failing, I wasn't involved in the day-to-day operations, so I wasn't aware just how deep the issue ran. That changed today."

"Were you able to get it sorted?" Dorian asked.

"Not really. The books are a mess—mysterious investments never traced back to a legitimate source, wire transfers from shell companies and offshore bank accounts, anonymous contributions. It's a wonder we weren't investigated for fraud years ago." She fumed over her glass, anger flashing in her eyes. "But I did make one important discovery. Renault Duchanes? He's not the real buyer. He's simply the slightly more palatable face of a powerful backer."

"Let me guess," Dorian said, pacing before the fireplace. "The backer is the source of the secret cash flow."

Isabelle held up her glass in cheers, then took another deep drink. "Ladies and gentleman, may I present the backer, the source, the future owner of Armitage Holdings, and the leader of the most powerful demonic faction on the eastern seaboard—Nikolai Chernikov."

Dorian stopped pacing, nearly dropping his drink. "How did you determine this?"

"My brothers may have their heads up their useless asses, but fortunately, the majority of my father's executives do not. When the CFO and I found the anomalies, he brought the others in, and we pored over the records until we finally found the connecting point."

"Chernikov," Aiden said.

Isabelle nodded. "It took some time to trace, but the shell companies and foreign accounts eventually led back to him. Apparently, he's been investing cash for years, bribing a few unscrupulous employees to work on his pet projects on company time, leveraging company assets and intellectual property. Security is looking into it, but so far they've only identified one of the culprits."

"But if the sale goes through," Charlotte said, "will it even matter? Chernikov will own all the assets anyway."

"That's exactly right." Isabelle's eyes darkened. "And we really, really can't let that happen."

"Have you told your brothers about this?" Aiden asked.

"Not yet. The executives and I agreed it was best to hold

off until we have more information about the situation. In their rush for a quick sale, my brothers will only confuse matters. And we absolutely don't want them to burden my father with this."

"What does a demon like Nikolai Chernikov want with your father's company?" Dorian asked. "As far as I know, none of Chernikov's business interests—legitimate or otherwise—have anything to do with illusion technology."

"He isn't interested in the business applications." Isabelle retrieved a tablet from her attache case and pulled something up on the screen, then passed it over to Dorian.

They were schematics for what looked like some sort of virtual reality program, but overlaid with something Dorian instantly recognized.

"This is Manhattan," he said. "The transit system maps, if I'm not mistaken."

"I wish you were," Isabelle said, "but that's precisely what you're looking at. And those blinking triangles? Cameras."

He tapped on one positioned at the corner of Broadway and Forty-Fifth Street, right in the heart of Times Square. It brought up the camera's live feed, giving him a view of the tourist throngs, their faces bathed in the harsh light of the animated billboards. He clicked through a few more cameras, getting a glimpse of a dozen street corners scattered throughout his city—the Upper West Side near the park, where he'd first met Charlotte. Canal Street in Chinatown, home to his favorite place for steamed dumplings.

Battery Park City, with its views of Ellis Island and the Statue of Liberty.

And the people. So many people—every race, every age, every walk of life. He could almost hear the cacophony—the constant rush of traffic, the car horns, a man hawking his one-dollar umbrellas, a jackhammer, laughter and arguments, snippets of conversations in a dozen different languages. It was the music of New York City, a soundtrack as comforting and familiar to him as his own heartbeat.

"I'm not sure I'm following," Dorian said, though a cold dread had settled into his stomach. "What does all this have to do with Chernikov?"

"Security brought in a vampire to compel the employee involved," Isabelle continued. "She hasn't yet revealed the names of the others, but she did give us some insight about the project. I followed up with a trustworthy dark witch I'm still in contact with, and together we were able to fill in the gaps." She downed the rest of her drink, then glanced up at Dorian and shook her head, her eyes filling with a fear he'd never before seen in the witch.

In *any* witch.

The dread inside him turned to alarm. "Isabelle?"

"You should probably sit down for this," she said.

Dorian did as she asked, taking the chair next to Charlotte, who reached over and squeezed his hand, her touch steadying him.

Isabelle drew in a deep breath, then said, "Chernikov and his allies—including his own demons, the Duchanes vampires, a ragtag assortment of other vampire and shifter defectors, and a large coven of witches who've delved so deeply into dark magic they're practically demons themselves—are plotting to take total control of the city. At first, they were working to bring in more demons through the portals, but they haven't been able to secure enough vessels to house them all. Same story with the grays—Renault's witch hasn't perfected the resurrection spells yet, and there simply aren't enough existing grays to use in a wide-scale operation."

"But we found evidence of Jacinda's work at Estas' place," Charlotte said. "Along with two grays they'd been experimenting on. Estas works for Rogozin, not Chernikov."

"It's likely the witchcraft items you found were stolen," Isabelle said. "Estas was probably trying to recreate her spells. With news of the grays spreading, I'm sure they're all looking for a way to profit."

"And we've already determined Estas isn't loyal to Rogozin," Aiden said. "For all we know, he's working with Chernikov now."

"I *knew* that bloody demon was full of shit," Dorian ground out. "Chernikov tried to convince me Rogozin was playing the same game."

Isabelle shook her head. "I don't believe Rogozin's involved in this particular plot. It sounds like House Duchanes was courting Rogozin demons only as a way to spy for Chernikov. Renault Duchanes' relationship with Chernikov goes back many decades, according to my witch friend."

Dorian sighed, his mind churning with the new revelations. He wished he could say he was surprised, but he'd seen the writing on that particular wall as soon as Chernikov had started feeding him the so-called intel against Rogozin. "All of this aligns with what Gabriel and I learned from the Rogozin demons we... *conversed* with... the other day. Chernikov is building his armies."

"He doesn't need armies," Isabelle said. "Just the illusion of them."

"That's why he wants Armitage Holdings?" Charlotte gasped. "To create that illusion?"

"His witches are attempting to fuse demon magic with Armitage illusion tech," Isabelle said. "They're not quite there yet, but they're getting close. Using our technology and their magic, along with a distribution system built over the existing transit infrastructure, they're planning to create a virtual reality overlay. From there, using the transit maps, the security cameras, and rider data from the transit authority, Chernikov can pinpoint the flow of people around Manhattan and the boroughs at any time, day or night. With that information, he can determine the most effective target zones and times."

"Most effective for what?" Aiden asked, his face pale.

"Using the virtual overlay," she said, "Chernikov can cast all manner of illusions—explosions, sidewalk executions, car wrecks, terrorist attacks, murderous rampages by family members as well as the monsters of their nightmares —anything you can imagine. It won't even matter that they aren't real—the illusion tech is so advanced, and the demon magic so invasive and manipulative, no human exposed to the combination will *ever* be convinced it wasn't real. They'll feel pain from illusory wounds, suffer post-traumatic stress, even die from injuries that never actually happened."

"And for those who survive," Dorian said, following the grim trail to its logical conclusion, "we're left with a weakened, terrified population that's easy to control and further manipulate. Especially if a charismatic psychopath steps in to lead them."

Horror descended on the room like a pall, and for several long moments, no one spoke, each of them sinking into their own gruesome visions of Chernikov's new reality.

Dorian's mind flashed back to the people he'd seen in the camera views. Tourists, bagel vendors, carriage drivers, immigrants from every country in the world, museum-goers, celebrities, drunken revelers, students, billionaires, musicians, hopeless wanderers.

Vampires, shifters, witches.

Children. Grandparents.

All of them doomed.

Dorian rose from his chair and fixed another round of drinks.

"Chernikov isn't ready to give up on bringing in new demons, either," Isabelle said when he passed her a fresh gin and tonic. "Apparently, he's been ranting about some sort of ultimate weapon that can create vessels out of humans without contracts. My friend didn't know specifics —just that he believes he'll have access to it soon. Which only makes the rest of his plans that much more terrifying."

Dorian exchanged a glance with Aiden, and from the look in his friend's eyes, he knew they both shared the same thought.

The Blade of Azerius.

Terrifying didn't even begin to cover it.

"What of the other supernaturals?" Charlotte asked. "Won't you guys be immune? Isn't there anything you can do?"

"Some of us might be able to resist the demon magic," Dorian said, "but at that scale, and paired with the technology, it's hard to say. We've never been exposed to anything like it. Demonic energy has always been kept in balance by the dark witches."

"So they've all gone rogue?" Charlotte asked.

"Not all," Isabelle said. "There are plenty of dark witches who know how to toe the line—witches who appreciate the balance of light and dark, and can delve into either without losing themselves."

There was a hint of pride in her tone that spoke to Dorian of a much deeper knowledge—and a much greater power—than he'd suspected, despite her earlier expressions of interest in the darker arts.

Dorian caught her gaze, and a new understanding passed between them.

A new trust.

Isabelle Armitage was a formidable witch. One he was grateful to have on their side.

"Chernikov has been involved with the Redthorne line for centuries," he told her now, deciding it was time to let her in—fully. "Based on what he's told me—reading behind the lies, of course—and additional information we've recently discovered in my father's personal effects, I believe Chernikov has always wanted to be king. Not just of the demons, but of all supernaturals and humans alike."

"What information?" she asked.

"Nikolai Chernikov helped my father slaughter House Kendrick in England—the first play in what I now realize is a *very* long game." He sipped his scotch, resuming his position next to Charlotte. "As long as vampires remained the most powerful of the supernaturals, Chernikov knew a demon would never be recognized as a king—not without an army backing him. He needed my father to ascend and come to America, where he could establish the Redthornes as the ruling supernatural family, and install Chernikov in a position of power. Together, they forged the Shadow Accords, carving out territory for demons, establishing just enough ground rules to keep supernaturals from killing each other or revealing us to the humans. And then, he bided his time."

"Sounds like his time is coming," Aiden said grimly.

"He still needs the weapon," Dorian said. "All the tech in the world is still just that—tech. And tech has multiple points of failure."

"But we have no idea what the weapon is, or when he'll acquire it," Isabelle said. "At this point, it's just a rumor passed on from dark witch to dark witch. Frankly, we don't even know if the weapon exists, or if it's just another trick Chernikov conjured to keep his own people in line."

"It exists." Dorian drained his glass, then rose from the chair, extending a hand to the witch. "Isabelle? How would you like a tour of the crypts of Ravenswood?"

CHAPTER TWENTY

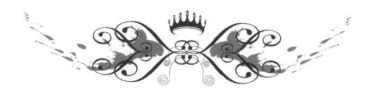

The eerie magic of the Book of Lost Souls illuminated the dim cavern as Isabelle inspected its pages, her eyes shining with the same endless curiosity as Colin's.

"I thought it might be a demonic grimoire," Colin told her. "But I've only a passing familiarity with demonic symbology." He looked even more wild and disheveled than when they'd seen him earlier, and the blood bags Dorian had brought him remained untouched.

Dorian fought back his worry, reminding himself that Colin was a medical doctor—one who'd been practicing in one form or another since they were children spying on their father. He certainly knew how to take care of himself.

"You're not far off the mark," Isabelle said. "It *is* a sort of grimoire, as well as a personal accounting."

"*Whose* person?" Dorian asked. "Azerius?"

She glanced up at him, her gaze reflecting the book's

silvery-blue light. "The Book of Lost Souls tells of his descent into madness and corresponding ascent to power."

"Always a good combination," Aiden said.

"The demon Azerius," Isabelle whispered, shaking her head as if she couldn't believe it. "All this time, I thought the book and the blade were myths. At the very least, long-forgotten relics never to resurface again."

"You're familiar with him?" Dorian asked.

"Oh, yes," she said. "He's venerated as a god by many demonic factions, including Rogozin's organization."

"Rogozin's... Bloody hell. The tattoos," Dorian said, recalling the demons he and Gabriel had tortured. "Some of the Rogozin demons had white birds tattooed on their inner forearms. They must've been ravens."

"The Great White Raven is allegedly one of the forms Azerius takes in dreams," she said. "Your father mentioned it in his notes."

"So he's a Russian demon, then?" Colin asked.

"Not exclusively. Stories of Azerius cross hundreds of magical and cultural traditions, though the Russians likely feel a close kinship—their soldiers were the last humans known to wield the blade."

"The blade of the *Bessmertnym Soldat*," Charlotte said.

Isabelle looked impressed. "You're familiar with the history, then."

"The *human* history, at least," Charlotte said. "All this demon stuff is new territory for me."

"Perhaps we can trade stories over tea one night." Isabelle smiled warmly, then turned her attention back to the book. "Azerius is known by many names—King of Blood and Ravens, He Who Slaughters the Blood of his Blood, He Who Drinks the Blood of the Fallen, He Whom Before All Mortals Weep."

Aiden rolled his eyes. "I bet *he's* fun at parties."

"By Azerius' own accounting," she continued, "his father was a disgraced god who devoted his life to starting human wars. He fathered seventeen sons, including Azerius, but lived only in service to his own bloodlust. Eventually, Azerius got fed up with the neglect. To secure his father's elusive attention, he slaughtered all sixteen of his brothers and their families, ensuring he was the very last of his father's bloodline, but his father didn't notice. So Azerius called upon the old gods of his father's time and made some sort of dark bargain—he sacrificed himself, only to rise to power in death with a bloodlust that rivaled his father's. He then declared war on all warriors, making it his life's mission to sow chaos on human battlefields and imbue soldiers with a limitless potential for brutality. In some cultures today, it's still believed that if a white raven appears in the encampment on the eve of battle, Azerius is present, and a prolonged, bloody battle will follow, with mass casualties."

"So you're saying he's got some anger management issues," Aiden said.

"That is an understatement." Isabelle closed the book, gently placing her hand on the cover. "People still call upon him for deals—deals so dark not even regular demons will touch them."

"Like Father," Colin said, "slaughtering the vampire royals in England."

"I still can't believe this is real." Charlotte reached for the blade. "This thing was literally forged in hell. It's—" The moment her fingers touched the bone handle, she swayed.

Dorian blurred behind her, catching her just before she collapsed.

"Damn it," she whispered, closing her eyes as he steadied her.

"Vertigo again?" he asked, and she nodded. "Colin, are you certain she hasn't suffered more serious injuries?"

"I haven't ruled it out." Colin came to stand beside them, pressing the back of his hand to her forehead. "Have you eaten enough today?"

"Yes." Charlotte opened her eyes. "Everything else feels totally fine. But it's exactly like before—the déjà vu too. I swear that blade has it out for me."

"What do you mean?" Isabelle asked, concern tightening her brow. "This happened before?"

"When we first discovered it," Charlotte said, "I got the same feeling as soon as I touched it, only it wasn't as bad. This time felt much more intense."

Isabelle exchanged a worried glance with Dorian, then asked Charlotte to join her at the table.

Dorian stayed by her side, afraid she'd faint again.

"Did you touch the book before?" Isabelle asked.

"No, just the blade."

"Place your hand on the book for me."

Charlotte did as she asked, but drew back at once, stumbling backward into Dorian's arms.

"Worse," she said. "Way worse."

Isabelle held her hand over Charlotte's heart. "May I?"

She nodded, and Isabelle pressed her hand to Charlotte's chest and closed her eyes.

After an agonizing moment, she lowered her hand and shook her head, whispering a single word that kicked Dorian's worry into overdrive:

"*Fuck.*"

"Isabelle?" he pressed, but she held her tongue. Dorian glared at her. "No shit-covered cupcakes, remember? Speak your mind."

She let out a deep sigh, then reached for Charlotte's hands, squeezing tight. "Charlotte, your demon mark... It's the mark of Azerius. I'm certain of it now—the energy signatures are the same. You're feeling the reaction of his mark—his power calls to it through the book and the blade. Your soul recognizes him as its master."

Dorian's entire body trembled as he fought to hold back his rage. He swiped the Book of Lost Souls from the table, his fingers turning white as he crushed it in his grip. "You're telling me the demon known as the King of Blood and Ravens, He Who Slaughters the Blood of his Blood, He Who Drinks the Blood of the Fallen, He Whom Before All Mortals Weep, He Whom Can Choke On My *Bloody* Fist... The demon who murdered his own kin... The demon who killed himself just so he could spend eternity tormenting human soldiers... *This* is the demon who's claimed the woman I *love*?"

"I'm sorry to be the bearer of more bad news," Isabelle said evenly, "but yes."

"If Azerius is the one who marked Charlotte, there's only *one* thing I need to know from this book." Dorian slammed it back onto the table, rattling Colin's test tubes. "How the *fuck* do I kill him?"

"I don't know, Dorian," she said. "He's a lord of hell, and that's his domain. He doesn't exist on the earthy plane."

"Then how do we *make* him exist here?"

"I suppose he'd have to be summoned, but I have no idea how to even *attempt*—"

"Read the bloody book!" he roared, but his anger wasn't for Isabelle.

He muttered an apology and turned away, shame heating his face, rage still swirling inside him like a tempest.

A soft touch graced his shoulder, and Dorian turned to find Charlotte smiling at him, her copper eyes full of love and kindness.

It disarmed him immediately.

He slid his fingers into her hair and brushed a kiss to her forehead, calming himself by the feel of her soft skin. "How is it you're smiling after what Isabelle revealed?"

"Because I'm channeling my sister, and she would *definitely* see the positives here."

"*What* positives? We've just discovered you've been claimed by one of the original demons of hell."

"Exactly." Charlotte curled her fingers around his wrists and gazed up into his eyes. "Last night—before we knew *anything* about this Azerius asshole—you promised me you'd find a way to break the demon bind. And after less than twenty-four hours, we already know who he is. We know about all his stupid names, his daddy issues, his bloodlust. We've got his toys. We know who worships him."

"And," Isabelle added, offering Dorian a warm, understanding smile despite his earlier outburst, "as a human promised to Lord Azerius, Charlotte will be safe from any demons who swear fealty to him. In their eyes, a soul bound to Azerius is untouchable—harming her would be like harming the demon lord himself."

Dorian blew out a breath, wishing the information brought him some measure of comfort. But what did it matter if she was safe from harm tonight, only to be dragged to hell tomorrow?

"We still don't know how to summon him," he said.

"*Yet.*" Charlotte turned and kissed his wrist, the touch of her warm lips further relaxing him. "Now, let's go back upstairs and get you another drink before you Hulk out on Colin's creepy collection of blood and bones and he has to recreate his research from scratch."

"Excellent point, Charlotte," Colin said. "And now that you mention it, I could use a drink too."

Finally granting his woman a smile in return, Dorian

leaned in and whispered, "You've convinced him to take a break, love. You really *are* a miracle worker."

As they made their way to the elevator, Dorian was overcome with the same feeling he'd experienced earlier—like someone had been watching them.

But just as before, the chamber was empty, save for the echoes of his dead father and the brutal lord of hell who would soon—one way or another—meet the same fate.

CHAPTER TWENTY-ONE

By the time they settled into the study and Dorian poured everyone another round, Gabriel had returned, the frustrated look in his eyes confirming what Dorian had already suspected—he wasn't able to trace the source of Sasha's call.

"It looks like whoever's holding her covered their tracks well." Gabriel returned Charlotte's phone and dropped into the chair closest to the fireplace, stretching out his legs before the flames. "The call bounced through several different cities, none of them in New York State. But," he added, "my source isn't giving up. I sent him the screenshot you took—he's analyzing it now."

"Thank you." Charlotte smiled—still channeling a bit of her sister, Dorian suspected.

"So what have you lot been up to, then?" Gabriel leaned back in his chair and glanced around as Dorian distributed the drinks. "No offense, but you look as if you've just emerged from the very dungeons of hell."

"You have no idea how right you are." Aiden lifted his glass. "Cheers."

There hadn't been time to get into the details of the blade and the book with Gabriel earlier, and now it spilled out in a mad rush, all of them trying to fill in the gaps with whatever information and hypotheses they had about Chernikov's dastardly plans and the demon Azerius.

They were all in agreement on one thing—Chernikov had to be dealt with, and quickly. They had no idea how much work had already been completed on his project, and no guarantees the other nefarious employees at Armitage Holdings would back off, even with their operation exposed.

"We need to take them out completely," Gabriel said.

"We can't take out Chernikov's entire organization alone," Aiden said. "We haven't the numbers."

"So we'll start with Chernikov himself," Gabriel said. "Cut off the head of the snake, then work our way down."

"And then we've got hundreds of pissed-off demon sycophants on the loose, with no obligation to honor the Accords," Isabelle said. "They'll be looking for blood and vengeance, and where do you think they'll start?"

No one said a word to that—no one needed to. In the wake of a Chernikov assassination, all those rudderless demons would be torching Ravenswood by dawn. And without an army of his own, Dorian had no way to defend it, especially when he considered Chernikov had the backing of House Duchanes, a coven of dark witches, and untold other defectors on his side.

At this point, he wouldn't be surprised if Malcolm was among them.

"I don't suppose you're any good with biological weaponry?" Aiden asked Colin. "Serious question, mate."

"If only I'd chosen my post-doctorate studies more strategically." Colin flashed a dimpled grin, then sipped his bourbon. "To be fair, I thought I'd be delivering babies and setting broken arms at this point, not trying to recreate a cure for vampirism, summoning a lord of hell, and plotting against an army of demons."

"You make it sound like drudgery when you say it like that," Aiden teased, then settled back into his chair, his eyes darkening with the same worries the rest of the group obviously shared.

For a while no one spoke, and Dorian allowed himself to be lulled by the comforts of a crackling fire, a fine scotch, and the company of friends and family. It'd been a long time since he'd felt anything close to it, and though Malcolm's absence left a particularly sharp ache in his heart, Dorian couldn't help but be glad for the moment.

Still, thoughts of Malcolm were never far, and now they clawed at his insides anew, filling him with a mixture of sadness, betrayal, and guilt—a cocktail of pain he'd associated with his family for far too long.

Bloody hell, he still wanted so badly for things to be different.

If only, if only, if only… A refrain as closely connected to thoughts of his family as the disconcerting feeling churning through his chest.

"I have a crazy idea," Charlotte finally said, bringing him back from his dark thoughts. He looked at her and smiled, warmed by the firelight dancing in her eyes. With a mischievous smirk, she said, "What if we got Rogozin to do it?"

"Rogozin?" Gabriel scoffed. "Yes, let's hop into bed with *more* demons, since my brother had so much luck bedding Chernikov. And wasn't it Rogozin's demons who attacked at the Tribeca penthouse?"

"Indeed it was," Dorian said, recalling the taste of Rogozin hellfire in his lungs as Duchanes had poisoned him and tormented Charlotte before his eyes.

"And Chernikov's who attacked us in Central Park," she countered.

"Your point?" Gabriel asked.

"Demons and vampires are mortal enemies, and right now, in the wake of your father's death, all of the demon factions are testing the boundaries. I'm not saying Rogozin is the perfect ally by any stretch, but there are no perfect options here."

"We can't trust him, Charlotte," Gabriel said.

"With this? I think we can," she said. "You guys said it yourselves—Rogozin is after territory, not human vessels. There's no way he'd want Chernikov's plan to succeed. If it did, Rogozin would be forced to give up all his territory and fall in line, just like everyone else. With his organization backing us, we've definitely got the numbers, right?"

"It certainly gives us better odds," Colin said.

"My enemy's enemy is my friend," Aiden said. "A classic strategy, to be sure. But I'm not sure that's enough to win him over. What's in it for Alexei himself? Why would he risk his own organization, his reputation, and his life to align with the royal vampires?"

"Because if he doesn't," she said, "the moles in his organization will sell the precious Blade of Azerius to his enemy, basically ensuring Chernikov's victory and sole dominion over all life on earth, human and supernatural alike."

Dorian sighed. As much as he loathed the idea of working with Rogozin—with *any* demon, for that matter, especially after Chernikov's treachery—Charlotte had a point.

"How are you seeing this play out, love?" he asked.

Through another cheeky grin, she said, "We offer him something no demon can resist: A deal."

"You're out of your bloody head," Gabriel said. "Demon deals are a one-way ticket to hell."

"Not if we read the fine print," she said, "and not if we're the ones making the deal."

"What is it you think we have to offer?" Dorian asked.

At this, the sparkle in her eyes dimmed, and she let out a long, slow breath. "Two things, actually, and you're going to hate them both."

Dorian took a long pull on his scotch, steadying himself.

"One—sell him the Blade of Azerius," she said. "Direct

buy, half of what he's supposedly paying Estas, none of the hassle."

"Why would I give up the one weapon we've got that can eradicate demons?" Dorian asked.

"Because it's not actually all that useful to you. Think about it—you can only use it on one demon at a time. If that's your grand plan against Chernikov, it's going to take a while."

"I agree," Isabelle said. "In the hands of a vampire—even the king himself—the weapon is more symbolic than anything else."

"A symbol of our power over the lesser supernatural beings," Gabriel said. "Turn that over to Rogozin—to *any* demon—and you may as well drop to your knees and offer to suck his cock."

"Even if we defeat Rudy and Estas and avoid the robbery," Charlotte said, "if you keep that blade, you're going to be hunted. The demons will never stop trying to take it from you, and eventually, they'll succeed. I'd bet my left tit they'll come after it the minute they figure out Rudy can't deliver it."

"I'd really prefer you not bet your body parts, love," Dorian said. "I've gotten rather attached to all of them. Furthermore..." He closed his eyes and rubbed them, wishing like hell he wasn't about to say this next bit, but seeing no way around it. "I actually agree with you."

"Fuck," Gabriel said. "So do I—about the blade being a danger to us, not about aligning with Rogozin. There *has* to be a better way."

"I'm all ears," Dorian said, but Gabriel had nothing more to add.

"Charlotte," Isabelle said, "what was the second thing?"

Charlotte sipped her gin and tonic, then turned to Dorian. "After Malcolm convened his council, you told me you weren't opposed on principal—only that you wanted to see other supernaturals represented."

"If and when I decide to form an advisory committee, then yes, I would want everyone represented. But... Wait. Surely you're not suggesting...?"

"That's *exactly* what I'm suggesting."

"You want me to extend an olive branch to the Rogozin demons? To invite them to the literal table?"

"I'm asking you to objectively look at the situation we're in. Even if we defeat Chernikov, you're still going to need more allies going forward. Your father has only recently died, and look at the chaos that's already come to your door. If we can secure an alliance with one of the most powerful demonic factions in the city—one poised to become *the* most powerful, if we can take out Chernikov—that can only help keep the peace."

"Are you serious?" Gabriel rose from his chair, glaring at Charlotte as if she were mad. "Rogozin is not our friend, Charlotte. He's a demon. You of all people should know that."

"*Gabriel*," Dorian warned. "Do not speak to—"

"No, he's right," Charlotte said. "I *should* know that—and I fucking do, Gabriel. *Believe* me. Rogozin's guys did unspeakable things to me as a kid. But I need to set my personal feelings about them aside, because what's happening now is so much bigger than me. War is coming, guys. Chernikov is the bigger threat right now—to House Redthorne *and* to Rogozin. But if your house and Rogozin's organization are united against that threat, Chernikov doesn't stand a chance. It's time to make a deal."

"Are you hearing yourself?" Gabriel shoved a hand through his hair, the air around him crackling with his anger. "Fucking hell, Charlotte. You find out your uncle's a demon, and suddenly you're an expert in navigating supernatural politics."

Dorian was out of his chair in a flash, but he stopped just short of putting his little brother through the wall. As much as he wanted to defend her from his brother's utter dickishness, Charlotte was doing a fine job on her own.

"Watch your tone, brother," he said instead, letting him off with a warning—the last he'd offer before mounting Gabriel above the mantle like a piece of art.

"Look, Gabriel," Charlotte said. "I don't pretend to know *anything* about supernatural politics. I'm just speaking as someone who's spent her entire life watching men swing their dicks around and play bullshit power games just to get one more slice of the proverbial pie. Vampires, demons, mortals… Corruption and greed rots everyone the same—from the inside out. So if you don't mind, kindly put your dick away before you break something, and give me a fair shot for once."

Dorian let loose a laugh, but Gabriel failed to see the humor.

Instead, he turned on Dorian with ice in his eyes. "I know you think you're in love, brother, but that's no reason to let this woman lead you into the wolf's den."

So much for Gabriel's compassion.

"In all your long years, *brother*," Dorian snapped, "have you ever cared for *anyone*? Or do you honestly prefer keeping your bed as cold as your heart?"

Gabriel slammed his drink onto the mantle. "Insults. Excellent strategy. In the meantime, I hope you like the feeling of hellfire up your ass. I'm sure Rogozin will pull out all the stops, especially after what we did to his demons in Woodside."

"You were supposed to pin that on Chernikov."

"I did what I could, brother. No guarantees. Had I known you'd be pitching him a deal, I might've suggested a different strategy in Woodside. Alas..."

"Bloody hell, Gabriel. This isn't a game. This—"

"This is a suicide mission! You can't possibly think you can walk in there and make a deal with the very demons we tortured! The very demons with the power to kill you in a bloody heartbeat!"

"What other options do we have? Chernikov is gaining power as we speak. We can't very well—"

"Gabriel's right, Dorian," Charlotte said.

"*Finally*," Gabriel said with a shallow laugh. "The human is talking sense again."

"He's being a total *douche* about it," she added, glaring at Gabriel with a look that would've set a mortal man on fire. Then, turning back to Dorian, "But he's right. You can't pitch a deal to Rogozin… But *I* can."

Dorian blinked. He couldn't have *possibly* heard that right.

"Charlotte," Aiden said, "while I agree you've brought us some ideas worth considering here, I'm afraid I can't—"

"*No,*" Dorian said, his mind finally catching up with her ridiculous suggestion. "Absolutely not. Out of the question."

"Come now, brother," Gabriel mocked. "Charlotte asked us to give her a fair shot. If she wants to get herself killed, that's—"

"Gabriel, I'm telling you *right* now, if you—"

"Rogozin *will* bite," Charlotte cut in. "I have proof one of his most trusted advisors is conspiring with my uncle—a longtime Rogozin associate—to double-cross him. And I'd be going in as an emissary to the vampire king, offering him the deal of a lifetime on the blade and a seat on the supernatural council. There's no way he'll refuse to see me."

"I'm not worried about him refusing the invitation," Dorian said. "I'm worried about him picking up where he left off when you were a child."

"That wasn't Rogozin. Those men were humans, or I'd already be dead. Besides, apparently I'm some kind of hell-bride for his precious raven king, remember? Isabelle said Rogozin's demons won't touch me."

"She's right, Dorian," Isabelle said. "I understand your concern, but I'm with Charlotte on this one."

"Charlotte..." he breathed, his heart already seizing with untold worries, but he feared he'd already lost the argument. He felt the shift in the energy—a sense of new hope rising among them, where moments earlier there had only been despair.

Even Gabriel seemed to be thawing out again, quietly nursing his drink in the corner of the room.

Dorian closed his eyes and sighed.

It was a terrible idea. The worst.

But also, a damned good one.

Dorian felt Charlotte's presence before him, and he opened his eyes just as she reached up to touch his face, a soft smile curving her lips.

"I can do this, Dorian," she said. "I'm asking you to trust me. I'm asking you to back me up. And I'm asking you to believe in me."

By the light of her beautiful, determined eyes, the last of his resolve melted away.

"I *always* believe in you, love."

"Then you'd better put on that kettle after all, vampire king. And we should probably get some Chinese takeout." Charlotte's soft smile stretched into a bright grin. "We've got a plan to hatch."

CHAPTER TWENTY-TWO

Charley had saved a single pair of Christian Louboutin stilettos from her pared-down wardrobe, and now those heels clacked against the cold marble floor as she strode purposefully across the hotel lobby, her chin held high, shoulders squared. Along with the shoes, she was dressed in a black pinstripe suit and cream-colored silk blouse, her hair in a loose twist. To everyone in the lobby, she probably looked like an ordinary businesswoman ready to make a deal over brunch, to pioneer a new venture, to take over a company.

No one there knew she was about to risk her life brokering a deal with the second-most powerful demon in the tri-state area.

The same demon who, eighteen years earlier, had sent his men to terrorize her in a pizzeria parking lot while her father and Rudy made some kind of shitty deal upstairs.

The silver scar above her hip burned at the memories.

But she wasn't that scared little girl anymore.

She wasn't her uncle's pawn, or her father's, or anyone else's.

She was Charlotte fucking D'Amico. Reformed con woman. Survivor. Jersey girl for life.

And today, she held the fate of far too many people in her hands to fuck this up.

Hiking the laptop bag up her shoulder, Charley followed the curve of the lobby toward the elevators, then took one up to the thirty-fifth floor. As the doors opened into the exclusive French restaurant in one of Long Island City's newest buildings, Charley steadied herself with a few deep breaths and a whispered reminder of why she was there.

Sasha.

Dorian.

Aiden.

Cole.

Colin.

Isabelle.

Even Gabriel made the list.

They were her family now. All of them. And she wouldn't let them down.

"Charlotte D'Amico," she announced to the maître d'. "I'm meeting some associates for brunch."

"Of course," he said. "Your party is already here."

The man led Charley to a set of double doors at the back of the dining room. He knocked once, and the doors swung inward, guarded by a bald, beefy man in a black suit and maroon shirt, no tie. Half of his face was covered in tattoos. The other half was covered in scars.

Charley forced herself not to stare.

The man dismissed the maître d' and shut the doors behind Charley, then gestured for her to open her laptop bag. She did as he asked, and he quickly examined the contents while she took in the scene before her.

The private dining room was large and ornate, bathed in soft light from the floor-to-ceiling windows that offered a view of lower Manhattan. The walls were a rich, buttery yellow that did nothing to warm the chill in her bones.

In front of the windows, one man remained seated while four others rose from behind the table, their eyes fixed on her as the guard patted her down with quick, precise movements. He finished up, then grabbed her by the elbow, delivering her to the table as if she were a prize the other men had won.

Not men, she reminded herself. *Demons.*

At her approach, the one who hadn't gotten to his feet— a demon who looked to be in his sixties, with a shock of thick white hair and piercing, steel-gray eyes—gave her the once-over. He didn't smile.

Rogozin.

"Ms. D'Amico," he said in his thick Russian accent, gesturing for her to take a seat directly across from him. "Please—join us."

She did as he asked, and the demons around him followed suit, settling back into their chairs. Every one of them had tattoos and scars—on their faces, their hands, peeking out of shirt collars—ornate symbols and words that mapped the stories of their lives, their crimes. She wondered if they all bore the white ravens.

She wondered—if things went south today—if she herself would end up as another tattoo in their long and colorful stories.

The thought made her shiver, but if anyone else noticed her discomfort, they didn't say.

Rogozin seemed to be considering his next words, while the rest of the group stared at her unflinchingly. A demon with barbed wire tattooed around his neck winked at her, and Charley had to clench her teeth to keep them from chattering.

But she'd come this far. She would *not* let them intimidate her.

Dorian and the others were counting on her.

All of Manhattan was counting on her, whether they realized it or not.

"Thank you for agreeing to see me, Mr. Rogozin," she finally said, as evenly as she could manage.

He gave a small bow of acknowledgment. "I was intrigued to receive Dorian Redthorne's message. For long time, I have sought way to meet with vampire royal family."

"He feels the same way," Charley said, the lie sliding smoothly from her lips. It was the first of several she'd probably have to tell today—mostly white lies, just enough to grease the wheels, but lies, nevertheless. Suddenly, she felt as if she'd spent her whole life training for this meeting.

All the cons, all the games, all the expensive outfits and the megawatt charm.

She was the complete package, and today, she'd work it for all she was worth.

"As Dorian mentioned," Charley said, "we've recently come upon some information we thought would be of interest to you. As some of that information relates to members of my own family, he thought I would be the best emissary."

Dorian had sent word to Rogozin through some of Gabriel's contacts—a mysterious network neither Charley nor Dorian himself knew much about. They'd told the demon that Dorian had learned of his interest in a piece of Scandinavian art in his collection, as well as the disloyalty festering in the Rogozin organization. Charlotte was to bring the demons a proposal—alone, unarmed, and in good faith—for a mutually beneficial arrangement between the two factions.

Now, Rogozin nodded, his cool demeanor revealing nothing. "I knew your father, Ms. D'Amico. He was... honorable man. I am sorry for your loss. Four years now?"

"Five years, sir," Charley said, fighting back the familiar sting of tears.

"And your mother?"

"She left when I was young."

Rogozin shook his head, his frown deepening. "Such shame. Beautiful young girl. No parents."

"Thank you, Mr. Rogozin. I appreciate your kindness."

"But you have vampire king to look after you now, yes?"

"Dorian and I have gotten close," she admitted, forcing herself to keep playing the game—a delicate balancing act of lies and truths, promises and threats. "He'd like to get closer to your organization as well, if you're amenable."

"I think he will need bigger bed." Rogozin and the other demons laughed.

Charley forced herself to laugh right along with them.

Oh yes, we're all friends here, ha ha ha…

"Coming to us was right thing to do," he said.

Charley nodded, pressing her legs together to keep from trembling. She was so parched, so thirsty, but she didn't dare reach for her water glass, lest she knock it over and cause an explosion of hellfire.

Dorian, Gabriel, Isabelle, and Aiden were at a restaurant around the corner, but that was little more than a show of support. It wouldn't do her any good if things went bad here.

Right now, there were only two things keeping her safe: the fact that she was promised to Azerius, and the assumption—the hope—that Rogozin didn't want to start a war with the vampires.

"Would you like a drink?" Rogozin gestured toward a decanter of clear liquid—vodka, she guessed.

Charley shook her head, then cursed herself for not knowing the custom. Was she supposed to politely decline the offer? Or was it rude not to accept? She was about to change her mind when one of the other demons let out another raucous laugh. He leaned over to the demon with the barbed wire tattoo and said something in Russian, making the rest of the demons laugh too.

Fear crept down Charley's spine, settling like a block of ice in her stomach. She had no idea what they were laughing about—killing her? Dumping her body out with the restaurant trash? Incinerating her? Did they all know she was promised to Azerius? Isabelle was certain they could sense the mark, and Charley was certain Rogozin had something to do with giving it to her, but still.

There were a *lot* of unknowns.

Nowhere to go but through it…

Charley closed her eyes and took another breath, deep and calming. When she opened her eyes again, they were all watching her, waiting. The room had gone so quiet, she heard the ice cubes shifting in their water glasses.

"Gentlemen," she finally said, digging deep to find her strength. An image of Sasha filled her mind, and she clung to it. "You are obviously very busy men." She pulled her laptop from the bag and set it on the table with a thunk, making the silverware rattle. "Allow me to get right to the point."

CHAPTER TWENTY-THREE

Charley laid out her case like a master prosecutor, presenting the evidence of Estas and Rudy's treachery, including Rudy's plans to escape to Brazil before delivering the artifact he'd promised Rogozin and Chernikov.

They might not have trusted her when she'd first walked in here today, but Rogozin and his demons couldn't ignore the evidence. It was too compelling, and much too complex a scheme for her to be making it all up.

"I always knew Rudy D'Amico was piece of shit," Rogozin said when she'd finished. "No offense to your family name."

"None taken."

"Estas? He surprises me. I thought he was loyal."

"I understand the feeling, sir."

"Yes, I suppose you do." He chewed the ice cubes from his water glass, considering her for a long moment. The other demons stared at her with blank eyes.

After a long, uncomfortable silence, Rogozin finally said, "You told me story of betrayal in my organization. Maybe I owe you story as well."

"I'd love to hear it." Charley forced a smile through a wave of nausea. Was he serious? Or was he stringing her along, only to deliver some terrible punchline at the end—something to amuse his brooding demonic sidekicks?

"Your father, Paul," he said, and Charley immediately stilled. Of all the stories he could've told her, she was not expecting one starring her father.

"He did not know about us," Rogozin continued. "About supernatural, I mean. Not until later. But Rudy, he always knew. He was working side jobs for me for many years—since he was schoolboy with broken heart. His girl-friend sleeps with his brother, he says."

Charley nodded. "I understand my mother was capricious. I recently learned she and my uncle had a longtime affair."

"Yes, and for all that time, he made deals to get her back. One day, he promised me some *very* valuable items. He brought your father to make delivery." He held her gaze a beat, ensuring she got his meaning, and Charley sucked in a breath.

He was talking about the Long Island pizza place.

Where you off to, little girl?

A chill gripped her spine, but she forced herself to remain still. Stoic.

"But when they made delivery," Rogozin continued, "I

discovered all items were forgeries. As you can imagine, I became upset."

So upset you sent your goons after a helpless kid?

"After that..." He shook his head, then took a deep drink of vodka, his eyes filling with something that looked a hell of a lot like shame. "Understand something, Ms. D'Amico. I did *not* send those men after you."

His eyes grew dark and imploring, boring right through to her very soul. The way he looked at her... It was as if he could read her thoughts. As if he needed her to believe him.

Strangely enough, she did.

"I did not know you were in car," he said. "Did not know you even existed. The men—two humans working for me—they acted of their own accord, thinking I would be pleased. I was not. But by the time I realized what happened, your father was..." He made a shooting gesture with his hand, and Charley flinched, remembering the popping sound as her father took down her attackers. "I respected him for protecting his daughter, but I could not let him go unpunished. I would've looked weak at a time when my organization did not have power it has today."

Bile rose in her throat, and she swallowed it down, along with a mouthful of curses. She knew all too well how power plays worked. Knew all too well that women and girls would always be used as pawns and prey, so long as the system was built to keep rewarding the predators.

"I made your father offer," Rogozin said. "That is when he learned of supernatural. I gave him three choices—I could kill all three of you, I could turn you into vessels, or I could spare your lives and souls, *if* he agreed to make an offering to—"

"Azerius," Charley gasped, the realization slamming into her with a clarity so sharp and bright, it made the stars dance before her eyes. "My father sold my soul to a demon lord?"

Rogozin raised an eyebrow—the only sign he was at all surprised that she knew.

From the moment Dorian had told her about the demon mark, Charley was certain it was her uncle's doing.

But her father?

Charley reached for her water glass, unsure whether she wanted to laugh, cry, or simply disappear.

"You were child," he said. "Your guardian had right to make deal for you. He thought it was best choice of three bad choices. He was honorable man, as I said. He made deal, but only because he believed he could find escape hatch. He had many years to make plan. Then one day, your uncle tells me Paul is going to do one last job, take money, flee country with you, and hire witch to break demon bind."

Tears blurred Charley's eyes as she recalled her uncle's words in the limo.

Do you know the most heartbreaking thing about the One Night Stand job? It was supposed to be his last job... He wanted you to have a normal life... He was planning to take his share and get you out of the country... Start over somewhere new...

"I was angry when I found out," Rogozin said. "Not because he could break the bind—that is impossible. Only

234

because it was betrayal of his promise. But before I could speak to your father about this, your uncle decided to take matters into his own hands. He wanted greater power, greater respect in my organization. Rather than earning it honest way, he went over my head. He called upon Lord Azerius and made deal to become demon host."

"How?" she whispered, though the end of this brutal tale was already coalescing in her mind, all the answers she'd been seeking for the last five years finally colliding in an epic, terrible conclusion.

"Is better if I show you this part." Rogozin gestured to the barbed-wire demon, who handed over a tablet. After queuing up a video, Rogozin passed it to Charley. "It will be difficult to see, but truth is better, no matter how painful."

The timestamp was dated the day before the One Night Stand job.

The day before her father's murder.

With a trembling finger, Charley hit play, holding her breath as the images and sounds came to life on the screen.

It looked like some sort of surveillance video—black-and-white, slightly out of focus. There were two men in the frame, but their heads were partially cut off.

Hidden camera, she realized. A third man was wearing it somewhere on his body, probably in a shirt button or tie tack. The others seemed unaware of it.

"He trusts me," one man said. "It's not even on his radar."

Travis. She'd recognize the snake's voice anywhere.

"Once you get through the tunnel," the other guy said, and Charley knew at once it was Rudy. Which meant the guy filming was probably Estas.

"Take I-80 West," Rudy continued, "and find a good, out-of-the-way place to pull off. Play it cool, and he won't suspect you."

"That fuckface won't have time to suspect me." Travis laughed, a sound that made Charley want to take a scalding-hot shower.

"Just make it look good," Rudy said. At his nod, Estas passed Travis a padded yellow envelope. "We need this to look like a gang hit, not an inside job."

"I know what I'm doing," Travis said. "What about your crew? You need to keep them in check. Last thing I need is one of those assholes asking too many questions."

"I'll handle them," Rudy said. "But watch out for his daughter. My niece is a *real* pain in the ass. One wrong move and she'll be sniffing around like a bitch in heat."

"Bitches in heat are one of my specialties." Travis laughed again, then peeked at the contents of the envelope. Seemingly satisfied, he tucked it into his pocket. Inside his jacket, right there under his arm, Charley spotted the holster and gun.

The gun that killed my father...

"This time tomorrow, gentlemen," Travis said, "the deed will be done. And we'll be officially in business."

Travis—a man Rudy had brought on as a forger, a man she'd later allowed into her bed... *He* was the inside guy.

The bastard who'd gotten close to her father, only to put a bullet in his head.

And he'd done it all on Rudy's orders.

Charley's head spun, the ground tilting beneath her.

It was one thing to suspect it—to *know* it, deep in her gut—after seeing the evidence Cole had found in the Estas files.

But it was something else entirely to hear the admission from their own mouths.

She returned the tablet to Rogozin and closed her eyes, not bothering to wipe away the tears. Anger, bitterness, grief... They hit her all at once, squeezing the air from her lungs.

"His brother's life in exchange for power of demon," Rogozin said. "That was deal Rudy made with Azerius. Unfortunately, like most humans making deals, he did not read fine print."

Charley took a deep, steadying breath, refocusing. If Rogozin was willing to spill some details about Azerius, maybe there was something in there she could use to find her *own* way out of this damn deal.

She opened her eyes, doing her best to appear as damsel-in-distress as possible, hoping it might keep Rogozin's guard down.

"What *was* the fine print?" she asked.

"Demon host becomes stronger human, this is true. But he cannot channel demon power until host dies and demon takes over vessel permanently. So Rudy is... how is saying?" He let out a low chuckle. "Shooting blanks."

The other demons laughed.

"I still can't believe this happened." Charley retrieved a tissue from her bag and pressed it to her eyes, buying herself a moment to think. Shooting blanks... Did he mean Rudy couldn't cast hellfire? Was that why her uncle still needed the gun?

If that were true, it gave them a huge advantage—one Rogozin probably didn't realize he'd just revealed.

But she needed more. Something about Azerius himself.

"Azerius," she said, forcing a note of reverence into her voice. "Do you know when he's coming to... to collect me?"

"I do not. It is miracle he's waited so long, though. Usually, it is shorter time."

"Is there a way I might summon him? A way to speak with him, maybe?"

His eyes sparkled with new light, as if he were entertaining the whimsical thoughts of a young child. "You wish to renegotiate, perhaps? Make better offer?"

"Is that possible? I mean, I know he's like a god to you, and maybe—"

"God?" He muttered something in Russian to the barbed-wire demon, and they both laughed. "More like... emotionally unavailable father with *very* bad temper."

Charley forced herself to laugh along with the others, but inside, her heart was sinking with each new revelation.

"Lord Azerius does not negotiate," he finally said. "As for how to summon him, well... He kills brothers. Like Cain. That is when he comes. But it can't be done without the..." He trailed off, then shook his head. "*Nyet*. It can't be done."

Can't be done without the blade.

That's what he was going to say before he thought better of it. Charley knew it, deep in her bones.

"So that's it? There's no hope? No way to contact him?" She lowered her eyes, playing every bit the naive human Rogozin wanted to see.

"Even if it could be done, he doesn't like to come. Summoning him binds him to vessel. It is too dangerous. He..." Rogozin sighed, then said, "I am sorry for your plight, Ms. D'Amico. But things could be worse, no? I'm sure Lord Azerius will show you *every* kindness."

At this, the other demons laughed again.

Lord Azerius will be too busy dealing with my boot in his ass.

"Thank you for your honesty, Mr. Rogozin," she said, sensing she'd reached her limit on gathering Azerius intel before they got suspicious.

Rogozin asked her if she'd like to take a moment to collect herself in the ladies' room, but Charley shook her head.

Her whole life, men had been making deals on her behalf. Her own father had bargained away her soul. Travis had taken him from her. Rudy had been manipulating her ever since.

Now, it was Charley's turn to make the deal. That's what she'd come here for. And she wouldn't leave this fucking table until she'd seen it through.

"I feel like we got a bit off track," she said, leaving the

naive little human behind and stepping back into the role of chief negotiator. "I'm here to discuss a potential partnership between your organization and House Redthorne. It's obviously no surprise to you that Rudy is planning to double-cross you. But what may come as a surprise is the fact that the object you seek is in fact in Dorian's possession, and he is willing to sell it to you directly for half of Rudy's price."

Rogozin's poker face was in full effect, but Charley could sense the shift of energy in the room, the greed and anticipation gathering among the demons like a storm.

She opened her laptop again, then pulled up the photos she'd taken on her phone when she'd first inspected the Mother of Lost Souls, right before she'd smashed it.

All of them gasped.

So much for poker faces, assholes.

"The Mother of Lost Souls has been secured at an out-of-state location," she lied, "pending the outcome of our negotiations. In addition to the sale, House Redthorne is extending another offer—a seat on the King's council, which will be reconvened shortly. It's important to Dorian that all supernaturals are included, and he feels your organization can best represent the interests of the demons in our community."

Rogozin folded his arms across his chest and narrowed his eyes, his suspicion growing. "Why would vampire king offer this honor to me, and not to Nikolai Chernikov?"

"Because." Charley shut her laptop and flashed a wide smile. "We need your help *killing* Nikolai Chernikov."

In the stunned silence that followed, the wait staff

finally delivered the meal, and as the demons shoveled in their ham and cheese crêpes and tuna niçoise salad, Charley took polite nibbles of her food and shared what she knew of Chernikov's plans and the allies he'd already amassed. This time, there were no spreadsheets, no photos, nothing but the story Isabelle had told them and the pieces of the puzzle she and the others had cobbled together.

But Rogozin believed her. She saw the suspicion slowly leave his eyes, replaced instead with something that utterly shocked her.

Respect.

"We are working on a plan," she continued, pressing her advantage, "but would like to know we can count on you when the time comes. Once the threat from Chernikov is neutralized, Dorian will happily conclude the transaction—with a few caveats, of course."

Rogozin folded his napkin and set it on his plate, eyeing her warily. "Caveats?"

"We know it's not the sculpture you're after, Mr. Rogozin. It's what's hidden inside." Charley held up her hand to cut off a string of sputtering denials. "Dorian understands it's a piece of cultural significance to you, particularly given your connection to Azerius. That's why he's willing to part with it. But you *must* agree not to use the blade on humans. I understand this may be part of its appeal, but as the ruling body over all supernaturals, House Redthorne is responsible for ensuring the safety of the humans who live amongst you. As such, he can't allow you to take shortcuts that would violate the existing Accords.

Demons have other ways of making deals—consensual deals. Using the blade on humans would constitute a breach of contract as well as a breach of trust. And trust *me*, Mr. Rogozin. The Royal Redthornes are not a family you want to cross."

Rogozin glared at her, scrutinizing every word for the lies within.

But Charley held firm, refusing to look away. Other than the little fib about the sculpture's location, she'd spoken the truth—about her uncle and Estas. About Chernikov. About the deal Dorian was offering.

She'd done what she could. Now, it was up to Rogozin.

"I'll give you gentlemen a moment to discuss this in private." She rose from her chair, but before she stepped away, Rogozin spoke.

"No need for moment," he said.

Charley held her breath, her heartbeat crashing against her ribs.

And then, after an agonizing eternity, Alexei Rogozin finally said the words she'd been longing to hear from the moment she'd first suggested this crazy-ass plan in Dorian's study last night.

"Tell vampire king Alexei Rogozin accepts proposal." He smiled at her—the first real one he'd offered—then gestured for her to reclaim her chair. "Now you must enjoy food. You eat like bird. Is not healthy."

Charley laughed, happy to accept the invitation.

After brunch, Rogozin escorted her back out into the main restaurant. As they awaited the elevator, he said, "So tell me, what are we to do about my two traitors?"

"I won't presume to tell you how to run your organization, Mr. Rogozin," she said. "But I would like to deal with my uncle directly. We have some unresolved... family matters to settle. Once that's done, I assure you, he won't cause you any more trouble."

An understanding smile spread across his face, and he reached out and touched her shoulder. "You are formidable woman, Ms. D'Amico. I understand why vampire king is so taken with you."

"I'll take it as a compliment."

"As it was meant." He gave her shoulder a friendly squeeze, then released her. "Tell him I look forward to hearing from him whenever time is right. We will be waiting."

The elevator arrived, and she stepped inside, turning around to meet his eyes once more.

"Forgive my presumption," he said, placing his hand against the doors to hold them open, "but if I may give you a word of advice?"

"Of course."

"As demon in hell, I saw many, many wars. Many deaths. As demon on earth, I have seen many, many wars. Many deaths. I know your father was great loss to you. But revenge... It does not fill hole inside you. It only leads to more holes." He shook his head, lost for a moment in his own thoughts. Then, glancing at her once more with a look she could only describe as pity, "Mourn your father, Ms. D'Amico. Avenge him if you must. But then? Let it go. Live your life. Enjoy time you have left, before..."

He trailed off and finally released the doors, smiling once more before turning away.

As the doors slid closed and the elevator began its descent, the unsaid words echoed through her soul.

Before Azerius comes to claim you.

CHAPTER TWENTY-FOUR

"Is there nothing you can't do, Charlotte D'Amico?"

Safely back in his bedroom at Ravenswood, Dorian cupped his woman's face and stared into her eyes, still trying to process everything she'd told him about the meeting.

While he'd been crawling the walls of a nearby restaurant, hoping for the best but fearing the worst, she'd been dining with demons, altering the course of Dorian's life. Of *all* their lives.

He'd been bloody terrified the entire time, cursing himself for allowing her to go through with it. Cursing himself for not turning her into a vampire when she'd asked, certain he'd left her weak and vulnerable. In those terrible hours, he told himself he'd finally do it—he'd turn her the moment they returned to Ravenswood, if only to give her that elusive advantage over all the enemies who might otherwise harm her.

But then, just when he was ready to storm into that hotel and steal her from the demonic clutches he was so certain had trapped her, she'd returned to him.

Safe. Whole. Overwhelmed, but relieved.

She'd done it. She'd succeeded in securing the deal.

Yes, there were details to work out and formalize. And no, they had no guarantees Rogozin wouldn't fuck them as swiftly and thoroughly as Chernikov had.

But Charlotte had gone head-to-head with a powerful demon crew with little more than a laptop and a prayer, and she'd accomplished exactly what she'd set out to do.

Dorian had never been more proud of anyone as he'd been in that moment.

And in that moment he knew, without reservation, he'd finally grant her wish. He'd turn her into a vampire—not because he was afraid of her human frailties, but because he saw in her a strength and determination that refused to be dimmed, no matter how much darkness life had thrown at her.

He wouldn't turn her to make her strong.

He would turn her because she was *already* strong, and becoming a vampire was *her* choice—one she'd made from the depths of the same inner badassery that had allowed her to face the demons. That had allowed her to survive her father's death and her uncle's cruelty. That had allowed her to look into the eyes of a monster and see the human soul inside.

His soul.

Dorian pressed a long, lingering kiss to her lips, then

pulled back to admire those beautiful copper eyes once more. He could lose himself in them. In her.

How had she come into his life? How was it even possible she was his?

"Only one thing," she said now, granting him the gift of a smile as she reached up to trace her fingers across his forehead. "I can't read your thoughts."

They were standing before the windows, and Dorian looked out through the glass, taking in the view of his father's lands. *His* lands. "I was thinking about fate."

"What do you mean?"

"For more than two centuries," he said, "the Book of Lost Souls and the blade of the demon Azerius were buried here at Ravenswood. And a mere eighteen years ago, in a moment of abject desperation no father should ever have to face, yours promised you to that same demon. And somehow, across all the years, all the twists and turns, all the different possibilities, fate saw fit to bring us together."

"So that's it, then?" she teased, trailing her fingers down to unfasten the top buttons of his shirt, her touch making him shiver. "You think this was all some twist of fate? A stage play where we're merely the actors?"

"Is that what *you* think?"

At his question, her fingers stilled over the next button, and the smile that had shone so brightly only moments ago faded. "I think we were both cursed with fathers who made terrible choices they convinced themselves were the right ones. And those choices—however terrible, however painful—set us on the collision course that ultimately brought us together. If you want to call it fate? Fine. Fate put me on your path." She glanced up at him again, her eyes flashing with new fire. "But fate did *not* make me fall in love with you. It didn't make *us. We* did this, Dorian. One kiss, one touch, one conversation, one heartbeat at a time. At least, that's how I feel. If you feel differently, I—"

"Charlotte." He covered her hand with his own and pressed it against his chest, his heart banging like a wild thing beneath her touch. "Do you feel that? For more than two hundred and fifty years, I scarcely remembered it even existed. And now, it beats again—because of you. *For* you. What I feel... My love for you... It's not some cosmic whim or trick of the gods. It's beyond explanation. Beyond words. Beyond all things. Don't *ever* question it."

Her smile finally returned, and Dorian touched his forehead to hers, breathing in her scent, her very presence.

It was time.

Dorian took one last deep breath, then said, "I have a proposition for you, Ms. D'Amico."

"Is that so, Mr. Redthorne," she teased, returning her attention to the buttons on his shirt. "Better make it a good one. Word on the street is I'm an excellent negotiator."

"I've heard the rumors."

Finished with the buttons, she pushed the shirt off his shoulders, letting it fall to the floor, then got to work on her own clothing, losing the jacket, the blouse, and the suit pants in quick succession.

He stared at her, his gaze tracing the delicate lace

outlines of her jade-green undergarments, his thoughts unraveling.

Charlotte arched an eyebrow, clearly aware of her effect on him. "You were saying, Mr. Redthorne? Or have you already given up?"

"Option *one*," he said firmly, sweeping his half-naked goddess into his arms. "You remain as you are—an impossibly stubborn, fiercely beautiful mortal woman whom I vow to love and protect for the rest of your life."

The meaning behind his words hit her instantly, and her smile stretched wider, her eyes shining with emotion. "What's option two?"

"Option two." He lowered his voice to a whisper, the words themselves feeling like a sacred declaration. "I will make you immortal, if that is still your desire. And from that moment henceforth, you'll be an impossibly stubborn, fiercely beautiful vampire queen whom I vow to love and protect for the rest of eternity."

Charlotte gasped, a new light dancing through her coppery gaze. "Sounds an awful lot like a real date, Mr. Redthorne."

Dorian was captivated once again by her eyes, and for a moment he said nothing—just allowed himself to get lost in them, memorizing the threads of gold, the light, the sparkle, the storm.

"Is this truly what you want?" he finally asked.

She took his face between her hands and smiled. "It's truly what I want, Dorian. But only if you want it too."

"I do, love," he said, and despite his lingering fears, that was the truth. "But you must promise me you'll do *exactly* as I say. Once I determine your heart has slowed enough— almost to a stop—you'll need to drink my blood. Your body may reject the taste at first, but you have to fight through it. If you don't take my blood, your heart will—"

"I'll take it. I promise."

"Maybe I… I should call Isabelle. Or Colin. If anything goes wrong, they can help—"

"No. Just you, Dorian. You and me." She put her hand over his heart again and smiled. "I trust you. I trust *us*."

Dorian let out a deep exhale. "All right, love. You and me."

They stripped out of the last of their clothing, then he turned her toward the window again, both of them gazing out across the rolling hills to the river beyond. In the early evening light, it was a copper vein drinking in the last golden rays of the setting sun.

It was beautiful.

It was perfect.

Dorian swept her long hair aside, blazing a trail of kisses down the back of her neck, the taste of her skin a remedy that chased away the last of his fears.

Bracing her hands against the window, Charlotte arched her back, and he slid his cock between her thighs, entering her from behind with a soft, slow rhythm as his hands wandered her luscious curves. He skimmed over her hips, up the sides of her ribcage, sliding forward to cup her breasts. She moaned softly as he grazed her nipples, teasing and tugging, dragging his lips down the gentle slope between her neck and shoulder, hovering over her pulse point.

It beat for him, singing to him as it always did, an invitation as blissful as it was dangerous.

Taste me, I'm yours... Taste me...

Dorian's cock thickened in anticipation, his fangs descending, everything in him throbbing with need.

Charlotte let out a sigh of ecstasy.

"I love you," he whispered against her pale skin.

And then...

He bit her.

She cried out in pleasure, in pain, her body tensing, her heartbeat kicking into a frantic thrum as Dorian's fangs pierced the artery. Warm blood pooled in his mouth, and for a brief instant he savored the unique pleasure, the richness, the utter decadence.

A possessive growl rumbled through his chest.

Mine.

He swallowed it down, the taste of it making him dizzy.

And then, at long last, he began to suck.

Charlotte finally relaxed into the bite, the pain receding as the intense pleasure took hold. He gripped her hips and slid deeper inside her, stroking her, teasing her, guiding her body through the wild sensations he knew she was now feeling—the rush of heat from the pleasure of the bite and the slide of his rock-hard cock. The lightheadedness as the blood loss set in. The unmistakable tug of a human soul desperate to flee a dying body.

And she *was* dying. Every second Dorian fed, he pushed her a little closer to that black, terrifying edge.

He held her life in his hands. In his mouth. If he took too much blood, if he didn't initiate the change in time, if her heart spasmed, she'd die.

Charlotte's hands slid from the window, her arms falling to her sides as her body continued to weaken.

And still, Dorian drank.

Taste me, I'm yours…

Deeper. Darker. More.

Taste me…

Her pulse slowed.

Taste me…

So faint, he had to strain to hear it. To feel it.

Taste me…

And then it was nothing more than a memory, and she let out her last breath, collapsing backward against his chest.

With one arm holding her upright, his cock aching for release inside her, Dorian dragged his mouth from her throat and bit hard into his wrist. He pressed it to her lips and whispered his command against her ear.

"Drink, love. Do it now."

He waited, counted to ten, held his breath, but still, Charlotte didn't respond. Not a struggle. Not a whimper. Not a twitching muscle.

Her body grew heavier in his arms.

"Drink," he demanded. Begged. "Bloody hell, Charlotte. *Drink!*"

Suddenly, her body jerked to life, and he felt the warm suction of her lips closing around his wrist.

And then—finally, blissfully, miraculously—she drank.

She didn't resist the taste. Instead, she sucked him hard, her velvet tongue lapping at his skin, her lips vibrating with a hum of satisfaction as she took her fill.

He felt the change move through her body, strengthening her muscles, warming her skin, bringing her back to life.

Back to him.

When she was strong enough to stand on her own again, Dorian released his hold and slid his hand down her stomach, slowly gliding between her thighs. Still feeding from his wrist, Charlotte moaned at his touch, her hips rocking as he rubbed slow, hot circles over her clit, fucking her deep from behind, bringing her closer to bliss with every long, hard stroke.

It was erotic and incredible, dangerous and seductive. But above all else, it was special. A deeply powerful, profoundly intimate bond that would eternally connect them. He was her sire now, but it wasn't a position of power or coercion. They'd created this together. From their love, from their trust, from all that they'd come to mean to each other.

Love. He still wasn't quite used to the word, to the taste of it on his lips.

For so long, Dorian was convinced love was a recipe for weakness and stupidity. But that wasn't the case at all. It was *fighting* love—resisting it in all its forms—that had damn near destroyed him.

Charlotte saved him. She'd stormed the iron gates, cracked open his heart, and filled it with a light so bright, he could scarcely remember a time when he'd suffered alone in darkness.

And somehow, despite everything she'd witnessed at Ravenswood, despite all she'd learned about his past, she still wanted this life with him. She'd chosen it. Chosen *him*.

She was his woman.

His vampire.

His heart.

"Dorian," she whispered, finally breaking free from his wrist. "Don't stop touching me. Everything is on fire and I'm... It's so... You're... *Dorian!*"

She came with a last, desperate gasp, her body clenching hard around him, trembling, pulling him in deeper, driving him right over the last fucking edge.

"*Fucking... hell...*" It was all he could manage before a wave of hot, pulsing intensity swept through his body, and he came hard inside her, his fingers digging into her hips, his face buried in her hair, his soul no longer broken, but whole.

When they finally stopped trembling, when the wound in his wrist finally healed, when he could finally breathe again, Dorian turned her around in his arms and pressed his ear to her chest.

Wondering.

Listening.

Hoping.

And there, at long last, it was.

The steady beat of a newborn heart.

A *vampire* heart.

It was the most precious, most beautiful sound he'd ever heard.

Charlotte slid her hands into his hair, gently tugging him back up to meet her gaze.

Her eyes were as red as the blood soaking her lips.

"Dorian? I..." Her lush mouth curved into a smile, and she ran her tongue over her teeth, gasping when she felt the fangs. "Holy shit. I think I'm a..."

The realization made her sway.

"Yes, I think you are." He swept a lock of hair from her face and drew her into a tight embrace, the beat of her strong, beautiful vampire heart thrumming against his own. "It's all right, love," he whispered. "I've got you. I've got you."

CHAPTER TWENTY-FIVE

Hunger.

It burned through her like battery acid, making her ache and itch and writhe.

How had Dorian survived this? How had *any* of them survived?

Would it always be this way?

Charley couldn't be still another second. She bolted upright in bed, shocked to find it was already dark.

Shocked to find her eyes needed almost no time to adjust.

"Breathe, love," Dorian said, still stretched out beside her. He reached up to rub her back, and she instantly relaxed at his touch. "That's it, Charlotte. Deep breaths. It will pass."

"I feel so... buzzy. Like... like my veins are full of bees."

He let out a soft laugh and sat up, pressing a kiss to her

bare shoulder. "You need to feed. We've got blood bags downstairs. I'll—"

"Don't you *dare* leave me like this." She turned toward him, and in a move so fast it made her dizzy, she straddled him, pushing him hard onto his back. "I *need* you, Dorian. Right fucking... *here.*"

She rolled her hips, desperate to feel the heat of his cock between her thighs.

Dorian dragged his thumb across her lips, grinning up at her in the darkness. "Good to see some things *haven't* changed, my insatiable little prowler."

"I feel like I'm on fire," she breathed. Every word vibrated through her mouth like a kiss, her nerve endings sizzling at his every touch.

"It's an effect of the vampire blood. Newly sired vampires often feel extreme—"

She kissed him, smothering him, reaching down to fist his cock. He groaned and stiffened at her touch, sliding his hands up her back and hooking them around her shoulders.

Before she could guide him inside her wet, aching core, Dorian tightened his grip on her shoulders and blurred her out of bed, slamming her against the wall.

Fuck, yes.

Charley grinned.

And then she pushed back with everything she had.

In a blink, they were clear across the room, Charley pinning her man against the far wall, her blood surging with raw, undiluted power.

"Did I just *blur*?" she asked through a giddy laugh. "That was fucking amazing!"

"Ah, the first blissful taste of vampire strength," Dorian teased, his eyes sparkling with light and love. He lowered his mouth to hers, stealing a breathless kiss, then whispered, "Devil help us, I've created a monster."

She tested her strength again, pushing him back to the bed in another blur and collapsing on top of him.

"All that time," she said, her hair falling into his face, "you were holding back."

"If I'd shown you even a *fraction* of my full strength, I would've broken you."

"I *want* you to break me." Pinning his wrists to the bed, she hovered over his mouth and whispered darkly, "Fuck me, vampire king."

A low growl rumbled up through his chest, and in another blur, he flipped them again, pinning her beneath his solid, muscular form. Without another word, he pushed his cock deep inside her, claiming her hot flesh in a single stroke that made Charley gasp.

She felt *everything*. Every inch. Every movement. Every red-hot pulse of blood running through his veins.

His kiss tasted like heaven, like sin, like the end of the world, and the raw, masculine scent of him pushed her desires to the depths of their depravity.

The *best* fucking kind of depravity.

"More," she breathed, arching up to meet his every thrust, her body demanding all of him.

He slammed into her, again and again, setting her every nerve ablaze.

And still, she wanted more.

"Harder," she demanded. "Fuck me harder, Dorian. I need it."

Dorian let loose another possessive growl, and Charley growled right back at him, crushing his mouth with another kiss as he fucked her madly, deeply, hot and hard and desperate.

Her entire body hummed like a live wire.

This wasn't slow and tender. This wasn't dirty talk and bedroom games and naughty, delicious teasing.

This was mouths and hands and breath and fangs.

This was pulled hair and nails raked down backs.

This was a bruising grip, a devastating kiss, blood drawn and licked and sucked and devoured.

This. Was. Fire.

"Holy *fuck*," Charley gasped, the orgasm building inside her so quickly, she hadn't even felt the warning tingle of nerves. "Dorian, I'm so close. I'm... I can't..."

Dorian pulled out and flipped her onto her stomach, lifting her hips and slamming back into her pussy from behind, pushing her right back to the edge. Sliding his hand up her back, he fisted her hair and pulled, fucking her harder, deeper, and then—with a final vicious thrust that made her cry out his name like a curse—she came, a white-hot explosion that ricocheted through her limbs and dragged him right along with her, and with her final breath of ecstasy, her vampire king shuddered against her backside, his fingers digging into her hips, her name torn savagely from his lips as if he'd been waiting an eternity just to say it.

Sex as a vampire had been fucking *incredible*—hotter and more intense than it had ever been between them, which was saying a lot, considering their mutual appetites and Dorian's many, *many* talents.

But now, all Charley wanted to do was consume.

Blood.

Fresh blood, not the stuff from the blood bags Dorian had been trying to feed her for the last fifteen minutes.

It called to her—its coppery tang, its particular saltiness, the warmth of it. She'd never noticed it before, but suddenly, she could smell it everywhere—running deep in her own veins, in Dorian's, through the bodies of the animals and birds that skittered through the fallen leaves outside.

But despite their decadent scent, none of those sources would abate her hunger. Her body knew it as well as her brain.

She needed human blood.

"Is it always like this?" she asked, her voice trembling.

She and Dorian were huddled together at the kitchen table, Charley staring down at the glass of cold blood before her. The scent didn't stir her senses to life, didn't make her mouth water in anticipation.

It only made her gag.

"Just for the first few days," he said. "You'll get used to the cravings and learn how to modulate them by alternating with regular food. Eventually you'll only need to feed about once per week. But Charlotte, you really do need to drink this. It's been hours since you've turned—you won't be able to go much longer without human blood."

She lifted the glass to her lips again, her stomach churning. The moment the liquid touched her tongue, her throat closed up again.

"It's all right, love," Dorian said patiently. "Just a few sips, and then I'll fix us a snack."

"Waffles?"

He smiled. "With extra whipped cream."

Charley nodded, determined to see this through. It was just a little blood, for fuck's sake. She's the one that wanted to become a vampire so badly.

Get over yourself, girl!

With a shaky hand, she picked up the glass again, held her breath, and tipped half of it into her mouth, swallowing it down in a single gulp.

Her eyes watered, and she gagged again, struggling to keep the contents down.

Somehow, she managed—but just barely.

When she finally met Dorian's eyes again, he was holding back a smile.

"What is so funny?" she demanded. "That stuff is horrendous. Why didn't vampires pick something better as their fuel source? Like hot chocolate or, I don't know. Whiskey. Hell, at this point I'd rather drink curdled milk."

"Bagged blood is an acquired taste."

A shudder wracked her body, and she wrinkled her nose, wondering how long it would take her to acquire it.

"Well, I guess we've ruled *that* out." Dorian finally let loose a laugh. "It was worth a try."

"What else can I do, though? You said I need to feed on human blood."

He took her abandoned glass and downed the last of it, then said, "I'll arrange for a blood donor for you."

"A human, you mean? A live human?"

"A *consenting* live human, but yes. Donors provide a service for which they're well paid."

"But you don't feed that way."

"It's... not something I wish to get accustomed to again. But it's not an issue for my brothers or Aiden. You'll likely find it much more palatable than—"

"Dorian, I don't..." She closed her eyes. As hungry as she was... *no*. The thought alone made her stomach turn even worse than the cold blood. She understood it was a natural urge for her now—for all vampires—and she wasn't judging any who went that route. Hell, maybe she'd change her mind eventually too.

But right now, she just couldn't bring her brain around to the idea of sinking her fangs into another human being and drinking their blood. Consensual or not, it just didn't feel right.

"I don't want that," she said softly, shame heating her

cheeks. She cursed herself, feeling like a spoiled child. What the hell was she expecting? "I'm sorry, Dorian. I don't mean to be so difficult. I'll figure something out."

"Charlotte, there's no need to apologize. This is all new to you. It's going to take a bit of time, is all. Right now, I just need to ensure you're getting the nutrients you need."

He slid his fingers beneath her chin and tipped her face up, bringing his mouth down to meet her lips in a soft, reassuring kiss.

"I'm right here, love," he whispered, just like he had earlier. Then, tracing his thumb across her lips, "I've an idea. I'll crack open another blood bag and fix us both a nightcap."

"Can you add some extra gin to mine? Like, *mostly* gin, with just a splash of the red stuff?"

Dorian laughed. "If you think it will help."

"Certainly can't hurt."

An hour later, Charley had it all figured out.

A few quick sips of blood followed by a shot. As a vampire, she now had a high tolerance for alcohol, so she could handle a bit of mix-n-match, especially if it helped her get used to the taste of her new primary food source.

They were sitting in the butter-soft leather chairs in the study again—one of her favorite spots in the manor, second only to Dorian's bed. She had no idea where the other Ravenswood occupants were, but for now, she was closed away with her vampire king, slowly coming to terms with her new form.

Her new forever.

She was a vampire. A fucking vampire.

She still couldn't believe it.

Charley downed another sip of blood and a shot, then flashed a half-bloody smile at Dorian. "I think I'm finally getting the hang of this whole bloodsucking thing."

"I'm thrilled to hear it." Dorian took some blood and a shot of his own. "Though I can't say I've ever turned feeding into a drinking game."

Charley set down her glass and crawled into his lap, straddling him on the chair. "I like introducing you to new experiences, Mr. Redthorne."

"Is that so, Ms. D'Amico?" The firelight flickered in his eyes, his lush mouth curving into a smile.

"Speaking of new experiences… You know what would make this blood go down even *better*?"

Dorian laughed. "I can *only* imagine."

She flashed a wicked grin, then slid down onto her knees before him, reaching for the button and zipper on his pants and freeing his cock.

She stole the glass from his hand and took a sip of blood, then lowered her mouth, slowly taking him in.

"Charlotte," he whispered, closing his eyes and sinking into the pleasure of her tongue as she teased his hot, hard flesh.

She sucked him for a moment, then pulled back just

long enough to finish the blood before descending on him again.

"*Fuck*, that's... perfect..." Dorian slid his hands into her hair and tugged, her eyes watering at the delicious sting.

She'd gotten her fill from the blood, and now, with her vampire's cock in her mouth, she wouldn't stop. Not until she fucking *wrecked* him.

She swirled her tongue over his smooth flesh, then took him in even deeper, licking and sucking, scraping her teeth lightly along the top as she pulled back, only to swallow him whole again. He pulled her hair and rocked his hips, desperate, as always, to take back control.

For a few hot, delicious minutes, she gave it to him, letting him fuck her mouth, harder and deeper with every stroke. She moaned softly, loving the taste of him, the way her mouth made him come undone, one deep kiss at a time.

He was getting close. She could feel it in the tightening of his thigh muscles, see it in the ripple of his abs, hear it in his hot, shallow breaths.

Fighting back for control, she slid his cock almost all the way out, then took him in deep again, sucking him hard, devouring him with her lips and tongue until her vampire king could no longer take any more of her delicious torture.

"Charlotte," he ground out, fist tight in her hair as he finally broke, bucking wildly against her mouth, coming down her throat in a rush.

With a soft moan of pleasure all for him, she swallowed, then rose from the floor before the crackling fire, and Dorian glanced up at her with wide, dazed eyes, his heartbeat thudding through his chest, his breath still ragged and raw.

She'd just dragged her thumb across her lips when the study door slammed open, and a drunken asshole crashed their party.

"Well, well, well," Malcolm slurred, stumbling into the study. His clothes were covered with dirt and blood, his hair matted. The stench alone was enough to turn her stomach.

Narrowing his eyes on Charley, Malcolm sniffed the air as if *she* were the offensive one. "Looks like you've been busy, brother."

Gabriel trailed in behind him, his jaw clenched in a tight grimace. "You'll never guess who I ran into tonight," he said to Dorian, rolling his eyes.

Dorian, who was still busy tucking himself back into his pants, glared at Gabriel. "Where did you find him? And better yet, why the fuck did you bring him back here?"

"He was feeding on some poor student on Prince Street. I thought he'd be safer at home."

"It was consensual," Malcolm said, unable to hide the smugness in his tone, even through his obvious inebriation. "Can we say the same about you, Ms. D'Amico?" Malcolm's lips twisted into a mocking smile. "A vampire pet for the vampire king. *Very* interesting development."

At this, Gabriel's eyes widened, and he fully took in the scene.

The blood bags. The scent. Charley figured even the sound of her heartbeat was different now.

Gabriel said nothing, his face unreadable.

But it seemed Malcolm was just getting started. "Are you hungry, little pet? I bet you could use a nice, thick, bloody—"

In a blur, Dorian slammed him into the wall beside the hearth, the fire poker pressed against his throat, his palm over his brother's heart. "Talk me out of it, Mac. Ten seconds."

CHAPTER TWENTY-SIX

"Relax, brother." Malcolm raised his hands in surrender. "I'm not here to fight, nor to insult your pretty little—"

Dorian pushed harder against his chest—another warning.

"—*vampire*," Malcolm finished. "In fact, I wouldn't be here at all if Gabriel hadn't dragged me back, kicking and screaming the entire way."

"Bloody hell," Gabriel said. "By the way he was carrying on, you would've thought I'd torn off his balls."

Dorian closed his eyes, a wave of exhaustion rolling through his body.

He was fucking *tired*.

Tired of the arguing. Tired of his brothers. Just plain tired.

He pitched the fire poker and released Malcolm, returning to his chair next to Charlotte.

"As you can see," he said, "we're otherwise occupied this evening. So if you don't mind, Malcolm, go fuck yourself off to bed, and we'll talk again when you've sobered up."

"Since I'm here, I'd rather talk now. I've news from the front lines."

Dorian shook his head, his rage kept in check only by Charlotte's gentle touch on his arm. "And your new friends, Dominic and Silas? Have you brought news of them as well?"

Malcolm's face paled. "Dominic and Silas? Hmm. I'm not sure I'm familiar with—"

"Save it, brother," Gabriel said, pouring himself a glass of bourbon. "We've seen the pictures in the paper. We know you're cavorting with the enemy."

"*Again*," Dorian added, still burnt about the council meeting.

"The paper. Right." Malcolm let out an indignant huff. "You can't honestly believe I'd—"

"Plot against the crown?" Dorian asked. "Conspire against your own brother? Betray your blood? Now, where would I get such an *outlandish* idea?"

"Betray my blood? Now *there's* an interesting turn of phrase." Malcolm helped himself to a bottle of Dorian's scotch, tossing the cap into the flames and taking a drink. Then, pointing a wobbly finger at Dorian's face, "Do you know what father's little rebellion against House Kendrick cost us?"

Dorian scoffed. "Do you have several days? A month, perhaps?"

"You have *no* bloody idea."

"For fuck's sake," Dorian said. "Say your piece and be done with it."

Malcolm strolled around the room, taking in the books on the shelves, the paintings on the walls as if he'd never seen them before. "Renault Duchanes is back from Paris," he said casually. "Oh yes, we caught up over a... *bite*. Or two. Like old friends."

He turned his gaze to Dorian, clearly waiting for a reaction, but Dorian refused to give him the satisfaction. Instead, he seethed in silence, blood simmering beneath his skin as he waited, once again, for his brother to get to the *fucking* point.

"Renault told me the most *fascinating* story about his sire. I mean, about our father. That is to say..." Malcolm took another swig from the bottle, then laughed. "Well, that's the punchline, brothers. Father sired Duchanes. Apparently, it happened in France long ago—some sort of favor to save his pathetic life, promises of servitude, all very hush-hush, you know how it goes."

"*Duchanes* told you this?" Gabriel asked. "And you believed him?"

"Not at first, of course. But the longer we talked... It seems Renault is suffering from the same afflictions as we are, brothers. Oh, don't look at me as if you don't know. The aching eyes, the blurriness, the constant hunger. Bloody hell, I've only just fed, yet I feel as if I've been starved for months."

He reached over for one of the blood bags Dorian had left on the table and tore off the top, sucking it dry in a matter of seconds.

Dread coiled in Dorian's gut, and he knew Malcolm was speaking the truth—about this, at least. He could see it in his eyes—the hunger. The weakness. The darkness creeping in around the edges.

Dorian glanced at Gabriel, but his youngest brother closed his eyes and tipped his glass back, giving nothing away.

"What does this have to do with Father and House Kendrick?" Dorian asked, still fighting to keep from throttling Malcolm where he stood.

"It's a curse," Malcolm said simply. There was no smugness in his tone, no bait upon which he'd hoped his brothers would bite.

He was speaking the truth again.

The dread in Dorian's gut sank deeper.

"After Father failed to deliver the Mother of Lost Souls as per their agreement," Malcolm continued, "*comrade* Nikolai had his dark witches brew up a *very* special punishment. They unleashed a terrible curse—not just on Father, but on our entire bloodline. Including..." He blurred into the space behind Charlotte's chair and leaned in close, burying his mouth in her hair. "...the vampires we sire."

Dorian was just about to take him down, but Charlotte

saved him the trouble, blurring out of her chair, spinning on her heel, and punching him square in the face.

It was a move straight out of Midnight Marauder, and it did wonders to brighten Dorian's foul mood.

Malcolm hobbled backward and laughed, rubbing his now-bloodied mouth. "I see the king's first sireling is already getting accustomed to her vampire strength. Better watch it, brother—she's feisty."

Charlotte glared at him. "Touch me again, and you'll need fucking *surgery* to remove my fist."

He held up his hands, his smirk firmly in place. "Save your strength, Ms. D'Amico. You'll need it once the curse takes hold."

"You and your lies are not welcome here." Dorian rose from the chair and pointed toward the door. "Take the bottle and go."

"You feel it, Dorian. Tell me you don't."

"Irrelevant," he snapped. "Once we've bonded with the witch, this won't be—"

"It's not the witch bond, brother. It's the curse. And now you've cursed the woman you claim to love with the same fate."

Dorian readied another denial, another command, another insult, but they all died on his tongue.

Despite the traitorous source of this new revelation, somehow, Dorian knew it was true. He could feel it in his fucking soul.

Bloody hell. Cursed by dark witches? Was there no land mine their father had left unplanted?

Dorian let out a deep sigh. "Is that all, Malcolm? Or is there some other darkness you'd like to spread at my feet tonight?"

"No need to be testy, Dorian. I only wanted to share the information."

"Consider it shared." He grabbed Malcolm's elbow and steered him toward the door. "Now leave."

Malcolm jerked free of his hold and glared at him. "You look at me with such contempt, all because I speak the truth. I would've thought you'd be more grateful."

"The fact that I'm allowing you to leave this manor in anything other than an urn is all the gratitude I can muster. Perhaps *you're* the one who should be grateful."

"Me? And yet Gabriel gets a free pass?"

"For all his faults," Dorian said, "Gabriel is not a traitor to the crown. To his own blood."

"Are you certain?" Malcolm met Gabriel's gaze across the room, his eyes darkening with new malice. "Certain in all our years as men and vampires, our little brother never once betrayed your trust?"

"*Don't*," Gabriel warned, but Malcolm only grinned.

Then, leaning in close to Dorian, he whispered, "Perhaps you should ask him about his relationship with Evie. As I understand it, they were quite… close."

He blurred out of Dorian's reach in a heartbeat, and Dorian turned to find Gabriel pinning Malcolm to the floor, hands wrapped around his throat.

"Charlotte," Dorian said through gritted teeth, "if you'll excuse us—"

"No problem. I'm more than happy to skip the testos-terone-fest tonight." She gave him an understanding smile and touched his shoulder, then left him to deal with his brothers alone.

Dorian tried to pry them apart, but Gabriel was enraged, his cold eyes boring into Malcolm with a dark hatred Dorian had only ever seen in their father.

Malcolm managed to get in a swift uppercut, which Gabriel was all too glad to return.

"*Enough!*" Dorian roared, yet still his brothers fought, throwing fists and baring fangs, tearing at each other like wild animals, destroying half the study in the process.

Dorian finally wedged himself between them, launching Gabriel into a chair and pinning Malcolm face-down on the floor, a knee jammed hard between his shoulder blades.

Gabriel was just about to jump back in for another go when Colin blurred into the room.

"*This ends now!*" Colin bellowed, a darkness rising from within, his eyes burning with wrath.

The spectacle of Colin's anger was so shocking, Dorian and the others immediately backed away from one another, retreating to separate corners of the room.

"The fighting, the insults, the blood..." Colin shook his head, his body trembling with rage. "Is this all we're capable of? We're brothers, for fuck's sake!"

Malcolm spit out a mouthful of blood. "And Father—"

"Father?" Colin's lip curled in disgust. "Always about Father, is it? His dirty dealings. His cruelty. His legacy. Well. If you're so interested in his legacy... *Here*. Here is what

Augustus Redthorne has left for his sons." He pulled a capped syringe from his pocket and set it on the mantle over the fireplace, where it rocked back and forth, the red-orange liquid inside catching the light.

"What is it?" Dorian whispered, already afraid of the answer.

"That, brothers, is the cure," Colin said darkly. "The miracle our father spent the better part of his immortal life creating. Distilled to its essence, slightly improved for quicker administration and effectiveness, but the cure nevertheless."

"How do you know it works?" Gabriel asked.

"I don't. It took me some time to find all the pieces scattered among his notes, but that *is* the formula, precisely as he recorded it, along with my modifications." He backed away from the mantle with his hands raised as if the syringe was full of poison.

It *was* poison, Dorian realized. It had killed their father and would just as surely kill them. Faster, if Colin's modifications worked as designed.

"So there you have it," Colin said. "An easy escape from all your many burdens—yours for the taking." He spun on his heel, glaring at each of them in turn. "Gabriel? Do you wish to try it? Malcolm? Dorian? By all means, brothers. I could definitely use a test subject, not to mention *some bloody peace and quiet!*"

Something dark and sinister flickered in Malcolm's gaze, and Dorian knew in an instant what he was thinking.

Dorian was there in a blur, swiping the syringe from the

mantle and shoving it into his shirt pocket a heartbeat before Malcolm got there.

"Tested or not," Dorian said, "*no one* is taking this cure. Not today, not next week, not in a thousand years. *That*, brothers, is an order."

Malcolm shook his head, so clearly repulsed by Dorian's attempt to spare his life, he couldn't even be bothered to hold on to his anger.

"You're no better than Father, Dorian," he said, all the fire gone from his voice. "And because of that, you have doomed us all."

There was a time when the words might've hurt, but Dorian had no more room in his heart for traitors. Especially not the traitors who shared his blood.

Malcolm had been pushing for an alliance with Renault Duchanes from the start. He'd gone behind Dorian's back to convene a council of imbeciles, the act alone further weakening Dorian's position. He'd been witnessed feeding on humans with a vampire who'd left Charlotte for dead in an alley full of grays. And he'd just admitted to seeing Renault again, despite everything the other vampire had done to their family and to Charlotte since the night of the fundraiser.

As far as Dorian was concerned, Malcolm was no longer his brother.

Grabbing Malcolm's elbow and dragging him out of the study and all the way to the front door, Dorian said, "I hereby revoke your royal title and standing, and forsake you as a member of the royal Redthorne family and as my brother." He shoved him through the doorway and out into the cold night, hardening his heart for the final proclamation. "Darken my doorstep again, Malcolm, and I assure you—that urn will be more than ready to accommodate your remains."

CHAPTER TWENTY-SEVEN

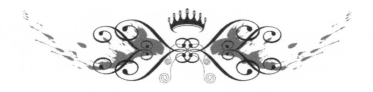

With one traitorous brother promptly escorted from the manor, Dorian stalked off in search of the other.

He found him pacing the gutted dining room, clutching a bottle of bourbon, as drunk as he was furious—quite an admirable feat for a vampire.

"Is it true?" Dorian demanded. "You and Evie?"

Gabriel laughed, his cold eyes glittering with mockery. "Oh, *yes*, brother. I was fucking your fiancée right under your nose. That's what you wanted to hear, was it not? Does it surprise you? You always knew I was the black sheep of the family. The wild one. Uncontrollable. Sounds like a traitor to me." He took a swig from the bottle, then hurled it into the wall just behind Dorian's shoulder. "*Off with my head!*"

"For reasons I cannot *fathom*," Dorian ground out, barely keeping his own anger in check, "you're lying to me." He knew it as surely as he knew the taste of his own bitter rage.

"What's done is done. Whether you believe me or not is irrelevant."

"*Believe* you? I'm not even sure what you're saying, Gabriel. Malcolm's innuendos clearly upset you. So if you didn't have an affair with her, what secret are you harboring? What was so terrible a crime you felt the need to hide it from me across two continents and two hundred and fifty years?"

"An affair. Right. If only my sins were so... pedestrian." Gabriel scoffed and turned his back, kicking a loose stone from the rubble at the hearth. "Sorry to shatter your image of me as a shameless reprobate, but no, I wasn't keeping your fiancée's bed warm. I was merely keeping her secret."

"*What* secret?" Dorian pressed, but of course he already knew. There was only one secret his brother would've carried in silent shame for so many years. One secret that had the power to destroy what was left of their nearly broken bond.

Still, he needed to hear Gabriel say it.

Dorian waited. Moments passed. Days, it seemed, before his brother finally turned to face him again.

And then it came, a whisper carried on a wave of sadness and remorse so vast it threatened to drown them both.

"I knew, Dorian. I knew she was a vampire."

"The *entire* time?"

Gabriel shook his head. "She confessed to me after I'd..."

He paused again. Took a breath. Opened and closed his

mouth a half-dozen times as the world continued to turn and time marched ceaselessly onward, and still Dorian was no closer to understanding his brother's darkness. To understanding *any* of this.

"For fuck's sake, Gabriel. After you'd *what*?"

"After I'd caught... It was late one evening. I was in the study, and I heard what sounded like an argument in the sitting room. But when I went to investigate, I..." He closed his eyes and grimaced, as if the memory still had the power to make him ill. "It wasn't an argument. Evie and Father were... entangled. Quite thoroughly."

Dorian blinked, waiting for the punchline that never came. "Evie and... and *Father*?"

"I waited in the shadows until he finally retired to his chamber, and then I cornered her, demanding an explanation. Naturally, I assumed the worst. Levied all manner of accusations, called her every name in the bloody book, threatened her, all in defense of my eldest brother's so-called honor." Another broken laugh shook loose from the deep well of resentment inside him. "And for *what*, Dorian? To stand here among the ruins before my king—my *blood*—and convince him I'm not a monster? So many years, so much bloodshed, so many secrets, and *this* is what we've come to." He pointed a cruel, accusatory finger at Dorian's chest, swaying on his feet. "Fuck off, brother. We're *all* monsters, carved in our father's image, just as he intended."

Gabriel's drunken speech quickly descended into a rampage about Augustus' endless machinations, but

Dorian could scarcely hear the words. His mind was stuck on the image of his fiancée and his father, thoroughly entangled.

His heartbeat thudded in his ears, the room spinning as the blood rushed to his head. "Evie was... She had an affair with... with *Father*?"

Gabriel's gaze sharpened, cutting straight through Dorian's heart. "Did you not know her at *all*?"

"Not as well as he did, it would seem."

"He was *blackmailing* her, Dorian! For months. Somehow, he'd uncovered her secret and forced her into the arrangement. He berated and demeaned her for what she was, then he took what he wanted from her, including the information that ultimately led him to the royal vampire family. He threatened to kill you both if she breathed so much as a word to you. So instead, she breathed it to me."

Memories slithered up from the depths, like corpses rising from the grave.

Evie, recoiling at his father's every touch or gesture as they shared a family meal.

Evie, crying in the sitting room, not realizing Dorian had been watching her helplessly from the hall, desperately seeking the right words.

Evie. Sad, complicated Evie, alone in a world of monsters she just couldn't escape.

Dorian held up his hands and tried to speak, if only to stop the rest of this dark tale from escaping his brother's lips. But when he took a breath, his throat closed upon the words like a fist, and Gabriel continued, every revelation stealing a part of Dorian's soul he knew he'd never get back.

"I promised her I'd help her find a way to tell you—to break Father's hold over her before he could solidify whatever dastardly deal he'd made with the king." Gabriel's voice turned thin and watery, as if he were swimming through an ocean of his own torment. "But I failed you both, Dorian. In the end, Father got *everything* he wanted. And here we are—the last of a dying legacy, one dark secret away from turning each other to ash."

Dorian collapsed against the bourbon-soaked wall behind him and slid down to the floor, unable to stand beneath the weight of Gabriel's confession.

Knowledge was its own kind of burden, ignorance its own kind of bliss, and in that moment, Dorian wanted nothing so badly as a return to the latter.

That the cold shadows of the past clung to Gabriel like a second skin was no surprise to him. None of the Redthorne brothers had escaped Augustus' reign unmarred.

But he'd never fathomed the true depths of his brother's anguish—a darkness that had chased him across the centuries and hardened his heart to ice.

There were no words of comfort to offer. Even if they'd existed, Dorian's mind wouldn't allow them to form; it was singularly focused on the story his brother had woven, searching for the loose thread that might—if only he pulled hard enough—unravel it all.

"You've made such an art of nurturing your guilt, Dorian, you've forgotten you weren't the one to invent it."

Through bloodshot eyes, Gabriel glanced around at the hollow room—the stripped walls, the broken floorboards, the temporary plywood Aiden had nailed over the shattered windows and doors. "Do you think you have a monopoly on this pain? That the horrors of what happened in West Sussex are yours alone to bear?" Gabriel blurred into his space, hauling him upright and slamming him hard against the wall, his voice trembling with rage. "Do you think I don't know what it feels like to look in the mirror and *hate* the man staring back at me?"

Gabriel glared at him with such malevolence, Dorian wondered if his brother might actually kill him.

It wasn't their savagery that connected them, he suddenly realized, but their suffering. Or hell, maybe they were one and the same. Like a snake consuming its own tail, where did one end and the other begin? Did it matter? Ultimately, both would destroy them.

Gabriel seemed to be waiting for something, but still, Dorian didn't respond. He was empty. Broken. And he knew, right then, if he uttered anything more than a breath, the last of his tattered soul would evaporate.

"I'm not the villain in this story, Dorian." Gabriel finally released him. "My sin was keeping Evie's secret. If I hadn't..." He let out a deep sigh. "Perhaps we would've died as mortal men of England, entombed with our forebears as nature intended. Perhaps we wouldn't be cursed to an eternity of choking on our own bitter lies."

Dorian looked up and met Gabriel's gaze, watching as all the cold, calculating rage faded away. For a brief moment, he looked like a young boy again, wild and reckless, but still innocent. Still trusting that his big brother would look after him.

Not since adolescence had he seen Gabriel so unguarded, and that—more than anything else—terrified him.

"You asked if I've ever cared for anyone," Gabriel said, his voice nearly breaking. "Evelyn Kendrick was my friend long before she was your betrothed. And our father *brutalized* her. Her own family executed her. The look of betrayal and fear in her eyes when her brother's blade bit into her neck… I'll never… I…" A tear slipped from Gabriel's eye, but he brushed it away before it even touched his cheek. "Not a day goes by when my choices don't haunt me, brother. But if given a second chance, I fear I'd only make the same ones."

At this, Dorian finally found the strength to speak. It was a single word, bearing the weight of everything that'd come between them. Everything that would keep them locked in this endless battle. "Why?"

Gabriel offered a sad smile that didn't quite reach his eyes. "Because it's what she asked of me, Dorian."

CHAPTER TWENTY-EIGHT

Not even a roaring fire and a bottle of scotch could chase the chill from Dorian's heart.

He longed for Charlotte, but while he was battling with his brothers, she'd fallen asleep in his bed, her body undoubtedly worn out from the abrupt changes it'd undergone today.

A vampire. He'd turned her, yet still, he could scarcely believe it.

Now it was just Dorian and Aiden alone in the quiet study, the scrapbook of the Crimson City Devil horror show lying open in his lap, his guilt and melancholy sitting beside him like uninvited guests.

A curse.

A bloody fucking curse.

"For how long will I pay for my father's crimes, Aiden? Another century? Two? Or will I carry the burden of his sins like an iron albatross for my immortal eternity?"

Dorian could scarcely carry the burden of his *own* sins, let alone those of the monster who's shadow still haunted his every step. He should've let it go—let *him* go—yet in the quiet spaces between all the arguments, in the sadness that lingered in the long hours that followed, Dorian couldn't help but feel his father's looming presence.

Aiden glanced at the book in Dorian's lap, his eyes skimming the headlines that echoed across Dorian's nightmares.

CITY STREETS RUN RED WITH BLOOD; 'CRIMSON CITY DEVIL' ELUDES AUTHORITIES

"I heard what you told Charlotte the night she found the book," Aiden said. "The whole story."

"You lived through the Crimson City hell with me, Aiden. It's not as if you overheard any state secrets."

Aiden nodded solemnly, nursing his scotch as if it were his very last glass. The fire crackled before them, and outside, a bitter wind howled against the windowpanes—winter's first harbinger.

Dorian didn't mind the silence. Aiden was one of the few people with whom he'd never felt the need to fill the void.

But his best mate clearly had something on his mind, and Dorian hadn't the heart to discourage him tonight.

"Out with it, Aiden," he said.

"We never talked about what happened." Aiden met his gaze, his eyes full of some new darkness. "After, I mean. With your brothers."

"No need. They abandoned me. Not that I can fault them—I certainly gave them good reason."

Aiden lowered his eyes and blew out a breath. "Your family is a tangled web of secrets, Dori. It always has been —long before the devils of House Kendrick turned us all into vampires."

Dorian nodded. His had been a noble family—six children, their parents wedded in a strategic alliance that had nothing to do with love, let alone mutual respect. Material wealth and status had never quite compensated for an absentee father and a doting mother who'd done her best with the cards life had dealt her.

"You've always treated me like a brother," Aiden continued. "Since that first day you caught me sleeping in your stables, pathetic little shite that I was." Aiden smiled at the memory, as did Dorian. "Even when the princelings saw fit to ignore me, you never looked at me as lesser."

"Because you never were."

"No, but I *was* an outsider. In some ways, I still am. It's granted me a unique perspective on your family—an observational distance, you might say."

"And what, pray tell, have you observed?"

Again, the silence gathered between them. Dorian sipped his scotch and gazed into the fire, searching the flames for answers they simply couldn't offer.

Gabriel's words taunted him.

Fuck off, brother. We're all monsters, carved in our father's image, just as he intended...

Aiden rose from his chair and poured himself another scotch, then handed the half-spent bottle to Dorian before settling back in. After a long, deep drink, he said, "When you were at your worst—when there was no talking to you —you'd vanish for days at a time. Weeks, even. All of us were mad with worry. It was the one time in our long, complicated history when your brothers and I managed to set aside our differences and unite under a common banner."

"*What* common banner? My brothers turned tail and ran, while you stayed behind and dragged me back from the pits of hell."

It was something Dorian would never forget; no matter how deeply he'd wanted to forgive his brothers, no matter how desperately he'd wanted to bring them back together as the royal vampire family, no matter how much he'd wanted to blame himself for their actions, the echo of that ancient betrayal was always whispering in his heart. Always reminding him he could never fully trust them—his own blood.

Yes, Dorian *had* been at his worst in those days. And of all his so-called brothers, only Aiden had stayed.

"Colin," Aiden continued, as if Dorian hadn't said anything, "followed a lead to Colorado, where he was able to use his medical credentials to get access to a lab. He spent months searching for a way to cure your bloodlust—a quest that eludes him even now, though not for lack of trying."

Dorian pictured Colin in a white lab coat, his hair tied back, his eyes glazed as he spent hours compiling data and looking at blood samples through a microscope, much like he was doing now. The thought tightened his chest, though he still couldn't bring himself to truly forgive him for leaving.

Dorian shifted uncomfortably in his chair. "Aiden, that's hardly a—"

"Malcolm walked away from his life in New York in a vain effort to ask your father for assistance. He followed Augustus halfway round the world, imploring him to return to Ravenswood and help his eldest son. Augustus—who insisted the Crimson City Devil's only mistake had been his lack of discretion—thought Malcolm should be ashamed of himself, begging for help like a worthless child. He beat your brother to within an inch of his life, waited for the wounds to heal, and did it again. And again. And again, for two long, excruciating months. 'A vampire is a violent creature,' he'd told Malcolm. 'He must make peace with his nature, or he will forever be dominated by it.' Yet still, Malcolm didn't give up trying to convince your father to return with him. Not until Augustus finally slipped away to Buenos Aires, and Malcolm lost his trail."

A pain lanced Dorian's heart, and he grabbed the bottle of scotch and took a deep swallow, desperate to numb himself, to block out Aiden's words, to convince himself it was all just another nightmare.

But in the end, neither alcohol nor denial could erase the truth from Aiden's eyes.

Bloody hell, Mac. I wasn't worth it.

"Which brings us to Gabriel," Aiden said.

Dorian closed his eyes and shook his head. Gabriel's part, at least, would offer no surprises. Since their reunion after their father's death, he and Gabriel had gone from sworn enemies to a somewhat tolerable nuisance in one another's lives, back to enemies once again. Under the threats of their common adversaries, they'd temporarily found some neutral ground, but Dorian wasn't fool enough to believe his little brother held any respect for him.

Especially not after what had transpired in the dining room.

Do you think I don't know what it feels like to look in the mirror and hate *the man staring back at me?*

"You don't have to say it." Dorian opened his eyes. "I know how Gabriel feels about me. I've brought him nothing but disappointment and agony, and every moment we spend in each other's presence only drives him further away. I'll be shocked if he's not gone by sunrise."

A heavy sigh escaped Aiden's lips.

"I love you, Dori," he said in a rare moment of complete seriousness. "You've been my brother and best mate for nearly the entirety of my life. There's nothing I wouldn't do for you. No stake I wouldn't step in front of, no fight I wouldn't wade into, no half-baked scheme I wouldn't volunteer for if it offered even a *chance* at easing your burden. But—"

"Do you think I don't know it, mate?" Dorian asked. "Of all my so-called *brothers*, you're the only one in the whole bloody lot who seems to understand the meaning of the word."

"*But*," Aiden pressed, "I'm *not* the one who brought you back that night."

"What are you saying?"

"You told Charlotte I tracked you down and brought you back, but it wasn't me." He glanced up at Dorian, his eyes full of utter anguish. "Devil knows, I tried. But in the end, it was Gabriel who found you. Gabriel who walked the streets day and night, forgetting to feed, forgetting to sleep, forgetting all else but his eldest brother. Gabriel who dragged you out of the very fires of hell and brought you home to Ravenswood."

"*Gabriel*? But... No. I remember *you* being here, Aiden. You never left my side."

"Yes, I was here. I was here the night Gabriel brought you home. Here through the nights of your withdrawals, when you begged me to tear out your heart and end your suffering. And I was here when you awoke from one of your nightmares and nearly killed your brother, simply for adjusting the pillow beneath your head."

"I... *what*?"

"By the grace of something I've never been able to name," Aiden said darkly, "I stopped you from beheading him. You can't see the scars, Dori, but he certainly carries them. I suspect he always will."

A chill seeped into the room, the wind screaming against the glass, the flames flickering in the fireplace. Dorian's very bones ached with it, his heart heavy as the darkest memories clawed their way into the light.

Gabriel, tending him at his bedside, night after night with Aiden.

And Dorian, out of his mind with bloodlust and a rage he just couldn't quell, lashing out at shadows. There was a knife, and somehow, he'd gotten hold of it and...

His stomach turned, and Dorian closed his eyes, hiding tears of shame.

"None of us knew whether we could actually bring you back from that darkness," Aiden said, "but I was willing to try. For whatever reason, I was always able to calm you in a way the others couldn't. Gabriel didn't understand it any better than I did, but eventually he realized his presence here was only causing you pain."

A hot tear escaped, slipping down Dorian's cheek.

"And so I remained at Ravenswood," Aiden said, "while Colin and Malcolm continued their desperate quests from afar, and Gabriel walked out the doors of his home and into a new life in Sin City, where he remained until your father died and he knew—even though you'd never deign to ask—you'd need him by your side."

It was a long moment before Dorian opened his eyes again, and when he did, he found Aiden watching him closely—not with the look of shame and disgust Dorian had expected, but with a look of love and brotherhood. Understanding.

"You say your brothers abandoned you, Dori," Aiden said, "but they didn't. They merely left. Leaving someone isn't the same thing as abandoning them. Sometimes, walking away is the kindest, most compassionate thing you can do for someone you love."

For the second time in as many hours, Dorian's memories spun and blurred, then sharpened again, rearranging themselves to make room for a new version of an old story that had shaped his life for decades.

The old stories, the things he'd told himself, the things he'd thought he remembered... He'd set the cadence of his life by those things. Used them to forge the iron gates around his heart, walling himself into the impenetrable fortress only Charlotte had truly managed to break through.

In so many ways, those stories—the old versions—had made Dorian the man and vampire he was.

Without them, who would he become? What was left of the Redthorne vampire king when the light of truth shone down on a legacy of lies?

He'd been wrong. About so many, many things.

He glanced down at his hand, still curled over the pages of his dark book. A hand that had slaughtered so many innocent people. A hand that had nearly cut off his brother's head. A hand that had nearly torn out another brother's heart.

Fuck off, brother. We're all monsters, carved in our father's image, just as he intended...

"What do I do, Aiden?" he whispered, his own black shame nearly shattering him. "Where do I go from here?"

"Forward. As we all must go." He came to stand beside Dorian, reaching down to close the Crimson City Devil book. "When you spend your life reliving the past—whether by tormenting yourself or making amends for things you cannot change—you miss what's right in front of you."

"How do I move forward when I've still so much to atone for?"

"I don't have all the answers, Dorian. But I don't believe we atone for the sins of our past by dwelling there. We do it by living now, moment by moment. Every deed, every word, every thought is a chance to do better. To *be* better." He cupped Dorian's cheek, brushing away a final tear with his thumb. "Let it go, brother," he said gently. "It's time."

"And what of my brothers?"

"I don't know if or when Malcolm will find his way back, but Colin and Gabriel? They're *here*, Dori. Whatever happened in the past—whether it was two centuries ago, fifty years ago, or even an hour ago—they're still here. They need you as much as you need them. All of you deserve a chance to be brothers again—brothers as you *should* have been, not as your father made you."

"All of *us*," Dorian said, rising from his chair. He gripped Aiden's shoulder, holding him tight. "All of *us* deserve to be brothers again."

Aiden nodded, a smile touching his lips. "Oh, very well. But I *refuse* to adopt the title of princeling. It's beneath me, Dori."

From somewhere deep in Dorian's chest, a genuine bout of laughter broke free from the darkness, and with no more than a last, passing glance, he tossed the book—the brutal reckoning of his past sins—into the fire. Together, Dorian and his best friend watched the pages curl and blacken, just as they'd watched the remnants of his father's dining room do the same, and for the first time in nearly fifty years, Dorian felt as if he could truly breathe in his own home again.

Aiden was, as ever, right.

His brothers, despite their mistakes, despite the shadows that lived inside every one of them—Dorian most of all—were part of one another's hearts. No matter what challenges they'd faced—no matter what storms still gathered on the near horizon—they were stronger together.

"One thing's for certain," Aiden said, draining the last of his scotch. "If the presence of the princelings at Ravenswood is to become a more permanent arrangement, we're either going to need more booze or less drama."

"Perhaps a bit of both," came the response, and Dorian and Aiden turned to see Gabriel lingering in the doorway, his face inscrutable. "But the less-drama bit may have to wait another day."

Dorian had no idea how much, if anything, Gabriel had heard.

No idea what, if anything, to say.

Gabriel spared him the awkwardness of fumbling for his words by speaking first. "I just heard from one of my guys. Rudy and his man Travis slipped up. We've confirmed Sasha's location."

Dorian's heart nearly burst with relief, and a surge of adrenaline flooded his limbs. "Aiden, will you go upstairs and wake Charlotte? And phone Cole and Isabelle?"

"Already on my way."

Turning back to Gabriel, Dorian said, "Where is she?"

"They've got her stashed in the apartment above Blood-bath. Rudy and Travis are there with her now."

Dorian was already heading for the door, but Gabriel grabbed his arm, stopping him.

"My guy says the place is crawling with enemies, Dorian. Duchanes vampires, Chernikov demons, witches, grays. It seems they've turned the club into their own personal hideout."

"I don't care if they've turned it into a full-on army barracks. We need to get her back, Gabriel."

"Dorian…" Gabriel sighed and shook his head, and Dorian waited for him to try to talk him out of it. To remind him that no human was worth risking so much for. That he never should've gotten involved with Charlotte and Sasha in the first place.

He was already gearing up for another argument when Gabriel finally met his gaze again, and the briefest flicker of warmth shone in his steely eyes.

"I need to change into my demon-stomping boots first," Gabriel said. "And you, brother, need to make a phone call to our new Russian friends." He smacked Dorian on the cheek and grinned, then headed out.

Dorian pulled out his cell phone and thumbed through the contacts. He'd known he'd have to make this call eventually, but he hadn't expected it to come so soon.

"All right, *comrade*," he muttered, then hit the call button. "Let's see how badly you want this bloody blade."

CHAPTER TWENTY-NINE

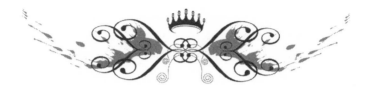

"Looks like they got her in the front room there," Cole said, passing the binoculars to Charley.

After Cole had called in a favor to his cop buddies to get the neighboring buildings evacuated on account of a so-called gas leak, they were all crowded inside the top floor apartment on St. Mark's Place, right across from Bloodbath —Dorian, Gabriel, Colin, Cole, a half-dozen of Cole's wolf shifters, Isabelle, and Charley herself—trying to piece together some semblance of a plan.

Peering through the binoculars, Charley got her first glimpse of Sasha—sitting on the couch in a sweatshirt and yoga pants, watching television and shoveling popcorn into her mouth.

"She's okay!" Charley nearly wept with relief. "Definitely compelled, but she looks unharmed."

"My guess is all the demons are on the main level with

the witches and the Duchanes vamps," Cole said. They really had no idea, as all the lower windows were heavily tinted, some of them boarded up after the cops raided the place and shut it down. "Grays are probably in the mix too. Gonna be one hell of a fight, Red."

Dorian nodded.

"Where's Rogozin?" Charley asked.

"He said he'd be here," Dorian said. "We have to hope he comes through for us, but either way, we don't have a choice. We need to get Sasha out of there tonight."

"And take down Rudy and those other assholes," Charley said, passing the binoculars to Gabriel.

Wordlessly, Dorian squeezed her shoulder.

"We've got some movement in the apartment," Gabriel said. "Looks like the gang's all here—Silas, Dominic, Rudy, and Travis."

Charley narrowed her eyes. "Those fuckers better not be messing with my sister."

"They're all in the kitchen," Gabriel said. "Looks like they're arguing."

"All right," Dorian said. "We can't reach the apartment from the bottom—they'll know we're coming. We need to get onto that roof, then head down through the rooftop entrance."

"The roof is unguarded," Gabriel confirmed. "Bloody idiots."

"Vampires go in from the top," Cole said. "The wolves and the witch will take the ground floor. Charley, you and

Aiden get Sasha the fuck out of there, back onto the roof and down to safety. The rest of you vampires—you work your way down to us after Sasha's out, and together we'll light these motherfuckers up."

"I can help subdue the witches with a muting spell," Isabelle said, "and keep some of the demons from possessing new vessels. But Cole, you and your team will need to guard me. I don't know how many we're facing in there, but I'm not powerful enough on my own to take out more than a demon or two at one time."

"We got your back, Isabelle," Cole said.

"If any of you are using the Blade of Azerius tonight," Isabelle said, "remember—do *not* let it cut you. We know it destroys demons and turns humans into vessels, but we don't know what that means for other immortals. Since vampires still have souls, we have to assume it will imprison yours, even if it doesn't kill you. One slice—one pinprick—and you're toast."

Dorian nodded, patting his side where he'd sheathed and holstered the blade before they'd left Ravenswood. "Noted. Now, is everyone ready?"

"Wait... That's it?" Charley asked. "That's the grand plan? Storm the castle, hope for the best?"

"It's decent," Gabriel said. "Not stellar, but workable."

"No more specifics?" she asked.

"We ain't got time for specifics," Cole said. "We'll just improvise like we always do."

"But what if—"

"Hey." Cole reached over and squeezed her shoulder. "You're not the only one with sweet-ass moves in this operation, Charles. We got this. All of us."

Despite his assurances, and Dorian's calming presence at her side, fear threatened to overtake her. But with another soft touch from Dorian on the back of her neck, Charley reined it in, forcing it down like a piece of hot coal at the bottom of her stomach. There it smoldered, the heat of it fueling her determination.

Sasha was in that building. And right now, everyone gathered here wanted the same thing—to save her.

Charley could *not* afford to get emotional and fuck this up.

She took another deep breath, then looked up at Dorian.

He smiled at her—just once, but it was all she needed.

A wave of emotion crashed into her so hard, she nearly stumbled. She was so beyond in love with him, so fucking gone for him, there was no room in her heart for a life where he didn't exist. He'd claimed her from their very first meeting at the auction, and though she never could've predicted the events that led them here, somehow she'd known, deep down, that she and Dorian were meant to be.

That they were meant to find a way out of this darkness —together.

Charley's heart nearly shattered in her chest. But instead of breaking, it expanded, filling up with so much love for him, so much awe at his boundless love for her, at his fierce protectiveness, at his bravery, at the risks he'd taken—and would keep on taking, no matter what came their way.

"Thank you," she whispered. Not just to Dorian, but to all of them.

And with that, they were off, heading back out into the dark night, ready to storm that fucking castle.

CHAPTER THIRTY

Charley had always dreamed of kicking down Rudy's door, and for the first time in her life, she finally had the balls—and the vampire strength—to do it.

No, it wasn't his door *exactly*—the building belonged to House Duchanes—but that was just a technicality. Rudy was on the other side, and right now, that's all she needed to know.

"On three," Dorian whispered, and they both began to count.

Charley got to two before she kicked that motherfucker down.

"Chuck?" Sasha jumped up from the couch, a wide smile stretching across her face as if her big sister hadn't just kicked down a door. "You came! Yay!"

"What the fuck?" Rudy bellowed, but before he or any of his goon squad could make a move, Charley was at her sister's side. As the other vampires filed into the small apartment behind her, she grabbed Sasha and blurred her to the back bedroom.

Sasha swayed on her feet, a giggle escaping her lips. "What was *that*?"

Charley pulled her in for a tight hug, barely holding back the flood of tears. But the second the chaos erupted in the main room of the apartment, Sasha started freaking out.

"Charley?" She looked at her sister with wide, terrified eyes, then clutched her head, shaking it back and forth as if she were trying to shake loose some terrible nightmare trapped inside. "What the fuck is... Oh my God. Vampires! They're vampires! And Rudy is... He's a demon! They took me and... Charley!" She was hyperventilating now, huge tears spilling from her eyes.

"Aiden!" Charley shouted. "I need your—"

Aiden was at their side in a blink.

"Sasha? Do you remember me?" He took her hands and gazed into her eyes.

For a moment, Sasha fell silent, blinking up at him in confusion.

"It's me," he said. "Aiden Donovan. Dorian's friend."

"Aiden?" A smile broke across her face, and Charley blew out a breath of relief.

"Listen to me, love," he said gently. "Before all this terrible business with the vampires happened, I made you a promise. Do you remember what it was?"

Something crashed in the kitchen, and Charley heard her uncle grunt in pain.

Good. Fucking serves you right, asshole.

Sasha took a deep, shuddering breath, then said to Aiden, "You said you'd teach me to play chess."

Aiden retrieved something from his pocket and handed it over—the ivory king piece, Charley realized, from the chess set Dorian's mother had given him.

"This is a king," Sasha said.

"Precisely. The first lesson in chess is that we must *always* protect the king. Now, I've got it all set up for us back at Ravenswood, but right now, I just need you to keep him safe for me. Can you do that?"

"I... yes. I think so." She sniffed back the last of her tears, her eyes filling with determination for her new mission. "Protect the king. Got it."

"Your sister and I need to take care of some things in the other room, but you can stay here and keep the king safe. We'll be right back. Okay?"

Sasha nodded and sat down on the bed, and Charley pulled Aiden aside, dropping her voice to a whisper.

"What's going on with her?"

"Either Silas or Dominic compelled her," Aiden explained, "and they're both dead now. The compulsion broke, and everything flooded back at once. It's too much for her mind to process—she just needed something to focus on."

"But... How did you know to bring the king piece?"

"I've been carrying it since the night I showed you the set. It reminded me of her. I thought... I don't know." He gave her a shy smile, his cheeks darkening. "I thought maybe it would help, somehow."

"You thought *perfectly*, Aiden, and I love you for it." She pressed a kiss to his cheek, then turned back to her sister. "Sasha? Listen to me, baby. I know shit is crazy right now, and we've got a *lot* to catch up on, but I need you to stay calm and trust that we're going to get you out of here."

Sasha looked up, her blue eyes wide, but clear. She was Sasha again. She was okay.

"I know you will, Chuck," she said. "And after this? You're totally getting another job, because your uncle is a fucking demon, and he sucks ass."

"It's a promise, Sasha."

Silas and Dominic were no more than piles of gray ash in the kitchen, but on the couch in the living room, two useless sacks of shit sat together, their hands and feet bound, their mouths taped shut.

Behind them, four vampires stood like Greek statues.

Aiden. Colin. Gabriel. Dorian.

It reminded Charley of the night she'd first met them— the Redthorne brothers, assembled outside the guesthouse at Ravenswood. Hard. Handsome. Intimidating as hell.

That night, she'd had no idea they'd become her family.

No idea they'd be here with her now, taking down the man who'd done his damnedest to destroy her.

Charley took the chair across from them and grinned at her uncle. "Guess Rogozin was right, Uncle Rudy. You're shooting blanks, huh? No demon fire. That's kind of pathetic for a demon host."

On account of the duct tape across his mouth, Rudy spoke only in grunts.

Charley turned her attention to Travis, glaring at his smug face.

Her stomach twisted, her hands trembling with rage.

"Are you certain you want to do this, love?" Dorian asked her. "I don't mind taking out the trash for you."

Charley continued to glare.

Travis. The man who'd pulled the trigger and ended her father's life. The man who'd crawled into her bed, making her feel again and again like she should be grateful for the opportunity to service his dick. The man who'd roughed her up, who'd taunted her, who'd threatened her.

"I'm certain," she said to Dorian. "I'll handle him."

Travis shouted something behind the duct tape, but Charley wasn't ready to hear it.

She got up from the chair and crouched before him, leaning in close.

"Hello, Travis," she said soothingly. Seductively. "Remember me?"

His pupils dilated as her compulsion took hold, and he relaxed, gazing at her with such adoration it made her teeth hurt.

She'd meant to remove the tape. Meant to ask him some questions.

How could you? Why? What the fuck is wrong with you?

But suddenly she was on top of him, her fangs burning

as she sank them into his neck, relishing in the taste of warm, coppery blood as it slid down her throat.

She hadn't planned on feeding on him—only terrifying him. But now that she'd started, she was pretty damn sure she wouldn't be stopping anytime soon.

And Travis, subdued by her words, by the shock of her new form, remained utterly still.

She drank.

And she drank.

And oh, *God*, she drank.

Her body felt strong and alive, and beneath her punishing mouth, his pulse grew faint—barely a whisper. She swore she could feel his soul, clinging to the last vestiges of life.

A gentle touch on her shoulder drew her attention, and suddenly Dorian was kneeling at her side, his hand on her back, a soft, imploring smile touching his lips.

"All right, love," he whispered. "Not too much."

Charley shrugged, not ready to break away just yet. For the man who'd murdered her father, there was no such thing as too much. Too much pain, too much fear, too much death—Travis deserved it all.

"Charlotte," Dorian said again, "I will back you up on *anything*. You must know that. But I also promised you if you lost your footing, I'd help you find your way back." He reached up and tucked a lock of hair behind her ear. "This isn't you. You're not a murderer. Come back, love. Come back to me."

Charley closed her eyes, not wanting to see the love in his.

You're not a murderer…

The words reverberated through her mind, hitting her again and again until they finally broke through the blood-lust, the vengeance, the grief.

But the voice in her head wasn't just Dorian's.

Suddenly, she heard Rogozin too.

Revenge… It does not fill hole inside you. It only leads to more holes.

Charley's resolve wavered. Could she do this? Kill a human being—even a piece of shit human being like Travis? He certainly deserved it.

But in the end, Dorian was right. Charley may have worn a lot of masks in her life, taken on a lot of fake identities to get what she needed. But she wasn't a killer. Not of humans.

Killing Travis meant her uncle had won. That he'd given her one more role to play, turning her into a vicious murderer.

Slowly, she came back to herself. Slowly, she pulled away from the artery and stepped back from the couch. Back from the precipice.

Beside her, Dorian let out a breath and got to his feet.

"Okay?" he whispered, and she nodded.

She was okay. She wouldn't kill him.

But she wouldn't leave him unscathed, either. Not after what he'd done to her.

She hovered over the half-spent body before her, gazing into his eyes once more.

In a soft, hypnotic voice, she said, "I want you to sit here in this apartment and *rot*, Travis. If by some miracle you survive the night, if by some miracle you ever make it out of here, I want you to remember this moment. Every day you wake up, every time you jerk off, every time you think to hurt another woman, I want you to remember *me*. Remember what I did to you tonight. Remember what I can *still* do to you, any damn day I please. You will live with that fear. That uncertainty. The constant looking over your shoulder, wondering just how close death really is, because *that's* what I've lived with ever since you put a bullet in my father's head."

She stood up again and wiped the blood from her mouth.

Glancing once more at Dorian, she nodded and held out her hand.

Dorian cupped her face, pressing a soft kiss to her forehead. Then, with complete trust, he handed over the Blade of Azerius.

Rudy screamed behind the duct tape.

"What's that, asshole?" Dorian asked. "I don't think she quite heard you." He tore the tape from Rudy's mouth, and her uncle continued mid-rant, as though he hadn't even realized he'd been muzzled.

"...practically raised you!" Rudy shouted. His eyes were demon black, his watch lost in the struggle, but Charley was no longer afraid of him. Even without the blade, she finally saw her uncle for the desperate, pathetic stain that he was.

"Paid your bills," he continued. "Bought your clothes. Kept a roof over your head after your father died. *He* was the one who sold you out to Azerius! He was the one who made the deal!"

"Because you fucked around with demons and backed him into a corner," she said calmly, refusing to let him get under her skin. "He did it to save our lives. And even *that* wasn't enough for you."

She pressed the tip of the blade to his throat, stopping just short of breaking the skin.

"We're supposed to be family, Charlotte," he said, his voice breaking, his black eyes full of desperation.

At the mention of the word *family*, Charley felt that hot coal ignite in her belly again, but she tamped it down. She wouldn't give Rudy the satisfaction of unloading on him— she'd given away too much of herself already.

Never again, asshole.

"Charlotte!" he shouted. "Think about what you're doing here. Please!"

"No," she said. It was a single word, spoken just above a whisper.

It felt like the first time she'd ever said it to Rudy, yet she knew it was the very last thing she'd ever give the man.

"Are… are you going to kill me?" he whimpered. "You said you weren't a killer."

Charley stared down at the pathetic man before her and tried to feel… something. She'd dreamed about Rudy's demise for so long that when the time finally came, she thought she'd be elated. Instead, there was only a quiet relief.

For years, Rudy had existed as her boss, her benefactor, her controller. When she tried to imagine him outside those roles—even as the uncle she'd known in childhood—she saw only a faceless form.

She felt neither remorse nor joy at his fate; for Charley, Rudy was simply gone.

Nonexistent.

She didn't know whether that made her cold-hearted and cruel, crazy, or perhaps just shocked and numb. At the moment, she didn't care.

Rudolpho D'Amico's story had come to its end.

"I'm *not* a killer," she said. "I'd never take a human life."

Rudy let out a rush of breath, his greasy lips stretching into a smile. "I know you're not, kiddo. You're a good girl. You—"

"Fortunately," she said brightly, "you're not human."

Then, without another word for the bastard who'd sold out his family, who'd hurt Charley again and again, who'd relished in her pain, she shoved the blade into his throat.

His eyes flickered like lightning, then turned black once more.

Seconds later, his body turned into charred ash.

Charley let out a deep sigh, and a new feeling rushed into her heart.

Freedom.

CHAPTER THIRTY-ONE

Leaving Travis to rot, Charley and the others slipped out into the hallway and headed straight for the exit they'd come in through—a metal door on the north side of the building that led back up to the roof.

But when Dorian wrenched it open, he damn near collided with a host of Duchanes vampires blurring down the stairs.

"Move! Now!" Dorian shouted as he jerked the door closed again. He jammed the fire axe through the handle and braced it against the wall—a temporary blockade that wouldn't hold the assailants on the other side for more than a minute.

The group rushed back toward the apartment, hoping to go out the windows instead. But as soon as they crossed the threshold, the windows in the apartment shattered, and a dozen more vampires crashed into view.

"Shit!" Charley gasped.

There was only one way out now.

Down through the club.

Charley grabbed Sasha, and she and the others blurred to the stairwell at the opposite end of the hallway, the newly arriving vamps closing in fast behind them.

Dorian fought off two vampires in quick succession while Charley got her sister down the stairs. They hit the ground floor and barged out through the doors that led into the club...

Straight into utter chaos.

The smell of brimstone and hellfire filled the air, and already the floor was slick with blood and ash. In her peripheral vision, Charley caught sight of one of the wolves charging at a gray, another taking down a demon. In his wolf form, Cole was glued to Isabelle's side, protecting her from would-be attackers as she struggled to manage both demons and witches.

Charley's heart sank. They were outnumbered ten to one.

"Hide!" Dorian shouted, touching her face once more, and then he was gone, blurring into the battle with his brothers.

Charley grabbed Sasha and blurred her beneath the bar, just as the front doors of the club exploded inward, ushering in a late arrival that nevertheless brought a smile to her face.

"Good evening, *comrades*," the demon said.

For a brief instant, the club fell silent as Rogozin strolled in, three dozen demons pouring in from behind him.

"So many pieces of shit before my eyes," he said. "Who is good guy, who is bad guy?" Rogozin laughed. "Well, how about we burn them all first, ask questions later, yes?"

There was no more talking after that. No more grand declarations, no more jokes.

Only bloodshed. Only fire. Only violence.

The demons were impossible to tell apart—outside of Rogozin and the men she'd met at the hotel in Long Island City, Charley had no idea who was who, which side was which.

She tried in vain to keep track of her vampire, of his brothers, of the wolves, but even that was an impossible task.

It seemed as if they fought for days—a great clashing of fangs and fists, hellfire and wolf bites, the blur of the vampires, the blood. So much blood she thought it might wash them all away.

There was nothing she could do in a fight like this—she didn't have the strength and coordination to take on so many adversaries at once. She would only get in the way.

On the drive down from Annandale-on-Hudson, Isabelle had given Charley the tattoos that would allow her to tolerate the sunlight—for a little while, at least. At the time, Charley wasn't sure why she'd needed them so urgently, but now she was grateful the witch had insisted.

It was going to be a long night—with a good chance she'd still be trapped there when the sun rose.

All she could do now was wait.

So there beneath the bar, she held Sasha close, singing a soft lullaby her father used to sing, rocking her as the glass and blood and ash rained down all around them, and deep in her heart, Charley prayed she and her loved ones would last long enough to see that beautiful sunrise.

"By proclamation of the royal family and the Shadow Accords, Bloodbath is now property of House Redthorne," Gabriel announced, although the Duchanes vampires who most needed to hear it were no more than ash beneath their shoes.

Charley knew it was probably just a formality, but she figured she ought to pay attention anyway.

She'd have to learn the ropes sooner or later.

She was one of them now. A Redthorne vampire.

The thought still filled her with awe.

Even the Rogozin demons were showing respect, heads bowed, hands clasped.

They'd kept their word and come through for Dorian, and now, thanks in large part to them, the battle was over.

They'd won.

Sasha was safe.

And her friends had survived.

Standing beside his brother, Dorian caught her gaze, giving her a quick, reassuring wink that filled her with warmth.

Soon, they'd be home, and all of this would be a memory.

Soon, Sasha would be in the sunroom with Aiden, learning how to play chess.

Soon, Charlotte would be in the arms of her vampire king.

She couldn't help but smile.

"All assets formerly belonging to Renault Duchanes have been seized," Gabriel continued, "including the witches who now stand accused of treason. They will be interviewed and taken prisoner for further questioning at the behest of the king."

A slow clap started at the back of the room, and all heads turned toward the sound.

There, from the darkest shadows of the deepest corner, a figure emerged, his clothes covered in blood and ash, his eyes wild with malice.

"Quite a speech, brother," Malcolm said. "I know *I'm* feeling inspired. Anyone else?"

"*Malcolm,*" Dorian warned, but before he could utter another word, Charley felt the heat of Malcolm's cruel glare and knew *exactly* who his target was.

Her.

She saw the blur of him.

Felt the rush of air on her skin.

Scented the foulness of his presence.

After that, there was only pain.

His vicious fingers, shoved deep into her back.

Her heart wrapped in his fist, beating only because he allowed it.

And across the space of the club, the man she loved let out a roar that rattled the windows, and she knew, in that moment, it was over.

Her brief immortal life had come to its end.

CHAPTER THIRTY-TWO

Dorian's heart fucking *shattered*.

It was all he could do to stand upright, to give voice to the words inside.

"Back off," he called out across the club. "All of you."

At once, the demons and allies surrounding him retreated, leaving him to face the monster alone.

Between them, the woman who owned his heart gasped for breath, her eyes never leaving his, even as the tears fell down her cheeks.

Dorian could hear the faint beat of her heart, struggling in his brother's grip.

"Malcolm," Dorian said, his voice a ragged whisper. "If you do this... You can *not* come back from this, brother."

"*Brother*? Wait, are you speaking to me?" Malcolm made a show of glancing around the room, as if Dorian's plea might've been directed at anyone else. "As I recall, *brother*, you banished me from House Redthorne. I'm a free agent now. Just... *Malcolm.* Nice ring, don't you think?"

"Malcolm, please... I was wrong. The title is yours. *My* title is yours. The crown. The manor. The cars, the artwork, the money. All of it. Just... *release her!*"

Malcolm shifted slightly behind her, and Charlotte gasped, her eyes wide with fear. She was utterly paralyzed. One wrong move, and it would end her.

"You would give up all that power just for this human?" Malcolm asked.

"You know I would."

"I do. Yet you would not give your own brother—your *blood*—the simplest courtesy or respect?"

Dorian held up his hands and took a step closer. "Malcolm, you—"

"*Don't!*" he roared. "Don't you fucking move."

Dorian stilled, catching Charlotte's gaze once more.

A smile graced her lips, and in a thin, watery voice, she said, "One percent, right?"

Dorian instantly recalled their conversation from the night of the battle at Estas' place.

"I took a risk... You can call it reckless or a death wish or batshit crazy if you want to, but that won't change how I feel. It won't change the fact that I'd do it a hundred times over if it gave me even a one percent shot at keeping you safe."

"Those are impossible odds."

"One percent is still a chance, Dorian. One I'll take over the alternative every damn night of the week."

"What's that, brother?" Malcolm asked. His eyes were

crazed. Gone. The eyes of a feral beast who no longer remembered he'd ever had a soul.

There would be no talking to Malcolm. No convincing him to do the right thing—the humane thing.

He'd lost his humanity long ago.

Dorian let out a deep breath, and with it, the last of his love for his brother.

With one more glance for Charlotte, one more smile, Dorian blurred into them, the bone handle gripped tightly in his fist as the Blade of Azerius sank deep into Malcolm's chest.

Malcolm's eyes went wide, and in that moment, all the haze, all the insanity cleared.

"Forgive me, brother," he choked out. "The only... way to... All the... And summon the..." A storm flickered in his eyes, and then he released her, collapsing to the ground.

His body didn't incinerate like Rudy's had.

Dorian had no idea what that meant for his soul.

Truly, he didn't give a damn. All that mattered was that Charlotte had survived his ruthless attack.

She stumbled into Dorian's arms, sucking in a strangled breath as the wounds in her back began to close.

Dorian held her upright, damn near choking on his relief. He'd only just looked into her eyes again when he caught the movement behind her.

A white raven perched on a cocktail table.

And there at its base, his brother's body rose from the ground, the blade still protruding from his chest, his eyes the color of midnight oil.

"Who has summoned me, and for what purpose?" the creature formerly known as Malcolm demanded.

"Dorian!" Charlotte gasped, clutching at his shirt. "The meeting with Rogozin... He said something about Azerius... Something about how he kills his brothers like Cain did, and *that's* when he comes. I knew it had something to do with the blade, but I didn't realize..."

Dorian blinked rapidly, still not believing his own eyes.

It wasn't Malcolm.

It was *him*.

Azerius.

The demon who'd claimed Charlotte.

Though his eyes were entirely black, Dorian sensed the shift of his gaze to Charlotte.

Dorian released his woman.

Without another thought, he grabbed the demon and blurred him up to the roof, far away from the people he loved.

Far away from Charlotte.

In the pale, pre-dawn light, Dorian and the demon Azerius circled each other upon the gravelly rooftop, sizing each other up. Dorian tried to think, recalling everything they'd learned about demon vessels, about Azerius, about the blade.

The blade to the heart wouldn't have killed Malcolm, he realized now—only a wooden stake would've done that. But it likely expelled his soul and turned him into vessel, which Azerius was now occupying. Rogozin had also told

Charlotte that summoning Azerius would bind him to the vessel.

The creature still had Malcolm's movements and gestures, which likely meant he possessed vampire power, but not demonic.

No hellfire, or Dorian would already be dead.

But it also meant he'd be a much stronger version of Malcolm, which put Dorian at a disadvantage.

"I am Azerius," the demon finally said, "King of Blood and Ravens, He Who Slaughters the Blood of his Blood, He Who Drinks the Blood of the Fallen, He Whom Before All Mortals Weep, He Whom Bringeth the—"

"Yes, and I'm Dorian Redthorne, vampire king of New York, brother to the royal princes, and blah, blah, *blah* with the pageantry. Frankly, I don't give a fuck about your titles. You're in *my* city now. Hitching a ride in my brother's body, looking at the woman I love. We need to have a talk about your choices, demon."

"A talk? How about a deal instead?"

"What are you offering?"

"I will remove the demons from your city—*all* of the demons, from *all* of your cities."

"And in return?" Dorian asked, already knowing the answer. Already knowing he'd say no.

"Hand over the woman," Azerius said.

"That's all you'd ask of me?" Dorian laughed. They were still circling each other like wild dogs about to pounce. "One human woman—a woman you've allegedly already claimed?"

"I cannot collect on that claim for another fortnight."

Dorian swallowed down his shock. His fear. "A fortnight is hardly a long wait."

"A fortnight on earth is several thousand years in hell. And what can I say? I find her... intriguing."

Dorian pretended to consider his offer, then shook his head. "A compelling offer, to be sure. But I've got a counter."

The demon lord raised an eyebrow.

"The woman claims herself," Dorian said. "And you can take your contract, your titles, and all the demons in all the cities in the world, and shove them straight up your arrogant ass."

The demon let out a deep, dark laugh that reverberated across the city. "A fight it is, vampire king."

He blurred at Dorian, taking him down with a force like a Mack truck. They rolled hard, and when they finally stopped near the edge of the rooftop, Dorian was pinned beneath him.

Azerius wrapped a hand around Dorian's throat, but before he could get a good grip, Dorian shoved his hands against the demon's chest, sending him reeling.

Dorian blurred to the other side of the roof for a momentary reprieve, but again the demon was on him, blurring in and out of his space, slamming him with an uppercut and a jab, the force of the blows making his head spin.

Another quick jab, a kick to the stomach, a fist to the face. Dorian took every hit, giving back just as many in return.

They fought like feral ghouls. They fought like grays. They fought until Dorian's ears rang and the world spun, and still, Azerius did not capitulate.

Neither did Dorian.

Azerius blurred in close again, sinking his fangs into Dorian's shoulder and tearing out a chunk of flesh, carving him clear down to the bone.

Despite the agony, Dorian landed a fresh series of blows to the side of Azerius' head, then dropped into a crouch, sweeping his leg out in a wide arc and knocking Azerius onto his ass. He leaped onto the demon, pinning his arms with his knees and grabbing his head, slamming it hard into the ground, caving in the back of his skull.

Blood poured from the wound, from his ears, from his mouth, but Azerius only laughed.

"You would kill your own brother for this woman?" he demanded. "This *human*?"

Dorian panted, his heart slamming against his ribs, sweat pouring into his eyes and nearly blinding him.

"You're not him," he breathed. "But yes, I would. Again. And again. And again."

The demon laughed again. Then, in a move so sudden and unexpected it made the whole world spin, Azerius blurred them back to the edge of the roof, pinning Dorian down once more.

He wrapped his hands around Dorian's throat, and this time, his grip didn't slip. It was unrelenting, choking off the last of Dorian's air, crushing his windpipe, fracturing the small bones of his neck.

Soon, he would pass out.

Soon, the crush of Azerius' grip would tear the head from his body.

Soon, Dorian Redthorne would reach his immortal end.

"You fought well, vampire king," Azerius taunted, blood leaking from an unhealed gash over his eye. "But only a miracle will save you now."

Miracle.

The word triggered something in Dorian's memory, just out of reach.

An argument with his brothers.

Colin, erupting in anger.

A glass vial flickering in the firelight. A deep, red-orange glow.

A miracle.

Colin's words whispering from the farthest corners of his mind.

The miracle our father spent the better part of his immortal life creating. Distilled to its essence, slightly improved for quicker administration and effectiveness, but the cure nevertheless...

A smudge of light as he'd blurred to the mantle.

His fingers closing on the cold glass vial.

The miracle, still tucked away in Dorian's pocket where he'd shoved it out of Malcolm's reach.

"I am Azerius," the demon said now, a grin of victory twisting his cruel mouth. "I am the King of Blood and Ravens. I am He Who Slaughters the Blood of his Blood. I am He Who Drinks the Blood of the Fallen. I am He Whom Before All Mortals Weep."

"You," Dorian choked out, "are a test subject." With his very last bit of strength, he flipped the cap off the syringe and jammed it into Azerius' neck, pressing the plunger and dosing him with the miracle cure.

Azerius released Dorian's throat, his hands clawing at the puncture wound.

The air rushed back into Dorian's lungs.

But for the demon, it was too late. The cure was already doing its work, turning the vampire body into a human, weakening him. Breaking him down.

With Azerius still looming over him, Dorian shoved his hand into the demon's chest and gripped his heart.

In that terrible, blood-drenched moment, the demon's eyes shifted from black to golden, his face crumpling in anguish as he looked upon Dorian with the face of his brother Malcolm.

"Please, brother," he said, stealing Malcolm's voice. "Don't do this."

A tear slid down Dorian's cheek, and though he knew it wasn't really Mac—knew it was just another of Azerius' tricks—he took the opportunity to say goodbye anyway, knowing it would be the very last time he could.

"I'm so sorry, Mac. For... for everything. But it's already done. I... I hope you find peace, brother."

He tore the heart from his chest, holding it for a brief, bloody instant before everything turned to ash in his hands, falling onto his face and scattering in the chilly Manhattan wind.

Dorian got to his knees.

He stared at his hands for what felt like an eternity, and all around him, a hush fell over his city.

And then Dorian Redthorne, vampire king of New York, brother to the royal princes, slayer of the King of Blood and Ravens, closed his eyes and wept.

CHAPTER THIRTY-THREE

It was Charlotte who saved him.

When she finally appeared before him on the rooftop, the sun rose over her shoulder, and for a moment Dorian swore she'd brought him the dawn.

"Charlotte?" His voice cracked, and he blinked up at her as if he hadn't seen her in years.

Centuries.

Eons.

"Dorian," she breathed, dropping to her knees before him.

He reached for her hair, the soft feel of it like a precious gift after all the vile things he'd touched.

"Malcolm...?" she whispered.

A question. A prayer.

Dorian could only shake his head.

The tears fell from her eyes, and she drew him into her embrace, holding his head against her chest, pressing her lips to his ash-coated hair as he steadied himself by the beat of her heart.

"What of the mark," he whispered urgently, still holding her close, terrified to meet her eyes.

"Isabelle says it's gone."

Dorian choked back a sob, fisting her shirt. "Tell me you're mine, Charlotte D'Amico. *Please*, love. Tell me you're mine."

"I'm yours, Dorian Redthorne. *Always*."

He crushed her in his embrace, and together they held each other until the city was on fire with the sunrise and the tears finally stopped and their wild hearts mirrored the same deep, perfect rhythm.

Back on the main floor of the club, Dorian watched in silence as the Rogozin demons, Cole and his shifters, and Gabriel worked together to sweep up the ashes and mop the blood from the floor. Behind the bar, several witches sat bound to high-backed chairs as Colin checked them for injuries and Isabelle ferreted out whatever intel she could.

Once loyal to House Duchanes, they were Redthorne prisoners now, and would need to be interrogated and punished for their crimes, but Dorian suspected most of them—like Jacinda Colburn, sitting at the end of the row—hadn't a choice.

He had no interest in further tormenting them. Only in

ensuring something like this wouldn't—*couldn't*—happen again.

Near the windows up front, Aiden and Charlotte sat with Sasha, Charlotte holding her sister in a tight embrace as the girl grilled them with a thousand and one questions. Aiden answered every single one with the patience of a saint, doing his best to guide her through her first trial-by-fire crash course on the history of the supernatural.

All things considered, she seemed to be taking it pretty well, just like her big sister had.

Dorian smiled at the memory of Charlotte's very first question.

Why the fuck didn't you tell me you're a bloodsucking vampire king?

They'd certainly come a long way since then.

Taking a seat at the far end of the bar, Dorian reached for an unbroken bottle of scotch and a glass, filling it to the rim. Before he took his first sip, a shadow fell upon his face, and a thick, blood-soaked arm reached for a bottle of vodka from the same unbroken stash.

"Mr. Rogozin," Dorian said, offering a small nod of thanks.

"Please," he said, filling his glass to the rim just as Dorian had. "Call me Alexei."

A few moments passed in silence, then Alexei finally said, "Seems to me, New York City is lonely place to be without allies—especially for Vampire Royals of New York."

"And for the most powerful demonic faction on the eastern seaboard."

Rogozin grinned. "Very true."

Dorian sighed and lowered his gaze to his untouched drink.

In the history of supernaturals on the earthly plane, he was certain there had never been an official alliance between the ruling vampire family and the Russian demons —*any* demons, for that matter. His father was likely turning over in the proverbial grave.

But Augustus Redthorne's reign was over.

Dorian's was just beginning.

He'd never asked for the crown. Never wanted it.

But for the first time since his father's death, he was beginning to see it as the honor it truly was—an honor he didn't have to bear alone.

Turning his attention back to Rogozin, he said, "Tonight was just a preview. There are still other demons in this city that need to be dealt with."

"Starting with Nikolai Chernikov." Rogozin grinned again. "Do not worry. Killing him will be great pleasure. Then, with Nikolai dead and vampire king backing us, we will quickly bring others in line."

Dorian nodded and took a steadying breath.

Considered his next move.

Searched his heart for the alarm bells he was certain he'd hear.

But they never rang.

Deep inside, there was only acceptance. Hope.

331

Things could be different now. Better. But it had to start with trust. A cautious trust, but a trust nevertheless.

Without further hesitation, Dorian handed over the Blade of Azerius. "This will probably make your job a bit easier."

Rogozin took it with both hands, his gaze as reverent as it was surprised. "But... What about deal? What about ten million dollars?"

"Keep your money, Alexei. Frankly, I'd rather the loyalty."

"You have already earned it."

"Really? Even though I felled your King of Blood and Ravens?"

"Felled?" Rogozin chuckled. "You were worthy opponent, Dorian Redthorne. But Lord Azerius is like cockroach in nuclear attack. He can not be killed—not even by king of vampires."

"Alexei, I trapped him in a vessel, turned him into a human, and tore the bloody heart from his chest. He's quite dead, I assure you."

"Not dead. Only banished for one thousand years."

Alarm flooded Dorian's chest. "But I thought... What of the demon mark? The witch said it's no longer—"

"Relax, vampire king. Through your bravery, you have broken demon bind. Lord Azerius granted you reprieve and will not come after Charlotte D'Amico again. You, on the other hand? I can't make promise."

Dorian blew out a breath and shrugged. "A thousand

years, though, right? Plenty of time to prepare for the rematch."

Rogozin laughed and lifted his glass. "So. Redthorne and Rogozin. What is saying? Best friends forever?"

Dorian shook his head and returned the laughter. "Let's start with mutually benefitting associates and see where it goes."

"Fair enough, King Redthorne."

They touched glasses and drank, Rogozin gulping down his vodka in one long pull.

When he finished, he set the glass hard on the bar and said, "I will notify you when Chernikov deed is done. Later today, with any good luck."

"Thank you. Oh, and Alexei?" Dorian held his gaze, a new understanding passing between them—the first, Dorian hoped, of many. "Please. Call me Dorian."

"So let's recap." Gabriel righted an overturned stool and took a seat beside Dorian. "The royal Redthornes are now aligned with Rogozin demons. House Duchanes has been decimated, but Renault himself is M.I.A. Cole is still getting reports of grays upstate. And we've got a dark witch's curse to unravel, unless we all want to die a slow, terrible death."

"Never a dull moment for House Redthorne," Dorian said. "Not to worry, though. I think I'm finally ready to make some new hires. Security guards or... I don't know.

Minions. Don't kings have minions?" He sipped his scotch and shook his head. "Bloody hell, this is a terrible idea. I *really* don't like people."

"Fairly certain the feeling is mutual, brother."

"You know, Gabriel, you're quite humorous when you're not being an asshole."

"If I had a dollar for every time I've heard that..."

"I can only imagine." Dorian took another drink, then said, "So what's next, little brother? Heading back to Sin City now that the worst is behind us here?"

"Right. About that..." Gabriel reached for a glass and poured himself some scotch, then topped off Dorian's glass. "Bloodbath was a terrible name with a terrible clientele, but the place itself has potential. Good bones, as they say. Plus, you really can't beat the location."

"Bloodbath? *This* Bloodbath?"

"It's ours now, brother. To the victor go the spoils, et cetera, et cetera."

"You're... staying?" Dorian could hardly speak through the sudden knot of emotion in his throat.

"Well, *someone* needs to keep an eye on you. Look what happened last time we left you alone for fifty years—you damn near destroyed the place. Besides, I think I already have my first employee. She looks good behind the bar, does she not?"

He grinned over at Jacinda, tied to a chair beside the other witches.

"Fuck you, bloodsucker," she spat. "I will bleed you dry and grind your bones into dust."

"See?" Gabriel said. "She'll be winning customer service awards in no time."

"If you say so." Dorian could hardly reconcile the fiery, angry woman behind the bar with the memory of the sweet witch he'd first met at the fundraiser, wandering through his gardens in search of rare herbs.

Herbs she'd later used to poison him, but still.

After a long silence, Gabriel turned to Dorian and lifted his glass, his gaze heavy and serious, his mouth pulled into a deep frown.

In that moment, Dorian knew they were both thinking of Malcolm. Of all the things they'd said and hadn't said, all the wrong turns, all the mistakes.

All the love.

There were no long speeches. No teary-eyed sharing of memories. But somehow, Gabriel managed to find the words that encapsulated it all.

"To brotherhood."

Brotherhood.

For so long, it had gone hand-in-hand with betrayal and loss. With regret. With anger.

But now, it gave Dorian strength.

He touched his glass to Gabriel's and smiled. "To brotherhood."

"All set, love?" Dorian asked as Charlotte finally returned from escorting her sister outside with Aiden.

Colin, Gabriel, Isabelle, Cole, and some of Rogozin's demons were staying behind to finish cleaning up and interrogating the witches, but Dorian was more than ready to get the hell out of there.

He wanted a shower.

He wanted to go to bed.

He wanted to make love to his woman—in the shower and again in his bed.

Charlotte nodded. "Sasha asked to ride back to Ravenswood with Aiden."

Gabriel let out a low chuckle. "I'll bet she did."

"Hey!" She laughed and smacked his shoulder. "That's my sister you're talking about, dickhead."

"And *my* brother," he added.

Dorian arched an eyebrow. "You *do* realize she's talking about Aiden, right?"

Gabriel shrugged. "I think he's earned it, don't you?"

"Nearly two hundred and fifty years ago, yes."

"Better late than never."

"Indeed." Dorian rose from the barstool and pulled his woman in for another kiss, breathing in her sweet scent, deeply buried beneath the blood and grime.

The shower would be long and epic.

His cock was already hard just thinking about it.

"You two are bloody disgusting," Gabriel grumbled, grabbing the last of the scotch and stalking off to find somewhere else to brood.

Charlotte finally pulled back, her eyes shining with emotion as she took Dorian's face between her hands.

Her touch, as always, steadied him.

"We did it," she whispered. "We got her back."

"We got you *both* back."

She stretched up for one more kiss, then whispered, "Take me home, vampire king."

Home.

Passing from her lips, the word was a balm on his broken heart, and he scooped her into his arms and carried her out of those bloodied ruins, out onto St. Mark's Place and into the bright hope of a brand new day.

CHAPTER THIRTY-FOUR

One Month Later

As the daughter of a professional art thief, Charley had experienced her share of endings. Broken promises. Shattered families. Deaths.

Every last one of her old endings had been abrupt and devastating, leaving her to pick up the pieces and move on as best she could.

But now, as she bubble-wrapped the last coffee mug from her kitchen cabinets and set it into the box with the others, Charley was experiencing a new kind of ending. One that set the butterflies inside her to flight, whispering in her ear about new beginnings. Possibilities. Promises.

Everything was changing so fast.

Thanks to a hacker friend of Gabriel's—another of his shady, mysterious contacts—they were able to transfer Charley's father's legal assets back into her name where they belonged. Once that was settled, she sold the Park Avenue penthouse in record time.

As beautiful as it was, she didn't want to stay there. The penthouse was part of another life—an old life Charley had long ago outgrown. The embers had already been smoldering within her when she first met Dorian, and in the time they'd been together, they'd exploded into a full-on inferno, burning everything in their wake.

Now, she was more than ready to emerge from those ashes.

To start again, *her* way.

Sasha had moved in with Darcy last weekend—a cute little two-bedroom apartment in Park Slope, Brooklyn, near some of their other friends from school. The girls had grown close, and after everything Sasha had experienced—everything she'd seen—she was ready to spread her wings a bit.

Next week, Charley would be moving out too—off to a third-floor walkup she'd found in Astoria, Queens, not far from the train. On a good commuting day, she'd be able to dash into one of the neighborhood's famed Greek bakeries en route, pick up a pastry and some coffee to go, and make it to Manhattan in less than half an hour.

Her new boss was pretty flexible with her schedule, but Charley didn't want to take advantage. She was beyond grateful he'd even considered her proposal and given her a real job, despite her lack of legitimate experience. But since the acquisition of Armitage Holdings, FierceConnect was growing like crazy, and Dorian needed all the help he could get. As of last week, Charley was officially a marketing assistant for a brand new division geared toward attracting and supporting women gamers, developers, and content creators. She also got to consult on some of the artwork with Dorian's graphics team, which she loved.

Mostly, Charley was tasked with getting coffees, scheduling meetings, making copies and travel arrangements— nothing too complicated. But she couldn't have been happier. It was her first real, paying, on-the-books gig, and she showed up every day with an easy smile.

Dorian had tried to give her a higher position, but Charley wanted to start small, to work her way up through the ranks without any special favors from the boss.

It was her first job, after all, and she still had a lot to learn. But she had so much fun being there, having lunch with her new friends, sneaking away for an occasional "appointment" in the boss' office. She even welcomed the stress that came with working for such a high-profile company. To her, every challenge was another reminder that she was finally taking charge of her life, doing things her own way.

Her personal life had its *own* set of challenges, and Charley was facing those head-on as well. She and Sasha had decided to start counseling—at least for their human problems. Considering their rocky childhoods and everything else they'd been through, they had a lot to work on, both individually and as sisters. After all the secrets Charley had kept from Sasha, and everything that had happened as a result, Charley knew it would take time to earn her sister's forgiveness and trust. She was ready to work for it, though. Together, they'd get through it, just like they always had—one day at a time.

That's what it all came down to now: one day at a time. Sometimes, even one *moment* at a time.

Charley was grateful for every one of those moments, no matter how many more she got. If she'd learned one thing from the whirlwind of her existence these past few months, it was that life came with no guarantees—and an awful lot of surprise twists.

With a satisfied sigh, Charley taped up the box of mugs and pushed it against the kitchen wall with the others, officially done for the day. She checked her phone, thrilled to find a text from her man. He'd been at Ravenswood all day, supervising the final touches on his remodeled dining room, including delivery and installation of a new painting he'd recently purchased.

Question, his text said. *Why aren't you in my bed right now?*

Hello to you too, she replied. *I take it the installation went okay?*

Come over and see for yourself. Better yet, come over and... come.

Mmm. Is there a guarantee on that offer?

Do you really need to ask? Don't make me start without you.

Charley laughed. *Okay. Let me shower & I'll call an Uber.*

Friends don't let friends shower alone, love. Especially hot, sexy friends like you. I need to see you. NOW.

I'm sweaty and dirty and no. Just no.

The sweatier and dirtier the better, Dorian replied. *I've already sent a car for you. Jameson will be at your doorstep in 5 minutes.*

You're impossible!

You love me anyway.

Charley smiled again, letting out a happy sigh. *Yes, Mr. Redthorne,* she replied. *I kinda do.*

Dorian greeted Charley in the Ravenswood foyer wearing nothing but a mischievous smile. The moment she closed the door behind her, she was in his naked arms, fending off a barrage of kisses.

"I'm filthy."

"Yes, you are."

"Stop!" Charley squealed, loving every minute of his attention. "What about the new dining room? Don't you want to show me?"

"I'd rather show you something else." Holding her tight, he blurred her up to the master suite. "Time to wash up, dirty girl."

Wordlessly, Charley stripped off her clothes, and together they stepped into the shower, steam filling Charley's lungs, the feel of the hot water on her skin instantly relaxing her. Dorian slipped his hands behind her neck and kissed her, and all the stress of the day's packing vanished, swirling right down the drain.

Charley was in absolute heaven.

"If I could start and end every day like this..." She trailed off into another happy sigh, her fingers gliding over Dorian's perfectly sculpted abs.

Dorian slid his hands down to cup her ass. "Let me speak to the owner, see if we can work out some sort of deal. I have to warn you, though. It's probably going to cost you. A *lot*."

"Is that so, Mr. Redthorne?" Charley wrapped her hand around his cock, already hot and hard for her. He groaned at her touch, and she stroked him, slowly increasing the pressure, knowing just how he liked it.

Dorian leaned his head back and sighed, exposing the corded muscles of his neck and shoulders. Charley pressed a trail of hot, wet kisses across his chest, then down his abs, following the line of dark hair that led to his cock. She sat down on the shower bench, settling herself between his legs.

"I bet we can come to an arrangement," she teased, urging him closer. As hot water streamed over their bodies, rivulets running down between her breasts and thighs, Charley parted her lips and took him deep into her mouth.

God, she'd never tire of the taste of him, the perfect fit of her lips around his smooth cock, the way he instantly fell under her spell as she stroked and sucked.

It was the same for her too. Whenever Dorian took control, whenever he touched her, kissed her, she was *his*. Completely. And she *had* been his, right from that very first kiss at the auction, giving herself over to him beneath a painting of a ship tossed about on a stormy sea.

"Bloody hell, woman. You're not playing fair." Dorian threaded his hands into her hair and guided himself deeper into her mouth, pumping harder and faster. She took him in —all of him—losing herself in his pleasure as he hit the back of her throat, the ache between her thighs growing unbearable. She slid forward on the bench and trailed a hand down her belly, her fingers dipping between her thighs, stroking her clit.

The sight of her touching herself made Dorian's cock thicken, and the slide of his hot, wet flesh against her tongue turned her on to no end. She stroked herself faster, harder.

Sex with Dorian had always been so hot, so effortless, even when they were strangers—even when she was still human. There had never been any shame or self-consciousness between them, whether they were exploring each other's bodies and boundaries or exploring their own. But things were different now. It wasn't just that they were both vampires, although that definitely made things hotter. It was that they knew each other so well—that they loved each other, deeply and madly. The sex had taken on a new intensity, a feeling that Charley could scarcely put into words.

She didn't have to.

She moaned against his flesh, sucking him harder, and when she looked up and met his eyes, she knew he was a goner.

"Charlotte!" He growled like an animal and gripped the back of her head, exploding in a hot torrent, his body shuddering with the pleasure of his release. She swallowed it down, moaning again as the wave of her own pleasure built between her thighs. Dorian slid out of her mouth, and she closed her eyes, circling her clit, bringing herself closer to the edge…

"No," Dorian said. "Not yet." He grabbed her wrist to stop her, and when she opened her eyes, he was on his knees. He dug his fingers into the flesh around her hips and slid her forward on the bench, then he dipped his head low. "I've been dying for a taste of you all day."

As the steam billowed between them, Dorian kissed her inner thigh, dragging his tongue along the sensitive skin, slowly making his way to her center. Her pussy ached for him, wet and needy as he traced her outer lips with his tongue, licking and sucking as his hands gripped her thighs, every kiss making her writhe in ecstasy.

She shoved her hands into his hair and pulled him closer, but Dorian was intent on teasing her, pulling away before she fell over the edge, diving back in before she lost her mind. He was an expert at this game, one she both hated and loved, building up the pressure inside her like a pot of water just short of boiling over.

But Dorian knew her body well; he sensed when she was about to lose control completely, and rewarded her for her patience by thrusting his tongue deep into her pussy, stroking her clit with his thumb until he brought her all the way there.

"Dorian, yes! Oh God, right there!" She gasped as her body clenched around his tongue, her legs trembling, her heart banging in her chest as the waves of pleasure slammed into her, sucking her out to sea, then carrying her right back.

After a long moment, Dorian finally pulled away, rising up off of his knees and bringing her with him.

Charley didn't have the strength to stand up on her own, but she didn't need it. Dorian lifted her effortlessly, pressing her against the shower wall as she wrapped her legs around him. He was hard again, ready for her, kissing her passionately as she slid down over his cock, his flesh filling her once again.

Dorian ran his thumb along her bottom lip, his eyes suddenly serious. He held her gaze for an eternity, water streaming down his face, dripping from his long lashes, pooling in the places where their bodies touched.

In his beautiful honey-brown eyes, she saw the soul of the vampire she loved, and knew she was right where she was supposed to be.

"I'm madly in love with you, my vampire queen," he whispered.

She wrapped herself around him even more tightly, her heart full and happy as they found their perfect pace together, whispering each other's names, kissing and touching until the sun went down and the seemingly infinite supply of hot water finally turned cold.

CHAPTER THIRTY-FIVE

Dorian had tied the silk scarf expertly over Charlotte's eyes, and now he placed his hands on her shoulders, carefully guiding her into the remodeled dining room.

It didn't even look like the same room anymore, which was how he'd wanted it. No longer his father's. No longer the room he loathed. But one he'd rebuilt, intending to fill it only with love. With family.

His family.

In less than a week, they'd be gathering around the table for their first holiday meal together as immortals—the inaugural Redthorne family Thanksgiving.

It was centuries in the making, and for the first time, Dorian actually felt the meaning behind its name.

He took one more glance around the room, wanting everything to be perfect for the big reveal. New hardwood floors gleamed beneath deep gray walls, the white woodwork and trim like icing on a perfect cake. They'd widened the glass doors and topped them with sheer window treatments that allowed in even more light. A blond oak table and chairs gave the room a bright, modern look, complete with a centerpiece of roses from Rosalind's garden. At the far end of the room, the hearth had been rebuilt by hand, with massive black and gray stones from a local quarry.

It was beautiful, and the thought of filling it with his raucous family again made his heart nearly burst.

Now, Charlotte held her hands out in front of her, as if she were afraid she might trip.

"I've got you, love." Dorian's lips brushed the shell of her ear, and beneath her thin silk bathrobe, he felt the quickening of her pulse. "Are you certain you're ready for this? Certain you absolutely, positively want to see this?"

"Oh my God, yes!" A nervous giggle bubbled from her lips, and she bounced a bit on her toes, reminding him of the proverbial child on Christmas morn. "I've been ready all day, Dorian. Come on!"

"You need to be *really* ready, though. Completely, utterly—"

"Dorian! If you keep building it up like this, it'll be a total letdown."

Dorian laughed, coming around in front of her and kissing her playfully on the nose. "Not possible."

"The suspense is killing me. Would you just—"

Dorian silenced her with a deep kiss, then slowly untied the scarf, letting it drape down over her shoulders instead. He held her gaze for a long moment, her eyes full of so much love and wonder, it made his heart hurt in the best possible way.

Bloody hell, I love this woman.

After one more stolen kiss, he finally stepped out of her line of vision, revealing not just the new dining room, but the gift he'd installed for her.

Charlotte gasped, pressing her hands to her mouth as the tears filled her eyes.

There, mounted above the rebuilt hearth, illuminated by museum-quality recessed lighting that erased every last shadow, was her painting.

Adrift.

"But how did you..." She shook her head, as if she still couldn't believe it. "That's impossible. I saw it go at auction. That night when—"

"Yes, I remember." Dorian grinned and took her hands. "Let's just say I made the buyer an offer he couldn't refuse."

Her eyes widened, and he rushed to add, "Quite legally, I assure you. I've got the bill of sale to prove it, along with the certificate of authenticity from the Smithsonian, who sold it to the family at the Salvatore years ago, all on the up-and-up."

Clearly relieved, she released Dorian's hands and approached the painting, admiring it up close. "Dorian, I... My God. It's so beautiful, I don't even know what to say."

"Say you love it," he whispered, pulling her into his arms again.

"I love it. I love *you*."

"It reminds me of you," he said. "Beautiful. Dangerous.

But when the storm finally breaks and that little sliver of sunshine slices through the clouds... All I see is the light, Charlotte. The hope."

Charlotte stretched up on her toes and kissed him, lingering in his embrace, and again he marveled that she was here. That she was his.

He'd never known a love like this, never felt anything so deep.

"It's amazing," she said, slowly turning to take in the rest of the room. "Everything looks so beautiful, and it's... God, I can't believe *Adrift* is here. Just... *here*, hanging in your dining room."

"*Our* dining room," Dorian amended.

She blinked at him and held her breath, tears filling her eyes once again.

Dorian took her face between his hands, gazing into those eyes.

Bloody hell, his life had changed so much in these last few months.

Charlotte had crashed through him with a force, bringing him out of the darkness and into the light, bringing him back to love, back to his family, back to himself.

Together with Rogozin's help, they'd eliminated Chernikov and dismantled his entire organization, quashing the immediate threat of the demonic takeover of New York City. They'd slaughtered much of House Duchanes, reclaiming Renault's assets for the crown, which Dorian was in turn funneling into projects toward the betterment of *all* supernaturals, guided by the new council they were just beginning to build.

After the Armitage Holdings acquisition became official, Isabelle followed suit, accepting Dorian's offer to become the Redthornes' bonded witch. In a new twist on an old tradition, she'd chosen to keep a workspace in the crypts next to Colin's, but live in her own home in Phoenicia, which was just fine by Dorian. He was more than happy for he and Charlotte to keep Ravenswood mostly to themselves.

Gabriel and Colin had established permanent residences in the city. Colin opened a pediatric practice in Manhattan, even as he still worked tirelessly to further their father's research, and Gabriel had made good on his promise to rebuild the club formerly known as Bloodbath—it would be opening in just two weeks.

Slowly, piece by piece, the Royal Redthornes were rebuilding.

But not all of the changes had been good, and many things remained shrouded in darkness and mystery.

Despite Gabriel's constant pressure, the Duchanes witch Jacinda was no closer to the cure for the curse Chernikov had placed on them for their father's treachery. The partnership with Isabelle had helped stave off the worst of the effects, but Dorian and his brothers were still struggling with light sensitivity and mental fog. They had to feed more often, and the tattoos faded quickly, despite Isabelle's best efforts to replenish them. It wouldn't be long before Charlotte and Aiden showed similar symptoms.

All they could do was keep searching. Keep fighting.

After the battle at Bloodbath, they'd searched the city for days for signs of Duchanes, but it seemed their elusive enemy had fled once again. Dorian had no doubts he was still working behind the scenes, gathering his followers for another attempted coup. While his alliance with the Rogozin demons had certainly bolstered their numbers, Dorian had no illusions that the Redthorne Royals were safe.

That they wouldn't have to fight for the crown again. For each other.

They'd already lost one brother to this battle. They wouldn't lose another.

For Dorian, the pain of Malcolm's death was as sharp as it'd been on that rooftop last month, and though they'd searched his room and belongings for an explanation, Dorian never found answers to the questions he sought. They haunted him still. Had Malcolm betrayed them after all, or had he been working to protect his family all along, sowing seeds of discontent only to gain trust among their enemies? Had he truly intended for Dorian to kill him, just so they could summon Azerius?

Now more than ever, Dorian believed the strange presence he'd felt in the crypts every time they'd discussed the blade and the Book of Lost Souls was Malcolm, quietly lurking in the shadows, plotting in silence to save them.

To honor his promise to their mother to look after his brothers.

But Dorian would never know the truth, and not everything in life could be wrapped up in a neat little bow.

He'd always found it disingenuous to only remember the best of a man in his death, as if the darkness had never existed. It *had* existed, and it was as much a part of Malcolm as it was a part of all of them. Discarding it might've made the memories brighter, but it would've been another lie. And lies were a part of his father's legacy Dorian was more than ready to bury.

So for now, he would love and honor his brother as a Royal Redthorne prince, remembering the light as well as the dark, embracing the former, slowly working his way toward forgiveness of the latter.

He took in the sight of the dining room again.

Yes, so much had changed.

And now, Dorian's life was about to change again.

"I've got a proposition for you, love." He slid the scarf from Charlotte's shoulders. "Two options."

She gave him a soft, devastating smile.

"Option one." He tied one end of the scarf around her wrist and leaned in close, his lips blazing a trail of hot kisses from her neck to her ear. In a dark, deadly whisper, he said, "I tie you up and do *very* bad things to you tonight."

Charlotte let out a sigh of pleasure, already melting beneath his teasing words. "And option two?"

"Option two." He kissed his way down her throat, then back up again, grazing her earlobe with his teeth, his cock already throbbing for her touch. "I tie you up and do very bad things to you *every* night, for however bloody long eternity lasts."

At this, Dorian tugged the scarf forward and brought her hand to his, then gently slid the ring on her finger. It was a stunning red diamond in an antique setting, as rare and beautiful as Charlotte herself.

"Marry me, my vampire queen," he whispered, dropping to his knees and pressing a kiss to her hand, his throat tight with emotion. "Be my immortal forever."

She stared at the ring, tears spilling down her cheeks, her heart banging wildly in her chest.

He'd rendered her speechless.

Dorian held his breath, desperate for her answer.

Outside, winter's first snow had just begun to fall, covering Rosalind's roses in a thick, white blanket.

Charlotte's eyes lit up at the sight.

Yet it seemed as if the spring had come and gone again before she finally sucked in a deep breath and dropped to her knees before him, wrapping her arms around his neck and claiming him in a devastating kiss.

Dorian ran his hand over her head, down her back, kissing her lips, her cheeks, kissing away all of her happy tears. She leaned into him, and he loosened her bathrobe and slid his hand between her thighs, finding her hot and wet and ready for him, as she always was. A soft moan escaped her lips—a music he would never tire of hearing.

But she still hadn't answered him.

"So what will it be, Ms. D'Amico?" he whispered,

teasing her with feather-light strokes as his lips brushed her collarbone. "Option one, or option two?"

Charlotte threaded her fingers into his hair and let out a delighted squeal, the first of many, many more he'd coax from her tonight. The snow continued to fall, enveloping Ravenswood in winter's diamond-white grace, but here in the dining room—in *their* dining room—Charlotte melted beneath Dorian's touch, her eyes shining with love, her legs trembling as he made her come, again and again and again, all for him.

"Option two, my vampire king," she finally whispered on a soft, breathless sigh. "Always, option two."

Thank you so much for reading Dorian and Charley's epic love story!

I hope you loved meeting the Redthorne Royals and falling in love with Dorian and his vampire queen Charley. Their story has come to a close, but don't worry—we're just getting started in the Vampire Royals of New York world, and there's lots more family drama, supernatural politics, and super hot romance coming your way!

So… whose story is next in this sexy supernatural lineup?

Gabriel Redthorne and Jacinda Colburn star in Heart of Thorns, a steamy enemies-to-lovers vampire romance and book one in the next trilogy in the Vampire Royals of New York series!

ABOUT HEART OF THORNS

Gabriel...

They say Gabriel Redthorne is the most ruthless vampire of all.

They say he tore out a man's throat just for spilling his bourbon.

They say his heart is so cold, the women he fucks turn to ice.

Good. Let them talk.

The vampire prince has always known it's better to be feared as a monster than loved as a fool, no matter how cold his bed is.

But then he meets *her*.

The witch who conspired with the enemy to take down the royal family.

Dark and devious.

Fire to his ice.

His prisoner.

And after one forbidden taste, the addiction that will utterly *ruin* him.

Jacinda...

For five years, dark witch Jacinda Colburn has been preparing.

Preparing to betray her half-demon bloodline.

Preparing to change her identity.

Preparing to disappear.

But for all her careful scheming, nothing could've prepared her for the heartless vampire prince—or for the punishment her wicked sins against his family have earned.

They say Gabriel Redthorne is vicious. Filthy. That he can kill a man with just a touch.

But now that he owns her, all Jaci wants to know is... What can that vicious, filthy touch do to a *woman*?

Find out in HEART OF THORNS, with appearances from all your favorite Vampire Royals of New York characters!

Vampire lovers! If you loved reading this story as much as I loved writing it, please help a girl out and **leave a review on Amazon!** Even a quick sentence or two about your favorite part can help other readers discover the book, and that makes me super happy!

If you really, *really* loved it, come hang out at our Facebook group, Sarah Piper's Sassy Witches. I'd love to see you there.

XOXO
Sarah

MORE BOOKS FROM SARAH PIPER!

Paranormal romance fans, I've got even more sexy books ready to heat up your bookshelf!

THE WITCH'S REBELS is a supernatural reverse harem series featuring five smoldering-hot guys and the kickass witch they'd kill to protect. If you like sexy forbidden romance, dark magic, and heart-pounding supernatural suspense, this witchy adventure will leave you spellbound!

TAROT ACADEMY is a paranormal, university-aged reverse harem academy romance starring four seriously hot mages and one badass witch. Dark prophecies, unique mythology, steamy romance, strong female friendships, and plenty of supernatural thrills make this series a must-read!

ABOUT SARAH PIPER

Sarah Piper is a Kindle All-Star winning urban fantasy and paranormal romance author. Through her signature brew of dark magic, heart-pounding suspense, and steamy romance, Sarah promises a sexy, supernatural escape into a world where the magic is real, the monsters are sinfully hot, and the witches always get their magically-ever-afters.

Her works include the newly released Vampire Royals of New York series, the Tarot Academy series, and The Witch's Rebels, a fan-favorite reverse harem urban fantasy series readers have dubbed "super sexy," "imaginative and original," "off-the-walls good," and "delightfully wicked in the best ways," a quote Sarah hopes will appear on her tombstone.

Originally from New York, Sarah now makes her home in northern Colorado with her husband (though that changes frequently) (the location, not the husband), where she spends her days sleeping like a vampire and her nights writing books, casting spells, gazing at the moon, playing with her ever-expanding collection of Tarot cards, binge-watching Supernatural (Team Dean!), and obsessing over the best way to brew a cup of tea.

You can find her online at SarahPiperBooks.com and in her Facebook readers group, Sarah Piper's Sassy Witches! If you're sassy, or if you need a little *more* sass in your life, or if you need more Dean Winchester gifs in your life (who doesn't?), come hang out!

Made in the USA
Las Vegas, NV
26 March 2021

20260237R00213